The Long Weekend

JENNIFER CHAPMAN

The Long Weekend

CENTURY PUBLISHING

LONDON

First published in Great Britain in 1984 by
Century Publishing Co. Ltd,
Portland House, 12–13 Greek Street,
London W1V 5LE

Reprinted 1984

ISBN 0 7126 0298 4

Printed in Great Britain by
St Edmundsbury Press
Bury St Edmunds, Suffolk

For Thérèse Tobin

Prologue

A dull thud from the front of the house indicated that Dan was home. Charlotte automatically felt a sense of pleasure and then checked herself for allowing habit to deceive her.

It was Dan's habit to linger in the hall for a few minutes, opening mail, mumbling over bills before coming through to find her. Only lately he had been forgoing this ritual and would be looking for her as soon as he was in the house. He searched her out as if he knew what was going on, or so it seemed to Charlotte, who was hypersensitive to every turn of phrase, seeing possible reproach every time she failed to avoid his gaze.

And yet old habits were hard to give up. They became instinctive like the immediate and undeniable gladness she had just felt to know that he was home. And tonight they were going out together – for the first time in months – so perverse that it should be now, when it was all too late and any pleasure in the outing was wiped away by suspicion. Why should he suddenly produce tickets for a concert if it was not a sort of doglike bribe? She was unfair to him, very unfair, she knew that and felt it hard, but then was it particularly fair of him to make an effort only now?

'Working hard?' he said, his face appearing round the door of the breakfast room where she kept her drawing board.

'Hello,' she said, with false brightness. 'Did you have a good day?'

'Not bad. You?'

'The same. Not bad.'

He waited in the doorway watching her while she fussed with the bits of paper she had been staring at unseen for the past hour. She had looked up at him when he came in, a brief, direct look in order to satisfy him.

'Been out today?' he asked next. What did that mean?

'Only to take Vicky to Audrey,' she answered truthfully, and seized upon an area of conversation that would not demand any deception: 'She was so excited about going. She had painted a picture for Audrey and another for James. You don't think she's getting precocious, do you?' Charlotte was fighting off Dan's watchfulness with prattle.

'She's only six, Lottie. A bit young for precocity,' he said gently.

'Maybe you're right. I hope so. I don't think I'd know how to cope with that sort of thing in my own child. When you see it in other children their parents just stand by and seem to think that it's endearing.'

'Perhaps it is to them,' Dan said. 'You know what they say, love is blind.'

And what did he mean by that?

Charlotte got up and went into the kitchen. The light was fading and the sun turning to amber low in the sky over the fields to the back of the house.

'Supper's about ready,' she called, but Dan was just behind her making her start as he murmured acknowledgement. He too was watching the horizon.

'I think it'll be a nice day tomorrow,' Charlotte said, a somewhat inane comment for her.

'Maybe,' Dan said after a pause. Every word seemed to be laden with overtones, undertones, but nothing was said. Did he know? It was not possible, Charlotte had been so careful, nobody knew. She would not allow herself to believe that Dan even suspected, and yet of course he must, just as she would if it were the other way

8

round and he was having an affair. It was ridiculous, but the hardest part was not being able to tell him in the way she always did about everything else; although, long ago, shortly before they were married, she had told him about another man, with cruel naivety asking him what she should do.

They had been lying in bed at the time. His bed or hers, or perhaps somebody else's, she couldn't remember. In those days they had taken advantage of every available bed to lie naked between sheets as opposed to the semi-clothed discomfort and risk attached to Dan's car. She had once even resorted to sticking her legs out of the window in an attempt to overcome the contortions of back-seat sex.

'I don't want to go off you. I'd rather stay with you,' she had told him in the bed. 'But I don't fancy you any more, if you see what I mean,' adding 'but I still like you,' as if the platitude could soften the blow. She had no right to demand his understanding but had assumed it and found it there; but that was ten years ago when she was eighteen and entitled to make mistakes and get away with it. The situation was different now. Dan had a right to expect more, although she had little doubt as to how he would react if she did talk to him about Nick: ultimately he would be magnanimous. The real difference this time was not with Dan but with Nick because Charlotte did not see the affair as a mistake.

Dan remained at the window, watching the last of the day while Charlotte put knives ands forks on a tray and took the casserole out of the oven. 'There's a good play on tonight,' she told him. 'We could put it on the video and see it when we get back.' Television, which she had come to detest for its regularity, was now a useful expedient to avoid Dan's slightly probing questions which she felt hovered between them all the time now, only needing a short space of background silence to become more searching and insistent. Or maybe she was simply frightened of what she might say herself, now that she had this perverse desire to be found out.

They ate supper with no time to talk as the concert started at

7.30. Dan fixed up the video recorder while Charlotte filled the dishwasher. They were busy all the time, busy and bright and careful of one another.

The concert was to take place in a converted barn in a neighbouring village. A mediaeval structure, it stood in the grounds of a large house whose owner had sufficient money to indulge his love of music to the extent of financing a semi-professional orchestra. Dan and Charlotte knew him slightly. He was lean and stooping and had huge hands with long bony fingers which dangled and swayed as he spoke. He appeared to be the absolute aesthete and his great barn with its warped struts and beams and appliquéd ancient farm implements against cobweb-laced walls had become a minor Mecca for the 'highbrow'. Not that Charlotte and Dan put themselves in this category, although Charlotte had always loved the arts, and Dan, he got a certain satisfaction out of a sense of being easy going. He had never minde´d going with her to look at pictures, to see a play, hear a concert, although they would have done none of it if she had not arranged the tickets. Tonight was the first time he had ever arranged them, which in itself was indicative of the creeping panic that he might now be losing Charlotte.

The great barn hushed into silence as the lights dimmed and the musicians sat poised to play. The concert began with Mozart. Charlotte tried to listen, staring ahead through the rows of motionless heads. She had a peculiarly lonely feeling that everyone else had gone into a trance and only she was thinking about something else. At one point she became aware of Dan watching her again, the glint of his eyes caught in the half light. Charlotte straightened her back and gazed harder at the violins, the poignant clarity of their sound suddenly penetrating her and making her shiver.

In the interval they were cornered by one of Dan's clients, who seemed to find it extraordinary that a solicitor should like music.

'Well I never,' he said, several times, accepting a drink from

10

them. 'And I hear you've got a clever wife,' he went on to Dan, looking towards Charlotte, at which point she went to the lavatory.

'Who was that buffoon?' she whispered to Dan when they were back in their seats.

Dan murmured a name and then added: 'He knows Nicholas Matthews, – that's how he knows you're clever.'

'Oh,' she said, briefly. 'I see.'

Neither of them wanted to talk about Nick, but on the way home they did, as if drawn to the subject by vertigo. Dan asked how she was getting on with the design work for him. He did not know that Nick was in America and Charlotte did not want to tell him. It was better to say that she had not seen him for a week without qualifying this by mentioning that he was away. She was sunk in deception, she thought, and felt an unfair sense of resentment against Dan for making it necessary. She generally preferred to be honest.

The first lie or half-truth was always compounded, she'd found. Once you started you had to go on, so that whenever Dan spoke of Nick she tended to say unpleasant things about him in order to assuage any suspicion. It was her defence strategy, but one that made her disloyal to both men and somehow to herself as well.

It was still quite early when they reached home. The house was oddly cold for the time of year, but you couldn't have a fire in August, so they took the television upstairs to watch the play in bed. It was about a woman who could not decide between her husband and her lover. They watched it intently, each making critical comments about the acting, direction, camera work, anything to emphasise the fiction – that none of it was real. There was a lot of sex in it, including a highly explicit scene under a bathroom shower. It ended inconclusively, and Charlotte and Dan slid down their bed and unavoidably began to re-enact the simulated passion of the play.

★

The clapping had subsided but Nick still felt hot, as if the surge of enthusiasm had generated a sudden heat that stung his face and neck. It would not show: long ago he had managed to catch sight of himself when it seemed he must be blushing but there had been no sign of redness and the sensation, though irritatingly involuntary, no longer worried him. He liked to think there wasn't much that troubled him any more, which was probably more true than he realised.

The hotel in Anaheim seemed to hum now with muted congratulatory sound. Air conditioning, 'pink' noise and a generally padded decor put its own restraint on any clamour, almost like being in church,Nick thought, and advancing the notion saw a kind of religious zeal in the American PR people, their over-firm handshakes pumping sincerity, catching hold of success.

Nick acknowledged it all with his slightly wry Englishman's smile, thanked the other delegates for their kind reception of his paper and made his way through the conference suite.

'Where do you think you're going?' Germaine Hartnell stood by the exit into the lobby, her gold-spangled bronzed arm a barrier in his path. Nick stopped and the arm stretched up, long red fingernails like blooded talons reaching round to the back of his neck.

'Darling boy, you were just wonderful,' she breathed at him, planting a moist kiss on his mouth.

He thanked her in the easy-going, slightly gracious way he had cultivated to the point of second nature, and attempted to extricate himself. He wanted to make a telephone call.

'Not now darling,' she drawled, taking his arm to lead him back. 'You've made it. You're big time now – you've got an obligation to your admirers, so give 'em what they want – you.'

Hesitating only a moment before Germaine's manhandling of him became unnecessary he went back into the body of the suite, carefully retaining that delightful edge of ingenuous surprise, modesty and reserve that in the English so appealed to his American colleagues. Three hours later he got to his room and the telephone.

Eight, nine hours ahead in England, Charlotte would be asleep in bed with her husband and if not asleep . . . he tried to dismiss the thought. He already felt proprietorial over her and vaguely annoyed, as if she was somehow to blame for his missing the chance to speak to her. He went to the drinks cabinet and got a static shock when he put his key in the lock. He took out a Scotch and several lumps of ice, trickling the golden liquid over the crystal cubes – just the look of the drink made him feel better. Not that he drank a lot. He didn't need it but he had developed a capacity for large quantities of Scotch without suffering. It was a necessary skill when drinking was part of business meetings – keeping up but staying sober. He had developed a lot of 'keeping up' tactics over the years and Charlotte – if he had thought about it – was one of them, but at the moment too strong a desire to be seen in context. He wanted her now for herself, which was dangerous, but then Nick did not consider the danger in what he wanted. He took and was positive about it, which was his strength.

Now he needed to relax after his triumph downstairs. His paper on the 'Gym and Tonic' campaign in Britain was good, he knew that, but the reception had been overwhelming, sent even him on a high. The Americans were generous with their recognition, more so than his own countrymen, and he had been taken by surprise – a new experience for him and one which was hard to contain; so that he wanted to tell someone – share it a bit. But he would not have told Charlotte. They would have talked slightly, of other things, nothing in particular, but heard each other's voices and felt the contact. If he wanted to tell someone there was only Marion and he had not spoken to her for a week. There had been no time and nothing to say. He hadn't thought to ring her and yet maybe she expected him to, even now.

That last night, before he left for America:

★

'You're late!' she told him as he wandered into the kitchen. She kept her eyes steadfastly on the mixing bowl in front of her, deliberately, self-consciously continuing with the process although she had no idea what had gone into the bowl and what had not. Her hands, the fingers suddenly stiff and awkward, just kept kneading away; the lump of heavy dough could have been clay and she would not have noticed or even cared.

'You know how it is,' he said.

She did, but once in a while she chose not to.

He did not kiss her. He did not go near her. That was what Marion had noticed above all. He no longer touched her in the spontaneous way he always had over the years. He was a man who liked and needed physical attention, both giving and receiving. It was a facet of his character Marion had always delighted in because it was so contrary to everything else about him. It was like knowing a secret and being the only one who knew.

'You seem to be coming home later and later these days,' she continued, quite unable to stop herself from chastising him even though it was not what she wanted at all, and knew it would only lead to the inevitable row.

'You didn't say you wanted me home early tonight. You weren't going out were you?' he said, still sounding conciliatory, which worried Marion even more. Tonight she wanted the comfort and security of a row.

'Do I have to ask you to come home early only when I'm going out?' she went on desperately, goading him but with no satisfaction. She did not want to be like this and despised herself for being unable to stop it. She knew she had never been clever with him and in a moment she would start using Paul as a weapon. Despicable and so predictable. She was too inadequate not to use their son as emotional blackmail.

'I'll just go up and see Paul,' Nick said, turning away from her.

'He's been alseep hours,' Marion shouted after him as he left the

kitchen. 'And I'd doubt whether he'd recognise you anyway.'
There. She'd done it now. He couldn't pass over that one. She was
frightened now. He had been in the wrong by coming home so late
but she had started the row and in so doing had made herself more
guilty than he.

Nick came back into the kitchen, but still he would not respond.
He went over to the oven and opened the door. Inside there was a
plate of dried up food which looked exactly the same as the meal
she had cooked the previous night and the night before that.
Unappetising. Unidentifiable. He had been losing weight lately
but not entirely due to Marion's cooking. After all, that had not
changed; nothing ever did with Marion, except maybe what there
was got worse.

He closed the oven door, leaving a fingerprint on the shiny
smoked-glass surface. The oven was new like everything else in the
kitchen, except Marion.

'Is there any cheese?' he asked, studying her back. He was losing
weight but she was putting it on. She looked grotesque in those
trousers. Horrible Crimplene things which showed every bulge.
He looked away, a great surge of guilt and distaste welling up in
his chest. He coughed.

'You can't expect me to start cooking when you get in,' she
remarked self-righteously.

'I didn't ask you to, I simply wanted to know if there was any
cheese in the house,' he retorted, suddenly losing his temper. He
had not wanted to, not any more, not now it was too late. He
wondered whether Marion knew this. He had been avoidng
watching her for weeks, at least it seemed like weeks but was
probably no more than a couple. The irony of the situation
suddenly struck him: he had done everything possible to prevent
Marion from knowing and yet he wished that she did. Oh, she had
by now undoubtedly guessed that something was going on, but
that was different to actually knowing, for sure. No words had
been spoken, but now they would have a row over the lateness of

his homecoming, the state of his meal, the lack of cheese, their sleeping son, anything but the real reason.

'Why don't you get yourself some new clothes?' he heard himself saying to her accusingly. 'Those trousers look awful. God knows what people must think.'

'God knows what they think about the time you come home,' she rounded on him. She knew the trousers were awful. She knew she looked awful in them, but her newer clothes did not fit any more and she did not have the heart to go out and buy more, a size larger. She meant to diet but was too miserable to motivate a determined effort. Her anger subsided into dejection and fear; she should never have let this begin. She sensed the dangerous ground she was treading.

'There's some cheese in the fridge. I bought some today,' she said quickly, trying desperately to steer away from the confrontation she had provoked. She was not ready for it and terrified that she never would be. Better to lie low and hope that everything would come right as it had before when she had suspected him of having an affair.

'It won't be worth eating if it's been in the fridge,' he declared, unwilling and unable to lose the initiative now he could see she was crumbling, an attitude which only served to heighten his irritation.

'I'm sorry,' Marion mumbled miserably. 'Really, I'm sorry.' She turned to face him. She would have liked to go to him and throw her arms about his neck. A reconciliation. But they were beyond that, and besides she had flour down the front of her jersey and Nick hated it if anything went on his clothes.

He had won again but his victory gave him no satisfaction. They stood facing one another for a brief moment which could not be sustained. It was too direct. They had to keep skirting round one another without looking. It was the only way to keep things going.

He went into the room which he called his study, and which Marion irritatingly insisted on referring to as his den. He closed the door gently, but firmly, shutting her out. He sat down in the wine-coloured leather chair which stood in front of the mahogany desk. Both pieces of furniture had been extravagantly expensive, but they were not the real thing he would have preferred. They were like him, he thought, a thin veneer of pretence covering the lack of authenticity. He experienced a shrivelling sensation somewhere deep inside and then he thought of Charlotte and felt better. She was authentic, plummy voice, the lot, and he had managed to fall in love with her. He allowed himself to dwell on this for a few minutes, thinking over the best moments, which surprisingly were not all sexual. He wanted Charlotte openly and not as a mistress. He had known this for some time but falling in love with her had complicated the issue. He had not expected it. Everything he had achieved in the last ten years had been without emotion: he had acted decisively, having discovered this to be rare in his rivals, who tended to accuse him of ruthlessness. Perhaps he was ruthless, but was that a bad thing? He had never really thought so but now he was no longer certain. Falling in love he was in danger of softening. He reflected on what had gone before; seeing his life in a different light, slightly rueful now that he could afford a degree of spiritual generosity.

He heard Marion going upstairs and the floorboards of their bedroom, which was above his study, creaked here and there as she moved about the room. He waited downstairs a further ten minutes and then went up himself. Their room was in semi-darkness but this night he did not turn on the main light to undress and hang his clothes. Marion had her back to him as he slipped out of his dressing gown and, naked because that was the way he always slept, got in beside her.

He lay on his back for a few minutes, realising almost immediately she was not asleep. America tomorrow, and they had not even mentioned his going. Away for a week. He did not like sleeping alone. He felt her stir. After all, it was Wednesday night and they always made love on Wednesday nights.

★

Again he picked up the phone by the bed but could not remember the sequence of the number. He dialled the code for the UK and continued what he thought was his home number but replaced the receiver almost immediately, doubting the sequence he had tried. Abandoning the impulse, he left the room and went downstairs to Germaine.

Marion, who had been sitting in front of a blank television screen (all channels having long since closed down for the night) biting the skin round her fingers, leapt up nervously when she heard the telephone ring – just once. She lifted the receiver all the same, but the connection wasn't there and hope subsided, leaving a nasty little vacuum.

CHAPTER ONE

Thursday morning – Charlotte

Half asleep, I felt Dan's kiss on my forehead, saw his dark shape move away from the bed, silently, as always, so as not to disturb me. He did not say anything. We never spoke at this time but communicated almost subconsciously, through this ritual of consideration and affection developed over countless mornings, always the same. Safe, secure and comfortable. The early morning before the rest of life began to intrude and destroy.

When he had gone I moved further down into the bed, relishing the warm comfort, savouring it for a little longer, but rolling over and pushing my head into the pillow to rub away the cold dampness of the kiss.

Fully awake now, I listened for the pattern of sounds that preceded Dan's going from the house. I listened as tensely as a burglar in a cupboard to the doors downstairs opening and closing and then his footsteps crunching into the gravel outside. The pattern never changed, but today I was fearful it might because for once it was necessary that it should not. You see, I suppose I had planned everything more than I care to admit. Dan falling down the stairs, his car not starting, such mishaps seemed much more likely to happen than was reasonably probable because somehow I expected to be thwarted. Even after the noise of the car had been swallowed down into the lane I listened to the silence, expecting any moment to hear a regurgitation of the engine sound. Poor, dear, Dan, to be the cause of this nervy heightened awareness as I set about deceiving him. He had done nothing to deserve it; he was never a jealous tyrant or in any way unkind, and I can say he was not to blame, and any sympathy must be for him. I have a horrid, compelling, selfish ruthlessness in the way I act when it most matters and all I can claim is honesty in the relating of how it was.

On Thursday morning, lying in bed, I did not know what was going to happen over the weekend. The plan, if I'm going to admit that there was one, extended only into Friday, before the compulsion to force a change, wreck the calm, make others unhappy, had fully taken over.

There is, after all, something desperately suffocating about certainty, and perhaps it was that more than Dan himself I was trying to escape. But I think I still believed on Thursday morning, lying in bed feeling wonderfully wicked and amazingly powerful, that all would yet be well with Dan and me.

When you are having an affair (oh dear, that word, it sounds so passé) the planning has to be careful and detailed, (unless, of course, you reach the stage of indecision where carelessness is deliberate). Snatched interludes of nothing in particular have probably been strategically plotted days in advance and whole nights require a major campaign.

There had been no whole nights with Nick, but that was the next stage and I suppose I had an instinctive feeling Thursday night would be the first. It was coincidence that Vicky should be spending this weekend with Audrey and James and their children and not out of the ordinary that I should be going to London to stay a night with Frances. Dan, as always, had acquiesced. If it made me feel better to go up to London every few weeks then it was a good thing. He would not have minded coming too but he didn't want to intrude, not unless he was asked, which, of course, he was not.

Frances had never really liked him. Frances, my oldest and dearest friend, going back years, to schooldays, an exclusive, critical friendship which has always allowed complete honesty without either of us having to worry about misunderstanding or disapproval.

'You've got to do something,' she said. 'You can't go on with things as they are. Dead and buried at twenty-eight.'

And so I had done something. I like to think it was not just because Frances prompted me, but it could have been.

'I suppose Dan will blame me for encouraging you,' she said when I told her, assuming – perhaps hoping for my sake – that he would find out.

'You don't mind, do you?' I had sounded apologetic but knew Frances did not mind at all and was probably pleased.

Frances, unmarried, career-minded and instinctively inclined to encourage 'doing something'. It wasn't that she actively disliked Dan. He wasn't the sort of person to have strong feelings about, she told me rather too incisively, in the early days of my marriage when it seemed terribly important to feel intensely.

'I may come to you on Thursday night, I may not, but if Dan telephones, I mean, I don't suppose he will as he never has before, but if he does and I'm not there . . .'

'If he does, I'll tell him you're in the bath. And who is this man? I want to meet him.'

'A man I work for. Nothing too serious. I don't want anybody to get hurt,' I said, wanting now to finish the call. Even to Frances I did not want to talk about Nick; I did not want to be like women I had met who relished the telling. And Frances would not pry, she never had.

I think then I did not want her to meet Nick. I was worried she would see all the things I had seen and disliked but which subsequently did not matter. With injustice to both of them I was afraid that Frances would instantly categorise Nick as a monied second-rater, clever in a non-intellectual way she would not admire, rough-edged but with a degree of trappings and pretentions to conceal it. It was because Frances and I had been friends for so long that I judged she would see Nick as I had in the beginning.

'Your husband tells me you dabble in graphics,' had been the first words I could remember him saying to me. Horrid man for using the word 'dabble', I had thought.

That was six months before this Thursday morning, the telephone call, indirectly emanating from Dan who evidently had told him that I was a graphic artist. How much Dan had said I was never quite sure, although I assumed his loyalty. It was unlikely he had told Nick how little work I had managed to find since setting up as a freelance after six years of being at home with Vicky. My old contacts, the studio in London I had been with before Vicky's birth, had suffered in the recession and could offer me nothing, not even encouragement, which was what I needed most. Working again was not so much a financial need as a means of regaining sanity and purpose, although I had a plan for the money – going to America for a month, maybe two, taking Dan and Vicky: it would be my achievement. Dan could afford to take us but that was beside the point.

So I could say it was my precarious state of mind that began the involvement with Nick. He offered me work.

'What sort of man is he?' I asked Dan the evening of the telephone call.

'Self-made and trying to hide it,' he said, sounding as if he meant to be accurate rather than give an opinion. 'He's got money, a nice car, he's just bought one of those vast new houses on the Old Rectory site. We did the conveyancing for him.'

'One of those nasty ones with neo-Georgian windows?' I had a tendency then to judge people by the sort of house they chose to live in, an absurd division into new house and old house types which amused Dan who did not really care about such things, having always lived in beautiful old houses as if they were his natural habitat and therefore finding nothing extraordinary or special about them apart from the fuel bills.

'They're not all that nasty,' he said.

'I think they're ghastly, especially as they caused the Rectory to be knocked down,' I went on, but railing more against Nicholas Matthews and his patronising 'dabble' than against the new houses.

'You didn't tell him that I dabbled in graphics – you didn't say it like that?' I asked, just to make sure. Dan gave me one of his long looks which said 'How could you doubt me?' The effect was almost theatrical. It was a mannerism that did not suit him and one which had become vaguely irritating.

It had been agreed that I should go to Nick's office in Cambridge on a Monday afternoon, early because of collecting Vicky from school, although I did not like saying that as it sounded unprofessional, and men never seemed to understand the importance of collecting a child from school at exactly the right time. Even Dan, in every other way so reliable, had a tendency to underestimate the length of an overdue five minutes to a child, but then he had been packed off to boarding school at seven. I knew the building where I had to go, remembered it as a blank-wall steel and concrete edifice, depressingly angular and somehow intimidating.

'I can't understand how people can work in a place like that, it's so uninspiring,' I had said, defensively, to Dan.

'They probably all live in new houses as well,' he had replied, gently mocking.

And I suppose that is how I set off on the Monday, defensive because I hadn't liked the sound of Nick on the telephone, worried about getting back in time for Vicky, and resentful over the meeting place because it was something solid on which to base my nervous fright. Pro-Publicity had a suite of offices on the second floor which contradicted the cold detachment of the building's exterior with over-plush decoration and furnishing. Nick's office, large and expensively tasteless, or so I thought in my defensive way that first meeting, was like a sort of operations room, a nerve centre with people rushing in and out looking determinedly purposeful. For half an hour I waited in the outer office, catching glimpses of a black leather sofa on a thick, cream-coloured carpet, a large, blackish picture on a white wall. I heard snatches of his voice but could not see him. I waited and worried and watched the time ebb away and because of all this and my dreadful lack of confidence at that period I became angry.

'Now,' he said when eventually I was allowed into the inner sanctum. It seemed that he expected me to take the initiative as if I had come to sell him something, which in a way I suppose I had. He was a big man in a gruff mood. (Later he told me he'd had toothache.) About forty, well dressed, slightly greying hair, uncompromising eyes and expression. A big, muscular man who looked out of place behind a desk. He did not smile or apologise for keeping me waiting, but stood up when I came in and asked me to sit down with a slightly unco-ordinated series of movements that emphasised a sort of awkwardness not uncommon in large people. And perhaps it was his size (not that he was a giant) which gave him an undeniable presence, overbearing I thought, even angry. I felt it at once, almost recoiling from the sensation he evoked, but then I'd had half an hour to work myself up into a state of hypersensitivity.

He was, I suppose now, rather frightening. I stared at him for a moment, determined to be indignant; put out because I was twenty-eight, a mother, married to a solicitor and, as much as I was lacking confidence at that moment, had allowed an insidious sense of status to influence the way in which I expected to be treated.

'Now,' he had said, and so we had to get on with it. He oozed impatient busyness, a man with no time to spare. I did not like him at all.

I told him the sort of work I did and showed him some examples, hoping he would not ask when I had done them, which was a long time ago. He didn't, but I had a feeling he knew all the same; that was another thing about him, he seemed to have that innate ability to perceive, watching with impatient but complete attention the whole time I was talking as if he was taking in a good deal more than the words.

When I had finished my bit he told me that the work he needed was a glossy brochure for oriental brassware: 'But if we like your work it could be an ongoing situation.'

Inwardly I winced, snobbish about buzz phrases. I thought him pompous. Behind his chair, on the windowsill, there was a photograph of a woman and a boy, obviously his wife and son. The boy looked serious, the woman pleasant but nothing special, and not the sort of person I would have imagined as his wife. Perhaps he was more human than he appeared, to have such a wife.

When he had finished explaining what he wanted, I heard myself start to mumble about not being sure how long it would take me and whether I was the right designer for the job. 'Am I mad,' I thought then, remembering how desperately I wanted the work. I think it is difficult for those who have never been through that awful lapse in confidence symptomatic of young mothers trying to get back where they were before, to understand the self-defeating hesitancy involved. It passes and is forgotten but at the time can feel near insurmountable.

Nick allowed a few moments of silence, an unnerving little trick I have since seen him use on others.

'Come on, you will have wasted your time and mine if you don't give it a try,' he said with a mixture of encouragement and mild exasperation which I considered unjustified as he had approached me in the first place. I still had it in my mind that he had called me 'a dabbler'.

'All right, I'll see what I can do,' I said, rather grudgingly.

'Good,' he said, as if he had never doubted that I would comply. 'It shouldn't take you too long. You're at home all day, aren't you?'

'Yes, at home all day with nothing else to do,' I added

sarcastically and then wondered what on earth I was saying, but the tone of the remark seemed to pass over him or he chose to ignore it.

'You'll let me have something in a couple of days then?' he went on.

I was about to say that I would, but stopped myself. It would be the end of the week. I had a lot of other work on. I think he knew I was lying.

'Friday then, if you can fit it into your busy schedule,' he said and for a moment I thought a smile flickered across his mouth.

It was then that I saw the time and leaping up like a scalded cat made a rush for the door, blurting out that I was late to collect my daughter from school.

'Here, telephone the school. Tell them you've been delayed,' he instructed with the sort of matter of fact good sense to make me feel an utter fool. Ignominiously I took the receiver from him and dialled the number. During this little scene he stood up to move away while I made the call and as he did so almost tripped over my folio which was lying on the floor by my feet. Automatically his hand shot forward and for an instant gripped the upper part of my arm. A sort of tingling shiver ran across my shoulders and for a split second our eyes reflected what I took to be mutual distaste.

For the next three days I struggled with the oriental brassware, rejecting one idea after the other, the shadow of Nicholas Matthews' doubtlessly high standards looming over the scattered sheets of paper. I was impatient with Vicky, telling her to go and watch television at a time when I would normally listen to her talk about school. By midnight on Thursday I felt that I had put together a reasonable design and was feeling quite pleased with myself. The following morning I took Vicky to school and went straight to Pro's offices.

'You managed to fit it in then,' he said as I took out my design and carefully laid it on the desk. It was no good, he told me, the concept was wrong. Better try again. But I had spent all week on it. He was surprised. He thought maybe I'd had to rush it with all the other work I had on. My eyes flickered round the room and fixed on the photograph on the windowsill. 'Poor, pleasant-looking woman,' I thought aggressively, but couldn't think of anything to say. The best form of defence was attack, Dan the lawyer had told me on more than one occasion, but I could not remember him ever using it himself and felt all the more aggrieved for being so ill-equipped to argue.

'How did you get on this morning?' Dan asked me that evening, unleashing the tirade of abuse I'd been bottling up all day.

'Why ever did you have to tell him about me in the first place?' I rounded on him. 'He threw out my design, said I had better try again, he's such a rude man, I just hate him, and he's nothing, a jumped-up nobody. He uses those awful phrases like "ongoing situation" and "at this moment in time" – the sort of stuff trade union officials use on the news. He's a Trog, Dan, an out and out thoroughgoing Trog.'

'You don't like him,' Dan observed calmly. 'Poor old Trog Matthews.'

I knew I was being disgracefully snobbish but it was the only sop left to my shattered ego. Trog had been the word used at Dan's school for the people who actually ran the place, cleaners, cooks and caretakers and the clever masters whose accents gave away their lowly origins. Such people, no matter how clever, would always be Trogs. A nasty, snobbish word, and one of the few aspects of Dan's expensive education I had always felt to be unworthy and demeaning. God, what a hypocrite I was after all and it had taken Nicholas Matthews less than a week to expose it in me.

'You're more pedantic about language than I am,' I said with unreasonable hostility. Poor Dan, for months he had had to put up with my bad temper which had grown out of a miserable despair I felt I bore alone, but which was almost certainly shared by a considerable proportion of my female contemporaries. There we were, isolated in our comfortable labour-saving homes, women who had grown up to get married and have children, and now that we had done all that were suddenly faced with the awful dilemma of choice. But whichever choice we made would be double-edged: stay at home and we did not do ourselves justice, go back to work and wear ourselves out worrying about slipping standards at home. The boring, familiar and poignant dilemma of my generation.

'So you have to do the work again,' Dan said.

'I don't see why I should,' I said.

'You can't let it defeat you,' he said.

'I wish I could,' I pleaded, as if Dan could give me exemption. 'I've a feeling that Trog Matthews is always going to be hard to please.' We left it at that and sat down in front of the television to eat our supper. We saw the news but then failed to find any other programme we could bear to watch, which was unusual for Dan. He was addicted to television and I preferred it to be on even if I was not watching; the room tended to feel dull without it. I took the dirty plates, my own still piled with food, out to the kitchen, and then went into the breakfast room. My drawing board, even with the discarded designs scattered over it, had a bleak, unyielding air about it. I sat down and began again. I eventually went to bed at half past three.

So you see, the beginning of it all was not so good, although perhaps you can understand how a feeling as strong as hatred might turn into something else. After all, there are not many people you meet who engender passion of any kind.

The beginning, as I told you, was six months before the Thursday morning I lay in bed pondering the mechanical details of my illicit plan.

Nick had telephoned me three times while he was in America, that was three times in seven days, enough to make me think, which for the preceding few weeks I had deliberately avoided allowing. It may sound odd, but during those weeks I'd felt at peace with Dan, as if it had become possible to drift over the deep-rooted sense of inadequacy in our relationship. We had always been friends, which is more than can be said of many marriages, and suddenly that was enough. It did not occur to me then that I might be one of those women who need a husband and a lover – I would have considered myself too honest and I really think the notion would have appalled me. So I was in a subconscious quandary and with a total lack of my professed honesty, had succeeded in postponing the issue. Quite simply I had stopped looking to the future and without really trying had achieved the best possible situation of living in a gloriously exciting present. And here I will be shamefully honest again in saying that there is hardly anything more invigorating than simultaneous love from two sources. I glowed in the way that some women do when newly pregnant, and was filled with a sense of wellbeing and new-found confidence. People said I looked marvellous, younger, thinner. Audrey asked if I had started taking vitamin tablets.

I had not, but how could your psyche make your hair shine?

I got out of bed on the Thursday morning, arched my back in a languorous stretch, pushed my toes into the skeepskin rug. Every sensation seemed pleasurable. I felt no guilt then, I was still in the present. I poured myself a Fenjal bath, and lay in the hot scented water, for once enjoying the silent loneliness of the house; and if there was any sense of justification for what I planned it was that opportunities should not be lost, and it was my turn, before it was too late.

After the bath I dressed carefully, although the clothes, apart from a more presentable set of underwear I had bought, were quite old. To have bought new clothes would have been too precipitate, too much a denial of what I was, and besides would have meant spending Dan's money.

I went downstairs to the kitchen and opened and closed the refrigerator. Breakfast was not only unnecessary but impossible. I went over to the window and stared out across the well-kept garden. It looked good and fresh with the dew still sparkling on the grass. It was a pleasure to look at because it was my mowing and weeding that had made it as it was. But part of me mistrusted it and remembered the lonely despair that had often preceded a sudden spurt of manic digging or pruning. The garden had been an outlet but also part of the trap, and wasn't gardening a middle-aged activity?

Beyond the lawn and flower beds there was a small field and I could just see the ridge of the donkey's back – Vicky's donkey, Tamara. Her head would be bent down to the grass, obliviously breakfasting. That was what mattered to Tamara. The idyllic setting in which she passed her days was of no matter, or so it seemed, although she was a continual enigma to me. I watched her sometimes and felt that she was watching me, and had the strange feeling she knew more of me than I of her.

Turning my back on those old daydreams I glanced round the still surfaces of my expensive kitchen, feeling oddly detached from it all now.

CHAPTER TWO

Thursday Afternoon – Nick

Charlotte was standing in front of a huge purple canvas which said nothing to me but seemed to please her in some obscure way; but then she saw the picture while I watched her – deliberately eccentric in her clashing colours, vast striped skirt which looked a couple of sizes too large and billowed as she walked, dreadful canvas espadrilles. And yet she got away with it, like the weird pictures in the gallery: twentieth-century art getting away with it at the Tate, not seeking approval but demanding a place as of right.

To have gone straight back to Cambridge, the office, home to Marion, jet-lagged as indeed I was, would have been beyond endurance; things had gone too well in California to descend to that so soon. I had asked Charlotte to be at the airport, almost bullied her into it, but the sight of her, bizarre and beautiful, produced surprise, not at her being there, but at the hedonistic sensation of seeing her. It was more than I had imagined.

The airport was crowded, people rushing together after long, maybe only short, separations, clinging to one another, hugging and kissing, cumbersome cases between them to accentuate the awkwardness of reunion.

Charlotte and I saw each other and took it slowly, carefully avoiding touching one another as if the illegitimacy of our relationship made it unseemly in such a public place to behave like everyone else. Stilted greetings were exchanged. 'Hello there,' I think she said in her BBC announcer's voice, 'Hello there, how jolly nice to see you,' she might have extended it. And in the same way I had spoken to her, lifting the quality of my speech as I always did with her.

It was a trick I had used for years; back in the days of journalism I'd drop a few consonants to encourage a candid interview with the hoi polloi, and put them back with emphasis to question the people who mattered. It had worked well, the chameleon tongue, and if there was something vaguely despicable about it, what did that matter if the results were achieved? And besides I had never seen any value in the 'I am what I am' approach, lowly origins shoved down people's throats with aggressive defiance and pride. I looked at it from that end of the spectrum because I knew what I had been and preferred to forget it. The trick had become second nature but Charlotte was the first person who, it had occurred to me, might not be fooled, and it had never greatly mattered before.

So I stood before her, ya ya-ing, on my guard against a slip of the old tongue, lifted, excited, entranced by what she did to me. Charlotte was 'class' I would have said at one time when the chasm between 'them' and 'us' had seemed greater. Now she was the embodiment of what I felt was my due, but standing there, in her crazy colours, a barely perceptible tremble in her jaw, the rhubarb voices all around us fading from existence, my temples buzzed, my hands felt clammy and my heart thumped out of phase. Or so it seemed in those first few moments of inane discourse while we each talked but didn't really hear the words the other spoke, only the sound of the voice as part of the whole presence.

A flash of white light cut between us and I swung round knocking my arm against something hard. It was a camera, still held poised between the photographer's hands. It clattered to the ground and the three of us stared down at it in dismay and then the picture-taker and I both began to talk at the same time: what did he think he was doing? what the hell did I think I was doing, smashing his camera? Why did he take our picture? Charlotte wanted to know. He thought she was someone else – well known, didn't he, and anyway why did we have to smash his camera, damn us to hell.

'Come on,' I said to Charlotte, moving close and taking her arm, steering her away. On the way out I saw a woman who looked like Marion. I thought it was her at first and instinctively quickened our pace. Guilty, furtive, jumpy, smashing cameras, hiding from my wife, I stopped short in the glass showcase created by the two sets of exit doors, dropped my bag, swung Charlotte into my arms and kissed her with enough force, passion and lust to make a picture worthwhile and the rhubarb people gawp and sigh.

'That was nice,' Charlotte said as we got into a taxi.

'Over the top, I'm sorry,' I murmured. 'I feel like a kid, you know, all this sudden lust.'

'I rather like it. It's so unexpected from you – the big businessman. You look so, I don't know, removed from that kind of thing in those clothes – with your briefcase.'

'You are funny, weird and funny,' I said, wanting to touch her again.

'Do you have to go back this afternoon?' I asked a few moments later.

'Not particularly.'

'Right, let's go somewhere.'

'London. I love London. Tea at Fortnum and Mason's and we could go to the Tate. There's an exhibition. I thought I wouldn't get to it.'

I had never been to the Tate before, never even thought of it. Art galleries were places you either grew up with or knew nothing about, kept beyond the bounds of comprehension through ignorance and prejudice by parents who felt threatened by anything more highbrow than a bingo hall. But that was no excuse, if excuse there had to be; it was just that there was never any time, not until someone like Charlotte came along and wanted to spend an afternoon looking at pictures. Then there was no question but that it should be done. Nothing else, apart from taking her to bed, was more desirable.

I glanced at the picture next to the purple mass and rather liked it. There was no meaning to be seen in it, none that I could fathom, but it was pleasing in an inexplicable way, maybe simply because it was part of the ambience of a place which belonged to Charlotte. And the time didn't feel wasted, not as it would in other circumstances. There was a sense of investment in the future, it was like watching the trailer to a film you intended seeing in its entirety.

That I had come to this point, of wanting the whole and not just the part that had dominated every other affair, gave an illogical twist to that sense of investment, as the sort of future I envisaged with Charlotte would mean divorce and all the awfulness that went with it: a financial mess that would probably drag on for months, years. The new house I would have to leave, Marion would have to be provided for, and I would lose my son. The ramifications of an afternoon spent in the Tate were colossal. But if I was aware of all this that afternoon the actuality was sufficiently remote and the moment too sanguine; the high-pitched optimism that accompanies being with the one particular person had put aside the other considerations.

How do you describe that feeling which, I suppose, is termed falling in love? It's akin to success, heady and colourful, it's there inside, energising, heightening awareness; the essence of being so that you wonder at how the black and white days that preceded could have been endured. But having realised it and accepted, I felt impatient to get on with it. I wanted to act and consolidate, to secure Charlotte and get on with the rest of life with her as a part of it. My success in California would produce new accounts. Pro-Publicity had to expand further.

This I told Charlotte in the penthouse flat above Pro's London suite as we lay in bed after tea at Fortnum & Mason. It was the first

34

time I had taken her to the flat. I had not even told her of its existence until that afternoon, deliberately, because maybe I had known early on that it was going to be different and had not wanted to risk attracting her with the trappings, which was probably unfair, but human enough.

'You never told me about all this,' she said.

'I didn't want you to run off with me for my view of London,' I said. From the bed you could see clear across to the other side of the Thames.

'You thought I might be a gold digger?'

'That's right.'

'Well I am, you know, and who said anything about running off together?'

'I did,' I said, watching her.

'Oh Nick. It's not that easy, is it?' she asked, as if I could reassure her that it was.

'No.'

'Well let's not talk about it, please,' she implored, climbing out of the bed and going over to the wall of smoked glass that divided us from the rush and buzz of the city far below.

'It's so peaceful up here. I feel more at ease than I do at home. Sort of tranquil inside. Serene you might say,' she said, stretching as if it was early morning.

'I think we must. Talk about, I mean.'

'Not now, Nick. Not at this moment. No intrusions.' She turned and came back to the bed.

'How many other women have you brought up here?' she asked with superficial lasciviousness.

'Oh, fifty or sixty. I thought you said no intrusions.'

'Is that all!'

'Give or take a few.'

'I bet there have been hundreds.'

'Probably. Does that bother you?'

'Nope.'

'Stay tonight,' I said.

'Yes. I'll stay,' she said, as I reached for her hand. 'Nick, you're going to have to decide things. I don't think I can. I didn't expect this to happen.'

Neither had I, not in the very beginning. Nothing could have been more unlikely.

There had been other affairs, most of them brief, sordid little liaisons which had started more by accident than design and then quickly degenerated into tedious sessions of guilt and recrimination. A couple of them had been Marion's friends, bored housewives at parties, full of booze or bravado, until the next time when they would start being silly, making demands, disappointing and predictable.

Sometimes I felt that Marion knew and I would despise her for saying nothing but when it was over there would be a period when the tranquillity of our home had renewed appeal. Marion had never been a demanding woman, she wanted little out of life other than a home of her own, and all day to be in it. Charlotte seemed to want neither.

I had not intended dealing with her myself that first morning when she came to Pro's offices in Cambridge. I was spending more and more time in London and it was only by chance that I happened to be there, but Charlotte had my name and insisted that her appointment was with me. She strode into my office, nervous and vaguely belligerent to counteract it, one of those arty crafty women, I thought, who parade originality with an inverted chic consisting of clothes bought from jumble sales, ethnic jewellery and plain speaking. I had begun to wonder why she had bothered to come at all as she appeared to have made up her mind to turn down the work before knowing anything about it. And then she had come back with a good design but totally the wrong one for the job, arrogantly ignoring the brief I had given her because she thought she knew better.

Why I saw her again myself, the second and the third time, even semi-subconsciously making a point of being in Cambridge the day she was due to come, made little sense to me then. If I had thought about it there was the likelihood she would not turn up the third time: she obviously did not like it when I caught her out over the lie about the amount of work she had and she could not need the money, married to a solicitor. But such supposition would have judged her wrongly, and even though I expected to see her again felt an odd sense of relief when she arrived with the revised design.

She was wearing a faded pair of jeans this time, and a ridiculous T shirt with a big smiling sun printed on it, although her own expression was wary and hostile as she undid her folio and took out the drawings.

I studied them for a few minutes but could see at once that they were right.

'This is more like it,' I said in a way that would irritate her. 'In fact, quite good,' I added, glancing up at her. I was surprised to see that her expression had changed to one of open relief, although she quickly recovered herself, adopting an insolent look of disdain.

'I think the first design was better,' she said.

My initial impulse was to ignore her, we had already been through all that, but her attitude was beginning to annoy me. It had been vaguely amusing at first but she was carrying it too far.

'It seems that I can't win,' I said.

'I beg your pardon?' she said, as if she had misheard me.

'I think you know what I mean,' I said.

I carried on looking at her, wondering why I was bothering to make something of her manner. Talented graphic designers were not that hard to find.

She stared back at me and for a moment I thought she was going to get up and leave; and then a curious little smile crossed her face and she said: 'Do you always have to be the winner?'

Still we looked at one another and smiling a little myself I said: 'But of course!'

The moment kept coming back to me for the rest of the day. I could not get it out of my mind, the slightly uneven curve of her mouth when she had smiled, the glint of recognition in her eyes.

And so we began to play the game, with semi-subliminal tactics not admitted, even to ourselves, I think, not until later when the time came that we wanted endlessly to talk about, and dissect, every little manoeuvre and how we had felt at the time, the uncertainties, were there any? Had that been possible? The naive relief of love made us childlike in mutual wonderment at what had happened to us, to two such unlikely people, but then those of us who have thought it impossible to experience such emotions fall hardest, as they say. We're taken by surprise by our own depths of feeling and part of the euphoria is in relishing the unlikelihood of it all.

Yet we do things which are contrary to our desires, even in the beginning, before the game has really started, because that is the way it is played. The next time Charlotte came to the office I did not see her but asked Piers to instead.

'What a dreadful woman,' he said to me the following day, 'but talented.'

'The talented ones are always difficult. They're the only ones that can get away with it,' I told him somewhat pointedly.

Piers Whitton-Howard was of the same mould. Insufferable a good deal of the time, he was none the less an asset to Pro and as such I put up with his supercilious arrogance, or at least managed to ignore it most of the time.

Piers wore his old school tie like an open challenge. I had employed him to widen Pro's range of accounts and to look after things when I was abroad. He had brought with him a big fat juicy account with a food manufacturer who produced a world-famous marmalade. Piers wanted partnership in Pro and had tried to use the Morgan-Mackie account as his lever. The fact that he had failed rankled deeply and he seldom missed an opportunity to accentuate the difference in our backgrounds. He would invite me to have dinner with him at his London club and go into long deliberations over the choice of wine, slyly asking my opinion in the hope of exposing the ignorance he assumed. Basically he resented me and the position of power I had over him. No family background worth mentioning. No birthright connections. No old school tie. All unforgivable because I had made money while the Whitton-Howards, now reduced to genteel poverty, had to earn theirs from the likes of me.

The Whitton-Howards of this world have always seemed like fair game to me, to be cultivated for their usefulness; or maybe it's just that ultimately chips on shoulders are as hard to remove as silver spoons. And so Piers and I resented one another and fought a constant battle beneath a veneer of civility and wit, although I think I enjoyed it more than he. I pandered to his vanity because it was amusing to do so, and he performed better puffed up. Occasionally he still angled towards the partnership question but I had ousted him from the marmalade account and he knew that had weakened his position. Without MM Foods – an account worth £200,000 a year – he could no longer dangle the threat of leaving Pro and starting his own rival firm.

Taking on the MM account myself had meant still longer hours working. I had tried to discuss the problem with Marion who would listen without really hearing, having closed her mind to the possibility of understanding anything to do with Pro. Inevitably she would merely complain that I spent less and less time at home as it was and another account could only make things worse.

It also made it a bad time to begin another affair which, by their nature, take up time which cannot be combined with doing anything else, although Charlotte continued working for me and this provided an easy alibi for both of us.

Dreadful and talented, she continued to argue about the work. Proud Charlotte, a pedigree person full of potential, and like Piers, somehow thwarted. It had given me a peculiar sense of power and retribution to employ him. Retribution for exactly what – the silver spoon syndrome, the sickening perpetuation of the accident of birth – it was after all hard to identify without admitting to the sort of foolish defensive prejudice I thought I had overcome. It was harder still to recognise the same motive in wanting Charlotte. Even now I can say that she is not really beautiful and that initially I did not find her attractive in that way. She was, as Piers confirmed, initially quite dreadful.

Spasmodic at first, our meetings then became regular and longer although they seemed shorter and shorter, filled with agile conversation which quickly widened beyond business. What we talked about I can hardly remember, only the quality of our comprehension, surprising and intoxicating.

But it was not enough.

One day in early August I had taken her to a pub for lunch. It was in one of the villages outside Cambridge, a low-ceilinged beamy old place with an unhurried atmosphere. I had chosen it deliberately because of its remoteness, as if discretion was already necessary, but by chance, or so it seemed, Piers turned up and joined us.

At first he had appeared mildly taken aback to find me lunching with Charlotte. He was polite and charming, but a touch wary as if remembering his pronouncement to me about her. But Charlotte, no longer so defensive about her ability, had long since shed her dreadfulness. The two of them, discovering that neither was as uncomfortable as they had thought, launched into a discussion about shooting – Piers' sport and apparently that of Charlotte's husband. Both had shot grouse in the Highlands the previous season, it transpired, and surely they had met? And did Mr Charlotte know so and so, yes, and Piers the Smuthers-Carruthers? And so on and so on. They verbally cavorted over shared acquaintances, ridiculously amazed at the smallness of their world – the exclusive world of the endangered species; and I listened and felt excluded and derisive and jealous.

'I thought you were in London this afternoon,' I interrupted to Piers in a way that suggested he should be. 'Perhaps you should shoot off,' I added, somewhat too acidly.

He and Charlotte looked at me in surprise, as if they had momentarily forgotten I was there. Both seemed slightly embarrassed, even a little put out. A pair of startled thoroughbreds. Piers quickly recovered.

'I'm on my way. I'm on my way!' he said, leaping up and backing off with exaggerated haste.

When he had gone Charlotte and I sat in silence, she fiddling with her empty glass, running her fingers up and down the stem. I felt angry with her, with Piers, with myself. I could feel a bearlike mood coming on and felt inclined to indulge it.

'We'd better go then,' I said, standing up. 'You'll be late collecting your daughter from school.'

She followed me outside. The sun was still hot and blindingly bright.

'I don't have to collect her today, she's going to tea with a friend,' Charlotte mumbled, brushing past me.

'Where are you going?' I called after her.

She stopped and spun round.

'The car's over here,' I said.

'I forgot I hadn't brought my own,' she said crossly.

'What's the matter with you?' I asked.

'Nothing.'

'Yes there is.'

'Well if you really want to know, I thought you were rather rude just now.'

We were standing about ten feet apart in the empty car park, glaring at one another.

'I thought you were bloody rude actually,' I said, trying to control my anger. Who the hell did she think she was with her assumption of the right to criticise?

We carried on glaring. It seemed that neither of us could think of anything sufficiently virulent to say next.

She spoke first.

'This is stupid,' she said, flinging her arms out in exasperation. 'I mean, why, what's the point? What do you want?'

I could feel the sun burning on the back of my neck. I felt incredibly angry with her still.

'I'll give you one guess,' I said, feeling my chest tighten. 'And it is stupid.'

Neither of us mentioned the fact that we were not driving back into Cambridge. We had gone to the car still enraged with one another but with a tacit understanding that things had moved on. We drove further into the countryside, passing fields full of ripe crops, golden and bristling in the heat of the sun. We stopped in a field entrance and got out of the car. We climbed over the stile into a grassy meadow. Still we said little, as if to talk now might lead us to reconsider what was in our minds. When we reached the far side of the meadow Charlotte halted and turned to look back the way we had come as if to make sure nobody had seen or followed. I put my hand on her shoulder and bent my head to kiss her. The sweet excitement coursed between us. We moved on and found a shady patch of grass under a solitary elm. Next to it was an old plough, rusty and embedded in the ground, cow parsley springing up between its shafts.

Charlotte sat down. The setting was hers in her flouncy skirt and bare legs, the diluted sunlight filtering through the leaves of the elm and flickering in her hair. That's how I picture her, anyway, when I think back, although it could be that I have built up the picture since to suit the memory. I remember feeling out of place in my well-pressed suit and Gucci shoes. I think I was more awkward than I care even to remember. I sat down beside her and somehow we bridged the awkward gap. We needed to be serious and engrossed and we were, although I remember more acutely the physical sensation of wanting her. But the grass was not the soft inviting bed it appeared to be. It was coarse and spiky and uncomfortable and distracting.

'What is it?' Charlotte asked, when I paused in mid-grapple.

'This is ridiculous,' I said, quite irritably. 'We're not a couple of kids.'

'I thought it was what you wanted,' she said. A smile came to her lips and she added, 'A roll in the hay.' It seemed that suddenly she found the situation amusing.

'Stop it,' I said, but I couldn't help smiling myself.

We looked at one another and laughed in relief.

'Back to nature?' I said.

'Yes, if you like,' she laughed again. 'It seemed nice here, less sordid than a bed in a hotel, or the back of a car.'

'Somehow it seems more natural to use hotels these days,' I said.

'I suppose so, but I still prefer a field in the sun.'

'You speak from experience?'

'Maybe.'

Charlotte was still sitting under the tree, her knees drawn up and her arms clasped round them. She glanced up at me and then looked away, half smiling in that peculiarly individual way of hers, the line of her mouth slightly uneven.

And so it happened the first time with Charlotte in a field. It was uncomfortable and probably undignified, half-clothed in the coarse grass, the sense of exposure making me take her with urgency and force. But that afternoon, only a couple of weeks before I went to America, did not really change anything, only speeded up what was already happening. Perhaps it would run its course and finish, like most affairs, in regret and ultimately cold detachment. There was no way of knowing, although it felt different. Urgent and necessary. Charlotte seemed filled with a bright, carefree energy. Everything delighted her, from driving the Jaguar (which she did at great speed, listening to opera) to looking at pictures in the Tate.

'Shall we go now?' she had said, taking my arm.

'But we haven't seen everything,' I pointed out, as if I really wanted to spend any more time in the gallery.

'No. It's better to look at only a few paintings otherwise they become a blur. Sometimes I've come here to look at just one picture.'

'How did you avoid seeing the others?' I asked, gently facetious.

'You think I'm mad, don't you, but it would be like spoiling a good meal by eating too much,' she explained earnestly.

'It's all right Charlotte, I think I know what you mean,' I assured her.

Tea at Fortnum and Mason – the same place I took Germaine when she came to London. Charlotte and I sat either side of one of the green marble tables in the Fountain Room. I soaked up her presence and we told one another about the places we had been and people we knew and mourned the fact that neither could be shared, revelling in the poignancy of it all. I was enjoying being in love with her, experiencing the intensity of such feeling. It was a bonus in life I was grateful not to have missed. But there it was, I saw it as an interlude and not something that could just run on indefinitely in its present form. There was the rest of life, and tomorrow, in just a few hours, it would be more pressing, more important than the luxurious intensity of today. That I wanted it to move on and into a different form was more clear when I took Charlotte to the penthouse flat and started to think about the future.

'Are you under suspicion?' I asked her as she lay beside me in bed.

'You mean from Dan?' she said. 'Maybe, although there's no reason for him to suspect.'

'People talk.'

'But nobody knows. Only Frances, and she wouldn't say anything.'

'They talk even more when they don't know but merely suspect. They do it to see whether they are right. People have seen us together – Piers, and there must have been others.'

'What about your wife?'

'I think she knows,' I said.

'But she can't,' she protested. 'We've never even met.'

'Oh I'm not saying that she knows it's you, only that she suspects an affair.'

'Isn't it funny,' she said next, 'but I've never really thought of it as an affair. Affair sounds so, over the top. Serious. Other people have affairs.'

'So what are we doing?' I said, deliberately losing patience to provoke her. 'Conducting an intellectual boxing match with time out for a quick poke now and then?'

'That's nasty. Why do you have to be nasty?'

'Because you exasperate me, Charlotte. You don't know what you want.'

'I suppose I don't,' she agreed. 'But is it strictly necessary to know what one wants all the time?'

'Yes, I think it is,' I said, 'there are too many people who don't know what they want.'

'But you haven't said either,' she said. 'You haven't really decided, have you Nick? Wanting and doing, there's the difference.'

CHAPTER THREE

Thursday evening – Frances

Venice – the Doge's Palace, St Mark's Square – I could almost feel
the warm stone and smell the air. Indulging the sensation, I sipped
the ice-cold Frascati, sunk further into my new Italian sofa and
allowed Vivaldi's *Four Seasons* to continue the illusion. And then
the telephone rang, the Venetian palazzi crumbled away and my
elbow sent the wineglass skidding across the room.

Shit, I heard myself say and as always felt somewhat stupid
swearing into an empty room, swearing at all. I picked up the
phone and recognising Dan's voice suddenly remembered it was
Charlotte's alibi night.

'Dan! How nice, just a minute, let me turn down the music.'
Having not expected the call to come I was completely
unprepared for it and after the brief conversation decided that Dan
had probably known none of it was true but had played his part just
as I had mine. The 'in the bath' bit had sounded rather thin but I felt
it unlikely he would call back and earnestly hoped not. Dan and I
had never really got on but I didn't particularly want to have to tell
him lies in finding answers to the sort of questions he might ask in a
second call. I didn't want to become involved in the Dan end of it.
It's always difficult when friends' marriages break up, as
Charlotte's surely would and should, although at one time I had
come to accept that maybe they did suit one another after all;

Charlotte's taste for drama, Dan's hearty dullness, the one balancing the other.

It had, though, been a delightful relief to find that Charlotte had not changed in spite of the years of uneventful married life. It was just as if she had been in hibernation for a time and then re-emerged with the old characteristics and personality which had made me want her as 'best friend' in our first term together at school.

Charlotte had been the first girl in the class to have a crush on one of the more senior girls. The first to say she was in love with a boy.

At the beginning of that first term we had been rivals. We had formed our separate opposing camps in the class, the serious and the stupid. Mine was the serious group, seen as stupid, of course, by Charlotte's gang, who were just as serious about being stupid: anyone could be serious but it took brains to be cleverly stupid. In fact neither camp achieved anything very impressive as far as the rest of the school was concerned and by the end of the term Charlotte and I had ditched our respective followers and formed our own exclusive alliance.

Together we went through all the intense phases of growing up, although I think Charlotte maybe suffered more, felt more, as even then I suppose I was already becoming a spectator in life.

We joined the Girl Guides so that we could go camping together and spent the best week of our lives tying endless knots, standing on parade in a field full of cow pats, our badges gleaming, our fingers black with Brasso. We cooked sausages and sang unintelligible Maori songs round the campfire. It rained every night and our tent leaked but the dampness added a wonderful pioneering mustiness to the smell of being under canvas. At dawn we went deer-stalking through stinging nettles but the discomfort and pain made it all the more worthwhile.

We counted the days and weeks in our blue diaries until the next camp but it was all quite different. We had both grown a lot during the intervening term and as the tallest girls in the company were allocated latrine duty. But we did not really mind and lumped the heavy metal containers across to a far corner of the field with a sense of stoical martyrdom which set us apart from the other girls, who treated us with a curious mixture of envy and respect. It seemed we could make anything desirable; that was our secret, and the latrine duty paid off handsomely when halfway through the week a group of Boy Scouts pitched camp in the adjoining field.

Captain, whose withered arm had made her hostile to men, immediately decreed that the piece of ground between the latrines and the far corner where Charlotte and I had to lump, was out of bounds to the rest of the company. The effect was to make the Scout camp, which otherwise would have been a matter of indifference to the Guides, a source of great interest and speculation.

Charlotte and I never caught more than a glimpse of the boys but were fiercely questioned by the others each time we came back from the far corner.

The boys, who were Rovers, seemed old to be Scouts and our overactive imaginations created an aura of sinister intrigue around their presence.

'I think they are undergoing special training. Probably something to do with the Foreign Office,' Charlotte told the girls who shared our tent. Her father sometimes visited the Foreign Office, she revealed, but instinctively we didn't ask why or what went on there. Nobody wanted to risk spoiling the thrilling mystery laid before us. We listened with awe, faces white and wide-eyed in Charlotte's torchlight.

'We mustn't tell anyone. They're probably training to be spies in Her Majesty's Secret Service,' she went on. We had a strong sense of honour to Queen and Country. The Guide promise, recited through trembling lips in front of the District Commissioner, had moved us deeply.

That was our last camp and the spies in the next field were soon forgotten. Boys took on a new fascination which dawned uncomprehendingly when the school started to build a new gymnasium. We found ourselves drawn to the makeshift wire fencing which surrounded the building site. Charlotte and I would go there at break, along with half the school, hanging about, feigning disinterest but within sight of the muscular labourers. But, like Captain, the headmistress (Reverend Mother as the school was a convent) quickly made an out of bounds rule to restore order and dignity.

If nature had confined me to conformity, in Charlotte it stirred rebellion and she then embarked upon the pattern of behaviour which was eventually to cause her expulsion from the school.

She discovered a route behind the tennis courts which, although it meant making a hole in the hedge, led round to the far side of the building site. I refused to go with her but felt an odd combination of disapproval and admiration as I kept watch by the hole. I couldn't really understand Charlotte's determination to break the rule. It seemed an unnecessary risk, even silly, and yet I envied her spirit and the sense of loyalty inspired by the cave-duty filled me with an emotional tingle. I was also aware of a new superiority in refusing to join Charlotte in this foolish adventure but thrilled none the less, as if by proxy. Added to all this was the sensation of what she was about being vaguely unwholesome, although I can see now it was not so much the force of nature but more the rebel without a cause, and understood by Charlotte no more than it was by me.

'What was it like?' I asked her, in a semi-interested, ungenerous tone, when she reappeared at the other side of the hole.

'Deva!' she said breathlessly, seeming not to notice the attitude I had attempted to adopt. Most things were 'deva' that term. It was our word, short for devastating.

'Really?' I said, forgetting my stance of indifference.

'Honestly. There was this man, he came over to speak to me. He was just dreamy, Fran, dreamy,' she said as I picked the twigs and leaves off her navy cardigan.

'What did he say to you then?' I asked, trying to regain a certain air of disapproval.

'Well, I couldn't understand everything he said. I think he was foreign. He kept calling me Colleen.'

'You didn't tell him your real name, did you?' I enquired anxiously, foreseeing the possible danger of being found out.

'No, I thought I'd keep him guessing,' she replied in an offhand manner and then, as if she had been saving the best bit, added in the same tone: 'He's asked me to meet him tonight.'

'You're not going to, are you?' I said, dismay preventing me from sounding as impressed as perhaps I might.

'Why not?' Charlotte demanded tetchily.

'I just don't think you should,' I retorted with an innate sense of what was proper and what was not.

'Well I haven't made up my mind yet,' she wavered.

We walked back past the tennis courts to where the rest of the school was taking its break.

'Why is virginity so important to men?' Charlotte asked abruptly as we went into the cloakroom.

'I don't know,' I said, trying to sound equally matter of fact but chilled by what might lie behind the question. 'All men want to marry virgins, I know that.'

'But what happens to the girls that aren't and how do men know, I mean, you could have an accident or something, you know, slip on a fence or playing hockey.' The notion seemed to trouble her.

'I don't think that would count.'

'Are you sure?'

'Oh, I don't know Charlotte, really I don't. Why do you want to know?' I had to ask, fearful that something terrible had taken place beyond the hole in the hedge.

'The man asked me if I was a virgin,' she answered simply.

My blood ran cold.

'He sounds horrid, this man. Rude and horrid. You won't go tonight, will you?' I pleaded.

'I suppose not,' she conceded, adding, as if to retrieve a little of the romance in the exploit, 'although being a foreigner he perhaps didn't know quite what he was saying.'

Instinctively I felt that he had, but said no more. Charlotte, however, needed further to satisfy herself that meeting the man would be a mistake: 'They do tend to be vulgar, foreigners, but I suppose it's not their fault. It's the way they're brought up, belching after dinner and that sort of thing.'

Fairly confident that Charlotte would not keep to the assignation I thought no more about it until the following day when Reverend Mother told everyone to remain in the hall after morning assembly as she had a serious question to ask the school. It had come to her notice that the hedge behind the tennis courts had been badly damaged and if any of the girls were responsible she asked them to obey their consciences and own up.

The hall went dreadfully silent. Everyone's eyes were on Reverend Mother, the inference of guilt infecting the entire school. The nun, her pale, solemn face scanning the rows of girls, waited. I dared not look at Charlotte for fear of incriminating her but then I felt a sudden movement beside me and saw that her arm had gone up, stiff and straight above the heads of the other girls. My own arm followed and I glanced at Charlotte who was staring ahead with a glazed look of stubborn rebellion.

A look of pious satisfaction passed over the Reverend Mother's face and she dismissed the assembly.

We were sent for during the morning, an undeniable sense of martyred injustice burning in my breast, and Charlotte, well, it was hard to tell.

'It was my fault. Frances didn't do anything,' she blurted out as soon as we were in Reverend Mother's study.

Reverend Mother, who wore a look of sin-weary sadness, rested her grey eyes on Charlotte and saw that she was telling the truth. I mumbled a protest and felt strangely cheated but there was not a lot I could say.

'I know where you went, Charlotte,' Reverend Mother began quite kindly, 'but why did you do it?'

There was a pause and Reverend Mother repeated the question. 'Why did you do it?'

'I suppose I wanted something to happen,' Charlotte said, sounding somewhat bewildered by her own answer.

The simplicity of her explanation seemed to exasperate Reverend Mother and what happened was that Charlotte was sent to the chapel for the rest of the day, although as a non-Catholic she did not have a sufficiently developed sense of sin to benefit from the cleansing process laid before her. But out of sin came glory. The friendship between Charlotte and me was set for life, that I had wanted to share the guilt and she had refused to allow it. It turned out to be one of those great and rare touching moments cemented in memory and cherished in heart for ever more, although never to be exposed or even mentioned again.

More immediately, life went back to uneventful normality for the rest of the term.

Just before Christmas Charlotte and I went shopping together one Saturday morning to buy presents for our families and each other. For my birthday Charlotte had bought me a tiny bear, a lucky mascot, and for hers I had given a blue plastic pencil case. For Christmas we bought one another lipsticks and mascara blocks, the lipsticks a lurid orange, the mascara navy blue.

Over the Christmas holiday we spent hours in each other's bedrooms practising with the make-up and listening to Radio Luxembourg's crackling heralding of a new era. Charlotte had been given a one-pound postal order by an elderly aunt and bought her first two records, one by the Beach Boys and the Beatles' 'She Loves You', which had just been released.

We began to despise the Guide movement but were too frightened of Captain to leave. I had been made a patrol leader, while Charlotte had not, which presented a problem as the slight was too great to ignore and although I was really rather proud of the new position bestowed upon me felt duty-bound to decry its importance and desirability at every opportunity. Secretly, I suspected Captain's failure to recognise Charlotte's leadership qualities had something to do with the mascara (my own attempts with the blue block had never been in evidence outside my bedroom as the wretched stuff made my eyes water terribly).

In the first week of the new year it was decided that the older Guides and Scouts should redecorate the Scout hut which both our groups used for meetings, although on different nights. With my new position of responsibility, which, in spite of all the decrying, had engendered a rather nauseating, priggish sense of duty and maturity, I felt there was a great deal of worthwhile purpose in the exercise. Charlotte, on the other hand, suffering from a touch of teenage sloth and the inexplicable misery of growing up, remembered that she was allergic to the smell of paint and pettishly brought a bottle of milk the first day which she poured into a bowl, explaining obtusely that it was the only antidote and in some obscure way supposed to soak up the fumes. Still treading carefully, I sympathised, but privately wondered whether it was the allergy or the cure that was psychological and then felt guiltily mean for the thought.

Whichever way it was, Charlotte forgot to bring the milk the next day and never mentioned feeling sick. The Scouts, who although none of them knew it, were some of the same boys who had been training as spies the previous summer, were much bigger and better than could have been hoped. It took most of the week to paint the hut, longer perhaps than might have been expected, but by Friday afternoon it was done although the sense of achievement was rather spoilt by the frustration of nothing having happened to continue the association. We hung about the hut, ostensibly admiring our efforts and checking for any bits we might have missed, and then Charlotte suddenly announced that we should have a party to celebrate and invited everyone to come to her place the next evening.

'It's all right,' she told me on the way home, 'my parents are going to stay with their friends in the country this weekend. I'll tell them I don't want to go.'

'Do you think they'll let you stay by yourself?' I asked.

'I'll tell them that you're going to spend the night. You will, won't you?'

'Of course,' I said, a little uneasily. I had no idea what was expected of one at a party.

I don't think Charlotte had either but somehow she had a notion of how it should be and that the chief requisite was an equal number of boys and girls.

At first she had thought it better not to tell her parents about the party but when I arrrived on the Saturday morning she decided to broach the possibility of a few friends coming round, without actually using the word 'party' which seemed to have overtones of noise and mess which might not help our case. Surprisingly, her mother seemed to think it a good idea although I gained the impression she was relieved Charlotte had not been planning something more dangerous. Coffee bars were the big worry and forbidden territory for both of us. A boy both families knew had been in the local dive when it was raided by police searching for drugs. He'd been caught disposing of a purple heart in his coffee cup.

Charlotte's parents left for the country and we skipped about the big flat, delighted with our freedom, no longer marred by any real deception. There were four bedrooms but we decided it would be fun to share a bed and more cosy, besides, there would be lots to talk about after the party.

By half past six we were sitting in the lounge, a jar of twiglets and three bowls of crisps dotted round the room, untouched to preserve our orange lipstick. Charlotte also had her eyelashes heavily blued but I had given up the unequal struggle, preferring a clear view of the world.

'I'm not going to wear any shoes,' Charlotte said, kicking off her flat brown slip-ons. 'The other girls are bound to have heels.' I had a pair of black Italian moccasins and thought it better to remain complete. Removing shoes seemed somehow suggestive, although suggestive of what I was not entirely certain.

The 'other girls' were to be two other Guides, both older than us, although not much, and a girlfriend of one of the Rover Scouts we had not met. At half past seven the two Guides arrived, both wearing heels and looking strikingly different out of uniform.

We all sat down, still eschewing the crisps and Twiglets with genteel restraint, and listened to 'She Loves You' three times in succession. By eight o'clock the room had fallen into an expectant silence. By half past things were getting desperate. Nobody arrived this late for a party, did they? And then, at twenty to nine the doorbell rang.

The lounge, which was a large room, too large a few seconds earlier, suddenly seemed to contract as the boys, who appeared devastatingly grown up in their Saturday-night clothes, fell into the room. One of them had two enormous cans of beer which he set down on the table and immediately began to open, calling for glasses as the first can exploded a spray of beer on to the ceiling. A loud roar of approval came from the others, none of whom seemed to have noticed us girls, watching on, rendered quite dumb by the overwhelming jollity of it all.

'Let's have some music!' one of the boys, the tallest and best-looking apart from a rash of spots on his neck, said to the room in general.

Charlotte, who I could see had been wondering whether beer left a permanent stain, hastened to put on the Beach Boys. It was all much better than we could have hoped although there were six boys and only five girls which presented a somewhat insurmountable problem.

The tall boy who had wanted the music asked me to dance and

two more quickly followed his lead and asked the other Guides. The boy who had brought his girlfriend had settled in a large armchair with a glass of beer in his hand and the girl on his knee.

Charlotte was now the only girl not partnered, a situation of which I was as conscious as she had to be. I ached for her, felt guilty for being partnered myself and even more so for the beastly sensation of triumph, although I didn't like the boy whose clammy palm oozed over mine.

The Beach Boys ended and Charlotte went to put 'She Loves You' on the turntable, an ill-disguised look of fed-upness across her orange lips. I was at a loss to know what to do for the best, relinquish my partner and chat to Charlotte or carry on jigging about and adopt an expression of boredom to make having a boy to dance with seem of little importance. I tried to imagine which I would prefer if I were in Charlotte's place and decided on a compromise; I'd have one more dance with clammy and look bored and then give it a rest.

At the end of 'She Loves You' I went over to Charlotte who pulled me out of the room in a conspicuous attempt at being nonconspicuous about it.

'God, what a load of drips,' she said in the hallway. 'How can we get rid of them?'

The lounge door reopened as she spoke and one of the boys asked where he could find the lavatory. Charlotte flashed her blue lashes at him and pointed out the direction.

Hope seemed to have been revived by this first piece of direct communication. None of us had ever spoken directly to one another, when we were painting the hut or even as the dancing had begun when it had been a case of grabbing rather than speaking. When the boy came out of the lavatory we followed him back into the lounge.

Things got going after that. Somebody turned out the main lights and as the Beach Boys went back and forth on the surf a sort of free-for-all took place with a lot of inept groping and giggling.

In the half-light I saw Charlotte locked in an awkward clinch with the boy I had danced with and a moment later a screwed-up pair of lips were pressed up against one side of mine, having slightly missed their target.

Everybody lay on the floor then, muffled yelps and protests and the squeaky wet sound of adolescent snogging taking over as the Beach Boys made their final surge over the wavy turntable.

My new partner, a blond boy and one of the two that had not danced earlier had, until now, worn a serious expression, slightly aloof, almost disdainful. At close quarters this had changed. His breathing had become alarmingly fast and heavy and the new look of discomposure about his face was quite off-putting. I closed my eyes so as not to see this but only succeeded in becoming more aware of what he was doing to the rest of my body. I didn't like it. It felt rude, added to which the floor was beginning to feel uncomfortable and the whole business somehow unseemly. One side of my jumper was being badly pulled out of shape and instinct told me that it would be dangerous to allow my partner's hand to penetrate my vest, although why it should be and how it might lead to 'going the whole way' in a room full of people, I had not rationalised. In fact, how exactly 'going the whole way' was actually achieved I was not entirely certain, the convent having omitted to include the more basic details of reproduction in the biology curriculum.

The floor, it seemed, was proving a problem for some of the others and two couples left the room. Seizing upon this precedent, my partner leapt up, indicating that we too should vacate the lounge and search out somewhere better to experiment with passion. In the hallway we met Charlotte and her boy. She and I glanced at one another, expressionless, full of adult impassivity, but as soon as she and her partner had disappeared into one of the bedrooms I told mine that I wanted to return to the lounge. Bedrooms were bad form and asking for trouble.

Later, when everyone else had gone home, the same sense of

decorum made me feel rather ashamed of telling Charlotte what had happened in the lounge. Rodney, my partner, who had said very little, was not really all that nice, I had decided, although I did not tell Charlotte this, only about the way he had eventually kissed me latterly, which had been revolting. He had kept trying to push his tongue into my mouth as if he meant to choke me. This, however, I ascribed to passion and therefore did not mention how revolted I had been. Lying side by side in Charlotte's bed we each wanted the other to believe in the romance of those kisses, the soul-delivering, lofty desire of their intent. Gordon, Charlotte said, had kissed her in much the same fashion and they had been very comfortable on the bed, her bed that we were lying in at that moment, she murmured with a tinge of romantic reverie.

The evening had been a great adventure and yet I had not really enjoyed it. Charlotte, I felt, was more in tune with such goings on, more eager to find the hot side of life and give herself over to whatever promised to be a new experience. To me the jumper-pulling and mouth-searching had amounted to an unnecessary encounter, and I felt a little sad to have made this discovery while Charlotte apparently had been transported to a higher plane of existence; although perhaps not entirely. Later on she again asked me for details.

'But how far did you let him go?' she persisted.

'Just kissing, really,' I said. 'That was far enough.'

'Not enough to get pregnant, then?' The question was earnest.

'No, I don't think so. In fact, I'm sure not,' I said, beginning to worry what she might tell me in a moment.

'They say you can get pregnant if you go to the lavatory after a man's been there. Do you suppose that's one of the reasons men and women always have separate ones?' She sounded worried herself.

'But they don't at home,' I pointed out.

'Oh, that's different,' she said obscurely, and that was the end of it. It was an illogical, late-night worry and she kept it to herself.

The innocuous little party turned out to become one of those events in life which take on greater significance than might have been supposed. The word quickly got round that Charlotte had organised an orgy. The boys, who had been quite amazed and probably shocked by the availability of bedrooms, could not be expected to appreciate the degree of naivety which had allowed them such access. Charlotte's notoriety was assured.

That such ignorance was possible in the early sixties seems hard to believe now but Charlotte and I grew up in the days when parents dealt with sex education, if they dealt at all, by offering their daughters booklets about banana flies. And schools, certainly the sort we attended, were still in the dark ages.

In the week that followed the party Charlotte and I were invited to the cinema by Gordon and Rodney. I accepted because I could not think of an adequate excuse to refuse and looked forward to the outing with dull dread and concern that there might be a repeat performance of gauche passion with all its inherent discomfort.

Gordon and Rodney met us outside and with awkward attempts at nonchalance extracted boxes of chocolates from their pockets which they shoved in our direction. A certain amount of confusion was created by these offerings as Charlotte and I felt it only polite to eat our way through them during the film, thus keeping our mouths full and unapproachable. The boys maybe thought this a deliberate ploy on our part but the possibility did not occur to us at the time and in the post mortem that followed we worried about our undesirability, especially as Gordon and Rodney had selected seats in the back row where we understood nobody was expected to watch the film. However, the next week we were again invited to go to the cinema although this time I did refuse. I simply couldn't eat Rodney's chocolates or worry about him not trying to kiss me when I didn't even want to breathe the same air.

Charlotte could not understand my refusal just as I could not her enthusiasm to accept. Gordon, I thought, was as awful and boring as Rodney and I made the mistake of telling her so. There was the suggestion of our first rift but after Charlotte's next date with Gordon she told me how she had noticed him surreptitiously breathe into his hand and sniff before he went to kiss her goodnight. Instantly she went off him and over the next couple of weeks was completely overwhelmed and obsessed by a revulsion which barely allowed his existence.

After that, boyfriends went into abeyance for some time. We decided to be scholarly and started Latin and Greek, but Charlotte did not take to the classics. She was good at art but that did not count for a great deal in the eyes of the school. She was also quite a good tennis player but the convent was not particularly sporty. She began to see herself as a misfit and complained that she should be so and yet it seemed as if she deliberately sought to be different from everyone else. Her school work was clever and highly original but not geared to passing exams. She was talked about a great deal and either admired or denigrated and in the difficult position of being both a conformist and her friend I found myself adopting an outward attitude of condescending tolerance.

And then everything started to change and Charlotte became different and special in a most wretched way. Her legs and arms developed nasty bruises and one day she came to school with a black eye. She did not explain it, even to me, and something in her manner, touchy and brittle, made it impossible to ask. For once in her life she desperately wanted to be like the rest of us, ordinary, safe and unmolested.

If she had known the cause of her father's sudden change of temperament, his morose moods and sudden, inexplicable, violent rages, she might have been able to confide in me. A dying father would have been inexorably poignant and the grief quite justifiably shared. But as it was she did not know that he was ill and found his outbursts not only terrifying but shameful.

And so she said nothing for a while and continued to smart with hurt pride and intense resentment each time it happened. Her mother, who refused to recognise the illness because she could not bring herself to accept its inevitable consequences, made light of the 'smackings' and constantly told Charlotte to 'cheer up and forget about it', but there was a sad quiescent preoccupation in her manner which frightened Charlotte and made her feel lonely and miserable to a degree that the memory of that awful time remained vivid and raw even years later when she eventually told me how it had been.

As the tumour grew and the headaches got worse her father became less and less coherent. Charlotte realised that he was going mad and felt bitterly ashamed of him. The illness, although she did not know it as such, dragged on and took its toll on her school work. She began to lose the ability to concentrate and the will to do so. 'Unco-operative and lazy' the form teacher wrote at the end of her report; she opened it in the cloakroom at morning break on the last day of term and contrived to make the comment illegible by tampering with the mistress's writing.

School was to finish at lunchtime after a special end of term mass in the chapel. Charlotte and I sat together at the back while the largely unintelligible Latin phrases spoken by the priest drifted over our heads. As a Catholic I accepted the service with a sense of routine awe and waited for the moment when I would have to get up and walk down the aisle to receive communion. That was the best bit. I was no longer fooled, but there was comfort and a sense of belonging in taking the bread, which I never chewed before swallowing. After all, one never knew. There was still a degree of mystery.

The moment came and I got up but it was not until I was more than halfway along the aisle I realised Charlotte had followed. An involuntary sense of outrage, inherited through centuries, filled me with shocked amazement as she knelt down beside me and the priest advanced on us. I saw her accept the bread and almost spluttered when the priest popped the next piece into my own gaping mouth.

Charlotte could not explain her great presumption to the Reverend Mother. She was expelled from the school. During the holidays her father died. The convent never knew but no doubt the nuns prayed for Charlotte. The ways of righteousness. The next term I was put up a year and no longer associated with our previous class. There was no one to talk to about Charlotte and anyway the shame of what had happened seemed better forgotten. I felt piously loyal and protective in not mentioning it or her to anyone.

With the benefit of hindsight and agnosticism I still feel pangs of guilt and indignation when I think of the episode. The nuns should have been told about Charlotte's father. It might have made a difference, although how I am not sure. Charlotte had already left, the course set, but could it have been changed? And now Dan. Supposedly I was being loyal and protective again, or was I? Perhaps he, like the nuns, had a right to be told and unlike them a chance to retrieve the situation.

CHAPTER FOUR

Friday afternoon – Dan

Coming home early had been a mistake. I had not expected Charlotte to be there but had half hoped. I hated the house to be empty, it was lifeless and cold when she was not there, which, to be fair, did not happen very often. A smile, a kiss, the smell of supper cooking, things you noticed only by their absence.

Damn her for not being home now, although that was not very fair either as I normally stayed late at the office on Fridays. It was no longer necessary but had become a habit, a ritual, and the staff expected to see me there, still at my desk as they all went home for the weekend; silly really, but part of the pattern of everyday life, secure and unchanging, until this Friday when I had come home early, the first Friday in months I could have used the extra time working.

It had been one of those days when everyone you telephone is out and all your letters have to be typed twice because there are silly little mistakes which you'd like to ignore but can't, and then have to plead with a disgruntled secretary who thinks you're making a fuss. I should have got rid of her but she had been with me too long and it would be difficult. She might take the firm to an industrial tribunal which would be bad for the us and for her – raking up all her shortcomings in public – terrible; but she was the sort to take it all the way. She might even leave of her own accord and still take us to task, pleading constructive dismissal because I had asked her to retype the letters. The wretched woman was always so defensive, snapping and snarling at the slightest criticism; perhaps she had problems at home, an unhappy marriage. Poor woman.

I went upstairs to take off the dark suit and change into my weekend clothes; surely Charlotte would not be too late, although she had not said when she would be back. She had been rather vague about it – rather vague about the whole thing.

I could understand that she needed to get away sometimes, although not so much now Vicky was at school. The difficult time had been when Vicky was a toddler; it would have driven me mad being at home with her all day. That was when Charlotte should have seen more of Frances but she had been in America those first couple of years. There were letters and postcards. Charlotte kept them all, the only correspondence she did keep, as if one day Frances might become famous. I knew that Frances did not like me, she never had. Oh, it was not obvious, she was too intelligent for that, always very civil and witty, but there was an underlying resentment. We would not have had anything to do with one another if it hadn't been for Charlotte, yet it was Lottie that caused the strain.

There was a time when I suspected a lesbian tendency in Frances but to say anything to Charlotte would have been cruel and insulting, and she would probably have told Frances. A seed might have been sown that had not been there after all. Pure, bloody-minded defiance, and a battle I did not want to risk.

Telephoning Frances last night was another mistake, like coming home early. It had broken the pattern. I had never phoned before when Charlotte was there, but I wanted to speak to her last night, as if there was a chance we could really say something to one another over the telephone. It was a sort of reverse logic, perhaps we could talk at a distance, in the way we had not at home for some time.

66

But Frances was there to bar the way. 'Dan, how are you!'

'Fine. And you?'

'Oh, not too bad you know.' And so it had gone on. Superficial niceties before I could ask to speak to Charlotte.

'Is it urgent, only she's having a long soak in the bath before we go out to eat.'

'No, not urgent,' I said, unable to put the lie to the test because I knew that Frances was lying, knew it and yet didn't want to know.

The telephone call, coming home early, they were both part of the same thing and yet there had been nothing to make me feel the way I did now, nothing Charlotte had said, no real change in the way she was. And she did seem much happier, although that was probably because she was working again. If only she had rung back.

I sat down on the side of the bed, facing Charlotte's dressing table. The mirror was tilted down and I caught sight of myself. I looked worried, more than I wanted to admit; and my hair, why hadn't I noticed before how grey it had become? But that was not the worst: I was looking distinctly overweight, not fat and it didn't show when I was standing up, but there was a spare tyre around my midriff. I looked ridiculous sitting there, dejected and flabby in my socks and pants. Why hadn't Charlotte said anything, she always used to: perhaps she had not noticed either. She had been almost detached lately, bright and breezy and detached. Amazing that she still fancied me but she seemed to. Sex had been better than ever recently; she had become totally uninhibited, even noisy, but she no longer talked afterwards the way she had in the early years. All that had changed. The first time she had cried.

I got up and changed the tilt of the mirror and then sat back on the bed, looking into the past rather than the present. It was almost painful to think about Charlotte but I could not do anything else, waiting, waiting in the silent house, alert for the sound of her coming home but knowing that the more I listened the longer it would be.

I wanted to see her more than ever in spite of all the years we had been together, the familiarity, and careless assumption that she was at home waiting for me. We had known one another so well. She had always been there, part of my life, even in childhood. But Charlotte as herself and not just one of the children who came to my parents' home to play upstairs while the adults talked, that had started just after the Christmas her father died.

Our families had been friends for years. Charlotte's father and mine were at school together and during the war the two couples shared a house. Afterwards they had each moved into their own homes, my parents into Lakeside when my grandfather died, and Charlotte's to a flat in London. But they had kept up the friendship, weekends in the summer when the sun always shone and in the winter, snow and log fires. Those weekends were always special: perfect moments suspended in time and memory. They carried on year after year until Charlotte's father became ill and died and everything changed although her mother continued to come with Charlotte.

There was a lot of sadness in the house the first few times, quite torturous really but inescapable because my parents felt it their duty to carry on as before and Charlotte's mother could not bring herself to reject their kindness.

Charlotte was sad too but there was a new kind of defiance about her. I felt sorry for her because of her father. She was fifteen but still seemed like a child to me, four years older and working as an articled clerk, whereas she was still at school.

And then the summer after that Christmas it all started to happen. The thin, pale schoolgirl had changed overnight into a leather and metal-clad monster who came to stay with us for a week while her mother was in hospital.

'At least she doesn't smell,' my mother, normally so tolerant and charitable about everyone, mumured after Charlotte had gone jangling and clanking up the stairs to her room.

'Poor Dorothy, it must be a trial for her,' she said when my father came in and she hurriedly explained the metamorphosis before he saw our guest.

'It must be that new school she goes to. Dorothy said it was "progressive" which I think means they can do what they like. It's very expensive,' she added with oblique justification.

During dinner, most of which she declined to eat, Charlotte talked non-stop while the rest of us sat silent and amazed, shocked and embarrassed.

'We went to Margate at Easter. It was great. Hundreds of Mods had to go to hospital. You should have seen them on the beach trying to run away from the Rockers. The best fight I've ever been in.'

'Do they allow you to wear your hair like that at school, dear?' my mother asked, as if she had not heard the bit about Margate.

'That shit heap!' Charlotte spat out.

My father coughed as if to clear the air and my mother got up to collect the dishes although none of us had finished eating. I stared at Charlotte, unable to take my eyes off the extraordinary sight she had become, her hair long and straggly and dyed jet black like her leather jacket with its silver studs and chains, her eyes with great thick black lines drawn round the lids and her mouth bright red. She caught my stare and suddenly opened her eyes as wide as she could in an overt glare. I looked away, acutely embarrassed and angry; how dare she come into our home like this and swear in front of my mother.

My father had already followed Mother out to the kitchen and I got up to join them, picking up the mustard pot as an excuse to leave the room. Charlotte, of course, was making no attempt to help.

'What does "shit" mean?' I heard my mother ask my father as I walked into the kitchen. He mumbled and coughed again, turning away from her as he saw me come in.

'Terrible. Terrible shame,' he muttered and then asked crossly: 'How long have we got to put up with her?'

69

'Now, dear, it's not long since she lost her father. We have to make allowances,' my mother replied, sounding anxious and conciliatory. 'Poor Dorothy, though. It must be difficult for her.'

'Um,' my father grunted, ill at ease in the kitchen where he rarely put in an appearance, but unwilling to relinquish the refuge and go back to the dining room.

After dinner I went up to my room to study, a nightly ritual which had started when I became articled and would continue for the next five years until I had taken my finals. Wednesday was the only night I had off, the night I went to Young Conservatives.

I had been reading for about an hour when my door burst open and Charlotte came in.

'Busy?' she said, quite obviously unconcerned as to whether I was or not.

'As a matter of fact, yes,' I replied, curtly. 'So be a good girl and go away.'

'So be a good girl and go away,' she mimicked, flopping down into the armchair on the other side of the room.

I ignored her, keeping my head down over my books but now quite unable to concentrate.

'Don't you find it a drag stuck up here working all the time?' she asked.

'No, not if I'm left in peace to get on with it,' I said, still without looking up.

She started to wander round the room. I could hear her picking up and putting down my things, making small bumps and bangs to disturb me and humming to herself, then a sigh and the twitchy little noises of boredom.

'D'you like my chains?' she said next, rattling the links together, deliberately trying to irritate.

'Not particularly. In fact not at all,' I replied pompously.

'I pinched them from a bog,' she went on. 'Anything to buck the cistern.' At this she went into paroxysms of laughter, rolling off the chair on to the floor.

'Do you enjoy behaving like this, trying to shock everybody?' I said, rounding on her as I gave up the pretence of studying. 'You're ridiculous. Do you know that! Just a silly little girl.'

She stopped in mid roll, blinked the big, black-rimmed eyes and stared at me. For a moment I thought she was going to burst into tears but instead she started to laugh again, a hard, coarse laughter which I wished she would stop before my parents heard.

'Me ridiculous!' she said after gulping for breath. 'Me! You should look at yourself. You're so straight and stiff you're ready for your coffin.'

'Oh get out and leave me alone,' I said, more nastily than I had intended. 'I'd rather be dead than like you. I don't know what your father would have said if he could see you now.'

I regretted the words as soon as I had said them.

'But he can't, can he, so it doesn't matter,' she said quietly, and getting up left me to my books.

I did not see her the next morning, a Wednesday, but all day at the office I kept thinking about her and wishing I had not said what I had about her father. Before his illness the relationship between them had been very close, much more so than she'd ever had with her mother. Once I had heard my parents talking about it: they thought Dorothy had been jealous of her daughter although they were too loyal to put it in so many words.

When I got home my mother cornered me in the kitchen.

'Dan, I know you won't like this but do you think you might take Charlotte with you tonight?' She hurried on before I could protest. 'She's been very subdued all day. I don't think she's really as bad as she likes to appear and she might enjoy meeting some of your friends.'

Guilt made me agree to my mother's request and I was thankful that the Y C's were going ten-pin bowling that evening – a setting in which Charlotte would not seem too out of place. Subdued she may have been but I could see that she thought it a huge joke when I asked her, as casually as I could manage, if she wanted to go.

'Super!' she said with heavy affectation. 'Absolutely super. Thanks awfully.'

'Don't mention it,' I replied acidly, wishing I had not let my conscience get the better of me.

'This is jolly, old bean,' she kept saying as we walked to the war memorial where the YC's were due to meet.

'Oh, do shut up!' I snapped at her just before the others were in earshot. I cursed my mother for inveigling me into this agonisingly embarrassing situation as one by one I saw my friends turn and glance at us, a ripple of astonishment and curiosity running through the group of sports jackets, floral-print summer frocks and white cardigans.

I was saved having to make any introductions by the arrival of the small coach we'd hired to take us to the bowling alley. Charlotte, hands thrust into her leather pockets, smiled gleefully at anyone who looked her way. The evening was going to be a nightmare, I just knew it.

As I had been at boarding school until the previous summer and had started going to YC's only in the last three or four months I didn't know the others that well, but there was a girl called Helen who I thought quite liked me and whom I had been thinking about asking out for a drink, on a Sunday maybe, after church, because I'd seen her at Evensong a couple of times. If Charlotte had not been with me I probably would have contrived to sit next to Helen on the coach; but now that she had seen me with the leather-clad monster I doubted whether she would be interested in me at all, which was another source of irritation.

Charlotte, idly playing with her chains, was, of course, totally unaware of the Helen possibility she had just destroyed. Neither of us spoke during the journey to the bowling alley but my resentment seemed to grow by the mile as I thought about Helen and how pleasant it would have been to spend the evening with her.

The plan was to split up into four groups for the bowling with

72

the idea that the winner from each group would play in a final at the end of the evening. At first this seemed the ideal opportunity to off-load Charlotte but then I decided I couldn't risk letting her loose on the others in case of what she might say. She'd had no compunction about using bad language in front of my mother so there was no reason to suppose she would bother to temper her tongue with my erstwhile friends.

The four groups had already been sorted out before we got there and Helen and I were to be in the same one, which in any other circumstances I would have viewed as a piece of good luck, but not tonight with Charlotte beaming facetiously at everyone I spoke to.

We changed our shoes for the special bowling pumps and went to select the bowls. Several times I tried to catch Helen's eye in the vain hope of retrieving the situation, if there had ever been anything to retrieve in the first place, but each time she seemed to look away until I was convinced she had decided to ignore me. Helen was a serious girl who had joined the Y C's because she was interested in politics, or so I thought. She was not like most of the other girls I'd met who seemed preoccupied with less weighty matters. Helen was not silly or empty-headed and not a bit like Charlotte in any way. She was also a year older than me which made her even more attractive.

The match began with Helen bowling first although her initial attempts missed the pins altogether, trundling off into the sides of the lane.

'Bad luck,' I said, over-heartily as she turned back to the group, but she was determined to ignore me.

The next two in the group did a little better but not much, and then it was Charlotte's turn. She needed only the first bowl to knock down all the pins: a clean, straight run down the centre of the lane, delivered with a great sweep of her leather-bound arm, chains flailing.

The same performance was repeated each time it was her turn, making her the clear winner from our group. Now I knew the reason for the gleeful smile but to be fair to her she was a worthy winner and, of course, went on to wipe the floor with the winners from the other groups in the final.

Suddenly she was the star of the evening with all the other chaps crowding round her.

At last Helen spoke to me: 'Your friend seems to be a very keen player. Personally I find this sort of thing rather mindless, don't you?' I had not noticed until then what a tight, thin-lipped mouth she had.

I was about to agree with her but something stopped me and instead I heard myself saying: 'No, not really, I think it's jolly skilful.'

Helen turned and walked away without another word, leaving me slightly disappointed about the possibility that had never been there after all.

The next evening, after dinner, Charlotte again came to my room.

'Thanks for taking me last night,' she said breezily after she had flung herself into the armchair. This time I looked up from my books.

'That's all right. You were quite a hit with the others,' I said. 'I mean, they seemed to like you.'

'You mean you didn't expect them to. You thought I'd be an embarrassment.'

'No, not at all,' I said, not very convincingly.

'I don't think the girls liked me. Very stuck-up some of them, aren't they, especially that Helen. You fancy her, don't you?'

I turned back to my books.

'No, as a matter of fact I don't.'

'No, as a matter of fact I don't,' she mimicked.

'I wish you'd stop that,' I said.

'I wish you'd stop that,' she continued, affecting the sort of plummy voice she'd had herself until six months ago.

I ignored her and wished she would go away although another

part of me wanted her to stay. Irritating as she was, the room came to life with her there, breaking the monotony of endless study, although so far that evening I had been unable to concentrate properly on the law tomes piled around my desk.

'Is there anyone you fancy?' she asked next.

'There may be,' I replied, 'but it's none of your business.'

There was a pause.

'Are you still a virgin?' she asked loudly. 'I mean, have you ever fucked anybody?'

I could feel blood rushing to my face, hot and red.

'I think you had better go to your own room,' I said, a little hoarsely.

'Go on. Have you?' she persisted lasciviously.

'As I said, it's none of your business.'

'I bet you never have,' she went on. 'You should, you know. It's great.' She got up then and left the room. After she had gone I tried to find some concentration but failed and went to bed early; but I couldn't sleep: my mind was full of her – resentment, distaste, she really was the most beastly girl.

She was due to remain with us at Lakeside until the Sunday evening and after lunch that day my mother, worried that Charlotte might tell Dorothy she had not had a good time now that my father was totally ignoring her, made another of her 'suggestions', this time that I should take Charlotte for a walk across the fields which stretched over the horizon behind our house.

'It's a lovely day and the fresh air will do you both good,' she said encouragingly. 'Tea will be at five, in time for Evensong.' I didn't know how she had the nerve to add the last bit as there seemed nothing very Christian about her scheme to lumber me with Charlotte for the afternoon.

We set out under a blazing sun. I strode ahead, tramping through the thick undergrowth which threatened to overrun the footpaths skirting the fields. It was mid-August and most of the fields were still bulging with their harvest, the stiff, ripe crops rustling and sighing in the afternoon breeze. We continued for about an hour, Charlotte a few paces behind and unusually silent, although I could feel her presence like a knife in my back. And then she called out to me to stop. Her feet were aching and she was hot, and couldn't we find a nice shady tree to sit under?

I ploughed on for a further five or ten minutes, obstinately passing several shady trees and then we came to Gadders Wood, a dense little patch of limes and elders two or three miles from Lakeside.

'Well I'm stopping even if you're not,' I heard her call petulantly, and turning, saw that she had flopped down under the first tree, her leather jacket discarded on the grass beside her.

Reluctantly I walked back to the spot she had chosen and sat down. I suppose I was almost afraid of her – of what she might say or do to embarrass me. She stretched out, lying on her back, her eyes closed. She had a thin white blouse on, peaked over her breasts by the dreadful pointed bra she wore, sticking up like a pair of cones.

Her legs were long and thin in black stockings, but the rest of her looked a terrible mess although, in a way, I envied her. Her's was a sort of uniform just as my tweed jacket and grey flannels were, but she could get away with whatever she liked – clothes, behaviour: she challenged the world to expect anything of her. It was a freedom I would have liked, although expressed in a different way, of course: but freedom to catapult the constricting expectations created by my upbringing, expensive education and worthy parents. And yet Charlotte's conditioning had not been that different so it had to be something in her, something I did not have. I envied her whatever it was but at the same time thought how badly she had used it.

Her eyes opened and saw that I had been watching her.

'It's so hot,' she said, and sitting up began to fumble for her suspenders under the tight black skirt. She rolled down the stockings and pulled them off.

'Why don't you take off your jacket?' she asked and then, as if seizing upon a sudden idea, added: 'I tell you what, for everything you take off I'll do the same.'

I had already begun to remove my jacket before she had said the second bit and felt if I tried to put it on again this would only incur the adolescent derision I had come to expect from her. So I threw down the jacket and pretending I had not heard, loosened my tie, my eyes fixed in a concentrated stare on the wheat field in front of us.

We remained like that for five minutes or so. I could hear her idly plucking at bits of grass and then she rolled over on to her front and said: 'Come on, Danny boy, haven't you ever played this game before, what's the matter, afraid you might lose?' She began to laugh and suddenly I was pulling at my tie, wrenching at the knot, but the force just made it tighter. She laughed more and if only to shut her up I rolled over towards her, pulled her up against my chest and clamped my mouth over hers in a clumsy demonstration of emotionless, animal lust that was completely overplayed in the attempt to cover up my total lack of experience.

It all happened very quickly after that. I was on top of her, pushing her skirt up and then grappling with the belt and zip on my grey flannels. Hopelessly nervous and angry I blundered on, hardly aware of Charlotte's trembling body until instinct told me that it was the first time for both of us, but by then, of course, it was all over, a brief, overwhelming sensation full of guilt and confusion.

I rolled away from her, pulling my clothes together, scrambled up and wandered a little way into the trees, leaving her still and silent on the grass. I felt dreadful, a contemptible wretch, and then I heard a soft whimpering sound which halted me in my tracks. I ran back to her.

'Why didn't you tell me? Why did you have to pretend?' I demanded accusingly.

She did not answer. I heard her sniff and then a great sob shook her body. I knelt down on the grass beside her and touched her shoulder.

'Charlotte?' I murmured in bewilderment.

'Go away,' she pleaded, her voice a pathetic whisper. 'It's your turn to leave me alone.'

I think there was probably a note of conscious drama in the desolate little utterance, but at the time I was too full of remorse and the conviction that I had behaved like a cad to allow myself any leniency in attaching the smallest degree of blame to Charlotte. She lay there, the innocent victim of my despicable lack of control, and I couldn't wonder at her wanting nothing more to do with me. I am surprised only that the word 'rapist' did not enter my head.

We went home the way we had come, in stunned silence at what we had done, me in front, Charlotte a few yards behind, home for tea in time for Evensong.

It was two years before I saw her again. Two years of law books pored over in a dull room. The weekends continued but Dorothy came alone and the possibility that Charlotte may have told her mother what had happened in Gadders Wood kept me closeted away with my studies while she was there. This meant that any news tended to be scant and rather watered down by the time it reached me, Charlotte having become an unmentionable subject in our house since her stay. Whenever her name did crop up it would be followed by 'Terrible shame' from my father and 'Poor Dorothy' from my mother.

For the first few weeks after she had gone I worried that there might be a letter or something, Dorothy confronting my parents with the news that her daughter was pregnant, but the weeks went by and nothing happened.

In spite of the tight-lipped episode at the bowling alley I did start taking Helen to the pub after Evensong, although it was all quite different to the way I had expected: Charlotte had changed things even if I had not yet realised how. Neither of us mentioned her but she was there, between us, somehow, making a space.

We went to the YC's' annual weekend conference at Eastbourne and made love in Helen's hotel room. She was a good sort really, patient and instructive in bed if a little dull out of it, but then I did not consider myself to be such stimulating company.

And then Charlotte got a place at the art college in the town near us. Mother felt duty-bound to ask Dorothy if Charlotte would like to stay with us during term time but to everyone's relief a place had already been reserved at the students' hostel, and Charlotte had spent half a term at the college before I saw her again and the second metamorphosis.

Boar Park Country Club was the 'in' place that autumn. It was a vast old house three miles outside the town, set in acres of woodland and meadow, part of which had been turned over to a golf course. My father was a member and spent most afternoons on the links, but it was Monday nights that people my age went to the club. Part of the labyrinth of cellars had been converted into a sort of nightclub and on Mondays there was a discotheque with drinks half price.

Helen and I had drifted away from the Young Conservative crowd. Her interest in politics had turned out to be less committed than I had at first imagined and although I had vague longer-term ambitions, the YC's had begun to seem a somewhat tortuous route to achieving them. Prejudice and intolerance combined with a priggish assumption of shared 'right thinking' had become more pronounced with the Wilson government in power and something to slam against; so Monday night had taken over from Wednesday and I had started taking Helen to Boar Park.

We didn't dance much, Helen suffered from asthma and never liked getting out of breath, although her dancing consisted of shifting her weight from one foot to the other while the rest of her body appeared to remain stiff. My own efforts seemed similarly inhibited amidst the fluid swaying movements of the other dancers and there were moments when under the influence of the flashing lights and pulsating music I longed for some sort of release, to break into wild contortions, to be loud and crazy. But, of course, I never did and after a couple of records Helen and I would retreat to some dark corner, to sip tepid drinks.

Why we kept going there I can't think except that it was an easy, mindless break from study and the music was loud enough for neither of us to feel it necessary to talk. We clung on to the relationship because it was better than nothing and there was nobody else.

And then one Monday night a crowd of students turned up and took over the tiny dance floor, spinning and weaving round each other in a dazzling display of over-the-top athleticism. It was late in the evening, about the time Helen and I normally left to find a quiet spot to park the battered Austin Cambridge I had acquired and go through the weekly ritual of groping one another in the back seat.

I glanced at Helen but she had not finished her drink. It was not often that I really looked at her any more. We saw each other twice, three times a week and yet I was avoiding her. After two years together the subject of marriage had crept up insidiously and with increasing regularity. We had been to three or four weddings, always invited as a couple: 'Your turn next,' well-wishers would say to us. I felt it creeping over me like a great convolvulus weed, taking hold, pulling down. I liked Helen, she was nice, but I could not bring myself even to contemplate the prospect of a lifetime together. Why did everything have to move on and change; couldn't things be left as they were, of the moment, without all the eternal strings? Perhaps I was being unreasonable to want the ease of familiarity combined with the stimulation of transience. Yes, I definitely was being unreasonable although the pressures from without seemed more so. Stubborn, that's what I was too, stubborn and unaccommodating, Helen had said so, weeping, when I failed to wear the signet ring she bought me; but quite simply, I did not like rings; my hands were not suitable.

I found it difficult to understand why Helen wanted to marry me. I had no money then, she did not seem to enjoy sex all that much any more and I felt sure she was no more in love with me than I with her. But there again it did not seem to me that the couples whose weddings we attended were very different: marriages not made in heaven but connived at in the ladies' lavatory at the Conservative Club, or so I supposed, with unkind cynicism.

Jaded thoughts such as these plagued me more and more as the convolvulus grew, stronger and more overwhelming as each week went by. I sipped my tepid lager in the Boar Park discotheque and waited for it all to get worse.

The Tamla Motown music the students had been dancing to came to an end and Roy Orbison began to sing. A tall girl with close-cropped hair, a polo neck jumper, mini skirt and long boots strode past the table where Helen and I sat, and then she stopped and turned back.

'Hello, Dan.' It was Charlotte.

She sat down and I introduced her to Helen.

'Yes, we've met before, about two years ago,' Charlotte said. Helen looked nonplussed.

'It's all right, I don't suppose you remember me. I was a bit different then,' Charlotte added, glancing at me, a wicked little smile crossing her lips.

'You could say that,' I said, taking in the amazing transformation. Charlotte looked almost ordinary now.

Helen, who had mumbled some sort of hello, got up then and went to the cloakroom to fetch her coat.

'It is nice to see you again, Dan,' Charlotte said when she had gone. 'Shall we have a quick dance before you go?' She had not changed completely, still the forthright manner.

'Yes,' I said, as if I couldn't find any reason to refuse. 'Why not?'

We got up and went on to the dance floor. The tempo was still slow and Charlotte put her arms round my neck and moved up to me.

We swayed to the music, our heads ear to ear.

'What happened to the chains?' I asked.

'They went rusty. What happened to the law books?'

'Oh, I'm still in bondage, I'm afraid,' I said. Charlotte laughed. We danced on into the next record.

'I think Helen's waiting for you,' Charlotte said. I glanced over to the table. Helen, her coat on, was sitting there watching us.

'I'd better go,' I said.

'Yes, you had.'

'Thank you for the dance.'

'Why don't we do it again next week?'

I hesitated: 'Yes, possibly. Good night.'

'Bye, Dan.'

'Enjoying yourself,' Helen said, icily, when I went back to the table.

'Are you ready?' I asked, pretending not to notice her mood.

She got up and went towards the exit.

'I think it was rather bad the way you just went off with that girl as soon as I wasn't there,' she said peevishly.

'I'm sorry,' I said. 'She's an old family friend.'

'I bet!' she scoffed unpleasantly.

Outside the night had gone cold. There was a clear sky and the moon shone brightly on the cars parked round the front of the old house. Helen shivered and as we walked towards the Austin put her arm through mine, clinging on.

'Is she really an old friend?' she asked.

'Yes.'

'I'm sorry.'

'It's all right,' I said, wishing she would still be angry.

We got in the car and drove off. I wanted to take her straight home but it did not seem possible and nothing more was said as I drove to the heath and took the Austin up a bumpy track to the highest point. When we got there I switched off the engine and turned to her.

'Not tonight, Dan,' she said, 'I want to talk.' I could see her face clearly in the moonlight. Her expression was intense, her eyes searching.

'Do you think we ought to call it a day?' she said.

'You're not still worrying about Charlotte, are you?' I said, leaning back in the seat and staring out over the lights of the town spread out below.

'No. It's us.'

'We're all right, aren't we?' I said, reaching for her hand, knowing she was after reassurance.

'You don't love me, though, do you?' she persisted.

'Of course I do.'

'But you never say it.'

Stubborn and unaccommodating, I could not say it.

'There you are, you can't because you don't!'

She began to cry and I felt wretched for making her unhappy. I started the car and backed down the track. I had a sense of urgency, to get away before I began to weaken, before pity got the better of me and I retreated back into a sort of sloth that seemed to have dulled everything for as long as I could remember.

We reached Helen's house. My heart was beating furiously but remorse was catching up with me.

'Look, I'm sorry. I didn't mean it,' I said.

'Yes you did,' she said miserably.

'I'm sorry,' I said again, rather lamely. She was already half out of the car. She pushed the door to and walked away. I let a moment go by and then leant across and wound down the window to call after her. But what was the point? I saw her standing by her front door, waiting, her back, slightly hunched, pathetic and accusing.

'I'm sorry Helen,' I murmured to myself and wound the window back up.

I drove home with a marvellous sense of freedom but

nevertheless suffered terrible pangs of guilt. I did not like myself very much for the way I had treated Helen, but retribution was waiting in the form of Charlotte.

Six months later Helen married the chairman of the Y C's, a big buffoon who is now an M P. Magnanimously she invited me to the wedding, but I was in France with Charlotte, heading for Paris in the battered Austin.

The convolvulus had been uprooted but was growing again and I was the cultivator. Why one thinks in such fanciful analogy (secretly – to oneself because to say it aloud would sound insane) I can only think is a way of softening reality: metaphysical comfort for the raw emotions that take over your life. To fit the mould cast for me it seemed I had to be a down to earth, a realistic plodder, solid middle-class, middle-of-the-road articled clerk, brought up to fulfil expectations of moderacy in all things. Not 'rocking the boat' seemed to be the main thing. Parting from Helen had been a small bit of rebellion but after the first flush of freedom I had to acknowledge that nobody really changes. We are what we have always been and six months with Charlotte should have proved it to me. I don't think she expected or wanted me to be any different, and it seemed not to matter to her that I didn't fit in with her crowd at the college, although I envied them in much the same way I had Charlotte two years earlier. It was an illogical envy I did not fully understand, although I think it was something to do with freedom of spirit.

I suppose I had looked to Charlotte to share it a little but instead she had looked to me for what she needed; she saw me as stable, reliable and uncomplicated. I was to be an 'always there' person for her, listener, mentor and lover; although at times it concerned me that the first two roles were more important to her than the third. I had to be patient I thought, even though that was not how I felt. Sometimes I would reach a pitch of frustration that became a physical burning sensation in my chest: the old feeling of wanting to break out even though I was the willing victim of Charlotte's expectations.

Taking her to Paris was an act of desperation. It goes without saying that I went back to Boar Park the Monday a week after finishing with Helen, although I very nearly did not, which seems incredible now. I had a law exam coming up and felt I ought to study more, possibly also because there seemed to be something cleansing and virtuous about sitting alone in my room, a sort of penance for Helen. But this had begun to fade by Friday, helped by frequent speculation as to how much Charlotte had really changed. Perhaps curiosity was the motive although I find it difficult to remember now, all the other emotions having long since made it impossible to think about Charlotte in objective terms.

She was there, that Monday night, with her friends from the college, girls and boys of varying ages and a lecturer, Chad, who was much older, grey-haired and balding, and inexplicably attractive to the college girls he taught, among them, Charlotte.

Chad, I found out later, had been a commercial artist who dropped out when he was thirty and, abandoning his wife and three children, went off to South America to paint pure art. Why he had returned to England was never fully explained, but he had come back and taken up a teaching post at the college, making himself a romantic figure with his stories about life in 'uncivilised parts' where you could get caught up in a revolution just by standing in a bus queue. Chad had a talent for telling stories and an eager audience in the anarchy-inclined students.

At first I told myself that the Charlotte crowd were an amusing lot. I felt as if I was standing back, as an observer, with a mild sense of superiority and condescension excusable by the conditioning process I had unwittingly succumbed to under the influence of the Conservative Club. But there was an ingenuous affectation about the students which was irritating and attractive at the same time. They were like a breath of fresh air after the stuffy young Tories. And then I began to realise that they were standing back from me. I was the odd one out; far more so than Chad, whose seniority lent him enchantment.

I thought about how I might change without appearing to emulate the students, but my role within the group had already been determined: the outsider tolerated because of Charlotte.

As a group we did all sorts of wild things, 'japing' it was called. 'Let's go on a jape,' they would say halfway through an evening, and we would all bundle into Chad's Dormobile and head for the coast to light an illegal bonfire on the shingle at Aldeburgh or Southwold and prance round it in sea-soaked clothes, or sit staring out over the night tide smoking shared reefers, but getting more of a lift from the salty sea air. There were indoor parties as well; impromptu gatherings after the pubs had closed when everyone would gravitate to an unknown house and dance till they collapsed or listen to Chad holding court on the concept of eternity or the sexuality of Peruvian peasant girls.

It was a very vivid period, almost unreal, and lasted only a matter of three or four months although it stands out in memory as having been much longer. And then it all began to change. Chad, who generally appeared to prefer group relationships and the privileged position he held within ours, as opposed to individual friendships, turned his attention to Charlotte. It seemed to me that the students had made him almost guru-like and responding to this he found it necessary to discourage other attachments such as the still tenuous one between Charlotte and myself.

He was clever about it, using little slights, smiling denigration. He started referring to me as 'the lad', accurately perceiving that his appeal for Charlotte was due considerably to his age. And there was nothing I could say or do that would not worsen the situation; I just had to ride it out and hope Charlotte would not succumb. I started smoking a pipe, even thought about growing a beard, without realising what I was trying to do.

The group lost its appeal. It had become like a dreadful amorphous mass, suffocating and somehow inescapable, although why seems hardly to make sense except that I suppose I felt I couldn't leave it myself in case Charlotte did not come with me.

86

Chad was relentless, and Charlotte seemed flattered and excited by his attention.

I waited for the Easter holiday, hoping and praying that there would be no drastic changes before the end of term. I thought that once the holiday came and the group split up for two or three weeks there would be a breathing space to consolidate things with Charlotte, who so far had shown no sign of wanting to get rid of me. The last day of term came and in the evening the group met in its favourite pub. Chad was there, drunk from the staff party at lunchtime. I had never seen him so full of booze. It had a strange effect on him, he was maudlin, morose, Silently I rejoiced and offered to buy him a drink.

'Gin. I'm on gin, lad.'

'No wonder you're so depressed,' Charlotte said.

'It's necessary to plummet to the depths sometimes in order to get a different perspective on life,' he said mawkishly. 'We have to suffer to perceive our souls.'

I laughed but Chad did not appear to notice. He had taken Charlotte's hand in his and was staring into her eyes.

'You do understand, don't you?' he said. 'You of all people must understand.' His voice was quite slurred but the moment was a sober one, and I could not mistake its meaning as Charlotte gazed back at him.

Later that night I suggested the Paris trip: 'You've always wanted to see Montmartre. I'll take you. We'll go over Easter.'

'Yes... yes, if you say so,' she had replied, her manner hesitant and vaguely distracted.

We arrived in Paris on Easter Saturday night and went straight to Montmartre. I parked the Austin some little way away and we climbed the steep streets to the small square where seedy second-rate artists parade their bohemianism to the tourists who buy their paintings. Some were doing portraits, reasonably skilful charcoal impressions of undistinguished people flattered into posing for a few minutes.

Charlotte said it was all quite magical and wanted us to buy a painting from a row of daubings pegged on a line of string under the trees in the centre of the square. They were too expensive really and more than I could afford but I bought one to please her.

We wandered around a bit longer and then went into one of the dark cafés which face out on to the square. It was crowded but we managed to find two seats in a corner next to a couple who were passionately kissing. There was a pianist on the other side of the room playing Edith Piaf tunes and an aproned waiter darting about with a tray of glasses balanced on one hand.

'Isn't it all wonderfully how it ought to be?' Charlotte said. 'I mean, it could have been spoilt, like everything else, by tourism and all that, but it's just as I imagined it would be – how I wanted it to be.'

I wondered how much of it had been orchestrated, whether after all the café was no more than a facade cleverly preserved by some big conglomerate which had long since taken over from 'le patron', but I didn't want to spoil the enchantment for either of us, and Charlotte enchanted was at her most enchanting.

The couple sitting next to us were still locked together, oblivious to everyone else, but their mood catching. I put my arm round Charlotte and she moved closer to me, resting her head against my shoulder.

'I think I could stay here for ever,' she murmured. I bent my head and kissed her, completely caught up in the atmosphere of the place.

We drew apart and I glanced round but nobody had taken any notice. The pianist started to play Piaf's greatest song, regretting nothing, and an old crone in a dirty blue dress and with socks rolled round her ankles began to sing the words, her voice amazingly similar to the original.

More people came in, drawn by the sound of the singer: the smell of French cigarettes mingled with something cooked in garlic, became stronger.

'Would you like something to eat?' I asked Charlotte.

'No, but you have something,' she said dreamily. I noticed that she had not touched her wine.

'Are you feeling okay?'

'Yes, just a bit queasy.'

'You should have said. We'll go if you like.'

'No. I'm all right. It'll pass. Usually it's in the mornings.'

The significance of this registered immediately. I stared at her but she looked away.

'Let's not talk about it now. It'll only spoil things,' she said, her eyes fixed on the ravaged singer.

My mind raced, thoughts tripping over each other, dismay, anxiety and a strange sense of relief – even, perhaps, triumph.

'We'll get married,' I said, quietly but firmly. 'As soon as we get back.'

'No. I don't want to,' she said, still looking away from me towards the singer. 'And besides, it might not be yours.'

That moment seems sharper now than it did at the time. It was numbing then, like a huge physical blow, so big you don't feel it at first but then when it does start to hurt gets worse before it gets better. It was years ago. Ten? It is something I will not think about for a long time and then I remember it, that moment and those words, recalled to mind when they can do the most damage.

CHAPTER FIVE

Friday Night – Charlotte

'Did you have a good time?' Dan said. I could feel him watching me, his eyes following me about the room as I fussed about with the things from my case, folding each garment two or three times, as a diversion and excuse to avoid meeting his gaze.

'What did you do today?' he asked. He was lying in bed, one arm behind his head, propping it up on the pillow.

'Oh, shopping. I didn't buy anything. I went to the Tate,' I replied, finding it irksome to lie, slipping in a bit of the truth, as much as I could.

'And how's Frances? Did she go with you?'

'Frances is fine, and no she did not come with me today, she's got a job you know,' I said, sounding a little exasperated, attacking to defend.

'Did she tell you I phoned last night?'

'What is this, an inquisition?' I turned to face him, using resentment to muster the strength needed to meet his eyes.

We looked at one another for a few moments but I refused to see the misery and anguish. I could not allow myself to recognise it. I did not want to confess or be forgiven, as I knew I would be. I needed to feel resentment and irritation to make it all bearable.

I turned back to my case.

'I assume Frances did not tell you,' Dan persisted, although less insistent and with a note of defeat in his voice.

'No, I expect she forgot. Why did you phone anyway?' I felt bound to ask and wished I had thought to call Frances before coming home.

'It doesn't matter. In fact I can't remember now,' Dan said unconvincingly.

I did not pursue it but went out to the bathroom to take off my clothes away from his gaze. Perhaps he would allow himself to be convinced there was no cause for his suspicions. It would be like Dan to turn a blind eye in the hope that all would be well again in time. Generous, self-effacing, he could do it and survive, justified and strengthened by his magnanimity, a crisis confounded. But then it all depended on me, did it not? I wanted some sort of crisis and could feel my heart hardening towards it, shutting out the inevitable awfulness, like craving a drug and disregarding the after effects.

Part of me had wanted the crisis to happen as soon as I got home, instantly before it had time to recede, but another part had hoped Dan might be asleep. Dear Dan, who didn't deserve the deception or the sense of antagonism and mistrust I felt towards him simply because he was there and had a right to question. Unwittingly he had become the enemy of my emotions: he threatened them and I was, I suppose, frightened of him because of them.

I had not meant to come home so late. Earlier I had thought about getting back in the afternoon and cooking a nice meal, making everything appear normal, but Nick and I had talked, a long intense talk which had brought the crisis nearer.

'I suppose we have fallen in love,' he had said, almost without emotion, making it sound more like a statement of fact than a declaration but it had been a monumental thing to say.

'Whatever happens. Whatever you decide. I'll go along with it,' he had said.

'Thank you,' I told him, although the two words sounded ridiculously inadequate.

92

I suppose it was Nick's businesslike approach to the affair, his general air of coldness and reserve contrasting to such extreme with the way he was in bed, that made the fascination so strong. I did not disagree with his statement about having fallen in love because perhaps I had, although love, real love, the only way I could equate it was to think how I would feel if the 'loved one' was killed or maimed and there was only one person for whom such a fate would seem intolerable – Vicky.

Powerfully, in the bathroom, I decided not to think about it, but shuddered in the cold shadow of that imagined divine retribution. On the way back to the bedroom I stopped outside Vicky's room. The door was open, the room dark, the bed flat and empty. I wished she was there, and was overcome with an unaccountable longing to touch her and feel her close.

Back in our room Dan, asleep or feigning it, had his back turned to me as I got into bed and lay down in the dark. I listened to his breathing, too shallow for sleep I thought. I don't suppose either of us had ever been more acutely aware of the other, stiff and alert, both wondering what, if anything, might happen next.

At some time during the night I must have fallen asleep because I got into my old recurring nightmare. I was in a strange foreign land which had been devastated. It was like a Salvador Dali painting although the surrealism was not so pronounced because the people seemed alive, rushing about, hiding, fearful, doomed, amidst dead trees on a scorched landscape. What had happened to create this scene was never clear but the atmosphere was fraught with catastrophe or rather the wake of it. Something terrible had happened and I was involved, as a victim but also, in some inexplicable way, as a perpetrator. I ran with the others but I was not one of them. They could turn on me at any moment although they all appeared remote and preoccupied and hardly seemed to notice I was there at all, but then why should they as they had their own problems. And then Dan would appear and seeing him I would rush to where he was, full of relief and gratitude only to find that he did not recognise me, did not even see me, as if I had become invisible, a figment of my own imagination.

Dan's appearance usually came at the end of the dream and I would wake up, startled out of sleep by the horror of it all. I would then be quite overcome with thankfulness because the dream, for all its strangeness, had felt utterly real and by far the worst bit had been not having Dan to turn to.

This night I awoke at the same point, my heart beating furiously, my eyes blinking in the dark, trying to find a chink of light so I could see Dan next to me in the bed, but he was not there. I reached across to touch his pillow as if I had to feel as well as see; perhaps I was still in the dream. I felt frightened and lonely but waited. Time seems different at night, long and short but never normal. You can lie awake for ten minutes and it seems like half the night or you can fall asleep and wake the next morning feeling as if only a moment has passed.

I lay in the lonely bed and knew that if Dan had been there I would have given way, told him everything; but I was quite unable to get up and search for him. The moment had been instant: I could carry on now and wait a little longer for the crisis. I realised that I was beginning to see the situation as if it did not involve me. It was as if I was waiting for some outside force to dictate what would happen. I had never felt this before. In all the old crises I had always relied on Dan to rationalise and point a way. I had always turned to Dan, instinctively, without hesitation as if being turned to by me was his purpose in life. I had never thought of him as ancillary, yet that was how he had been treated. It was shameful, although he had never complained. He had put up with a lot from me, maybe too much.

It had started even before Paris and that awful moment in the Montmartre café when I told him I was pregnant. He had allowed the Chad thing to happen. He stood by and observed. He allowed things to take their course rather than influence that course himself.

Chad was different from Dan in that he preferred to do all the wrong things while Dan seemed irrevocably righteous. The two were like opposite poles of a magnet and I felt pulled between them, from one to the other, back and forth. The contrast made them both irresistible and the flaw in my character prevented me from making an immediate choice. Like Chad, I found it stimulating deliberately to go the wrong way but at the same time I yearned for the comfort and security, the acceptability of conforming; so I played both and ended up in trouble.

Chad, of course, was much older than me. He had been married and there were children whom he had abandoned at tender ages in order to rid himself of any trappings alien to the irregular lifestyle he set about achieving. He was a weak man really and I eventually came to suspect that perhaps it had been his wife who had done the abandoning, taking the children with her. But I did not see this possibility until much later.

When I first went to the art college, post-Rocker phase, and into a new era of serious academia, or so I thought, Chad had stood out as innovator, leader, philosopher. Everything he said sounded amazing and original. He seemed to have a different perspective on life to everyone else but one that was instantly appealing to minds so receptive to any alternative view.

He gathered around him a privileged group, derided and envied by other factions within the college but exclusive and invincible.

For the first few weeks of the term I floated about without identity, an unknown quantity to myself and everyone else, as miserable as I had been in the beginning at the new school after the convent. I had to wait to find where and how I should be. And then suddenly I found myself in the Chad set.

I had been to one of his lectures. It was about light, Turner's use of it in particular, but then he had gone on to tell us about the different light in South America and how he believed the quality of light affected not just that of art but of life in general. We were spellbound by this nonsense, utterly taken in and illuminated to the secret of being. The lecture ran over time but nobody shifted until the caretaker appeared and broke the spell. The room cleared but I was at the back and became caught up with some of the students who were already part of Chad's group. They were all going off to a pub and Chad, suddenly noticing me, suggested I join them. And so I became part of the group and again felt special and different, made to feel so by Chad who seemed so special and different himself.

At first it did not occur to me to think of him physically and it came as rather a shock, like discovering that a favourite uncle no longer sees you as a niece, when it became apparent that he fancied me. It was soon after Dan came back into my life and sort of joined the group, uncomfortably like an interloper but with a kind of dignified persistence which I rather liked. On reflection it was probably Dan's entry on the scene as my friend that prompted Chad to want me. There were one or two casual relationships within the group but nobody else had brought in an outsider and I think Chad resented Dan, although I did not see that at the time, only that both men seemed to want me, a realisation sufficiently seductive and ego-boosting not to need reasoning or explanation.

Dan had been strangely reticent about restarting the relationship which had begun in the field beyond his parents' house two years earlier. I had rather assumed that as we had done it once, inevitably, now that we were together again, it would continue. After all, did not all men want sex and wasn't it supposed to be women who resisted and yet became anxious if they did not have the chance to do so? But Dan waited, allowing the relationship, now so different, to establish itself before we embarked upon the next stage, because that was how he worked things out, in stages, one properly following another.

After meeting again in the country-club cellar we saw each other every week, at first only on Mondays and then at weekends as well. We would go out to pubs with the group and then sometimes alone. On Saturdays he had started going shooting with his father who was involved with a syndicate which had bought rights over an area of woodland some miles away. On these days I would not see him until very late but he would always find me, usually with the group, and I would be pleased to see him. We would go on to an all-night party but sometimes, if there was nothing much going on, if Chad was elsewhere, Dan took me back to his home, Lakeside, after his parents were certain to be in bed.

I felt as if I was being smuggled into the dark house, which seemed silently disapproving. Dan never said anything about his parents' attitude and I guessed that they did not know he was seeing me again and would not have been particularly pleased if they had found me in the drawing room with their son, despite the long family association.

The room, which was vast with a high ceiling ornately patterned with plaster fleurs-de-lys and York roses, had a wonderful collection of old-fashioned sofas and button-backed chairs, casually arranged in little groups with the ones used most placed more or less in a semi-circle in front of the large red marble fireplace. Immediately facing it was a deep sofa with high back and sides held together at either corner by great silk tassels in faded gold. I would sit on this sofa while Dan made coffee in the kitchen and then brought it to me, without a word or a sound.

When we started doing this it was winter and his parents would have had a fire burning in the old cast-iron grate. By the time we got there the flames would have subsided but the embers still glowed and smouldered and sent off a soft warmth and enough light to leave the rest of the room in darkness.

The setting sounds, and was, romantically perfect but Dan, conscious of his parents in the room above, spoke in a soft whisper and gazing into the dying fire kept his distance.

We talked about Chad, but then everybody did. He was a conversation piece in the way people who inspire love and hate always are. But we talked about other things as well, including my visit to Lakeside of two years ago although never about what had happened under the tree. It was as if we wanted to pretend it had never happened, that it had been between two entirely different people, which in a way I suppose it had, as both of us had changed since then. We were both less extreme; we had grown up a lot. Dan had more confidence and tolerance and was very nice. I hoped that I was nicer too and thought I had to be; I could hardly bear to think about how I had been before, the embarrassment was too agonising. Dan, sensing this, insisted that I had been quite all right underneath it all and said even the bizarre exterior had been like a much-needed breath of fresh air in what must have seemed a rather fusty home. Dear Dan, so nice, but if only he could have shown a little open passion.

And then one night the fire had not been lit. Dan's parents had been out for the evening and had not used the drawing room.

'God, it's cold in here,' I murmured, huddled into the corner of the great sofa as Dan came in with the coffee.

He put down the mugs and standing in front of me took off his jacket. Instantly I remembered the episode under the tree which had begun with him doing the same thing, although this time he handed the jacket to me.

'Have this,' he whispered.

Suddenly and in the same uncontrollably mischievous way I had provoked him that summer afternoon I said: 'My legs are cold too: can I have your trousers as well or will the sound of the zip wake your parents?' God, what had I said! I had meant it to be a sort of joke but it had come out sounding brazen and bitchy.

He stared at me, amazed, shocked, disgusted, probably all three, but then he smiled: 'You haven't really changed at all, have you?' he said. 'Not one bit.'

'I suppose not, basically,' I said, a little defensively, wishing I had not upset the gentleness of our new relationship.

'Are you sure this time?' he said a few minutes later, holding my face between his hands and searching my eyes in the dim white moonlight cast across the room.

'Quite,' I said, unable to believe that we could stop anyway, lying naked in the deep sofa, trembling with cold and excitement.

Afterwards and quite stupidly I asked him if it had been his only concern. Perhaps I would have behaved better later on if I could have remained uncertain, although his tenderness should have been enough to tell me and probably would have if there had been anybody else to judge him against, but there was not, because it was only the second time for me.

The sofa, after that, became a major part of our first ritual, the first of the many rituals destined to form the pattern of our life together; and if there was predictability and a certain loss of spontaneity in it all, there was also a sense of belonging.

It was the other part of me, the bit that said my legs were cold, the bit that takes over and compels me to bring about changes, create risks and problems, that allowed Chad to take me to bed about a month before Dan took me to Paris.

I had been to one of Chad's lectures in the morning. His theme had been even more abstruse than usual and at lunchtime he offered to take me to the pub to expound further on the finer points. It was the first time I had been alone with him and I suppose I knew, almost straight away, that this was going to be it.

Chad, leaning back in his seat, one leg at a right angle over the other, his big hands giving added expression to everything he said, was at his most mesmerising. His brown eyes never left my face and all the time he was talking about the lecture they seemed to be saying something entirely different. He was alive with sexuality, it sizzled and threatened, heightening awareness, demanding recognition, challenging resistance.

It was a sort of visual and psychological foreplay, just beneath the surface of our conversation and entirely dominant although the actual words we spoke were only about art.

The pub cleared and as if there were no choice in the matter I went with him to his flat. I had been there before many times, with the group; Chad rented it from the council and it was on the top floor of a fairly new tower block. Inside he had turned it into what he optimistically termed his 'den of iniquity'. There was one large living room, the walls draped with brightly coloured Indian cotton and the floor awash with huge oriental cushions. There was no solid furniture, apart from a record player which stood on the floor amidst a scattering of Peruvian artefacts.

'Let's not mess about,' he said almost as soon as we were in the flat. 'Take off your clothes, Charlotte,' he commanded and obediently I did as I was told, quivering and entranced by such manifest dominance.

Chad's lovemaking had a violent intensity that terrified me at first. I could not stop trembling and finding this rather tiresome and embarrassing kept saying it was cold in the flat.

'Shut up and try to relax,' he murmured, not unkindly. At this stage we were still standing up, he taller than me and seeming even more so than before now that we faced one another shoeless and naked.

He ran his hands down my body, accelerating the trembling, and then he used his tongue. My muscles stiffened with revulsion but then I began to experience unimagined sensations and an involuntary craving for them to continue. I closed my eyes, and began to moan and sway and jerk, hardly aware of what I was doing as the sensations inside me took over, insistent and uncontrollable until they reached an unbearable pitch and suddenly seemed to explode and disperse.

My body went weak and my legs seemed to lose all strength. I thought I would collapse to the floor but Chad held on and lifted me up against his chest. I threw my arms around his neck and buried my closed eyes in his hair as I felt him push up into me. I clung on, pinioned and breathless as he lifted my legs to go round his back.

'You bitch, you beautiful bitch,' he cried out a moment later.

★

'Don't you have a bed?' I asked him later as we lay in the great soft cushions on the floor.

'I don't need one,' he said. 'That's the trouble with Western society. It thinks it needs beds and three-piece suites and tables and chairs in order to be civilised but carpentry has nothing to do with civilisation. It's a state of mind, clouded by materialism in countries like Britain.'

'But aren't these cushions simply a different sort of furniture? I mean where do you draw the line? How do you justify living in this flat and not in a mud hut or a tent in a field?' I asked, somewhat facetiously because it seemed to me there was something not entirely ingenuous about his parameters of civilisation and I suppose it occurred to me for the first time that he was striking a pose.

'Ah, but would you have allowed me to seduce you in a mud hut?' he answered. 'I think not, dear Charlotte. Sex, the great antidote to western civilisation. It's the only thing that makes it all bearable. We all have to compromise our ideals to satisfy the more base human needs. Ultimate civilisation, that would be akin to perfection. We strive for both but rarely stop to think how sterile and boring it would be if either were ever truly achieved. Perfection cannot exist. It contradicts itself.'

An uneasy sense of confusion began to take hold of me. It was not that I failed to understand what Chad was saying but that I no longer heard him in the same way as I had with the group when everything he said had sounded profound and meaningful. Base human needs had exposed him to me as fallible. To hear him grunt and cry out and see his face, red and blotchy, beads of sweat glistening on his balding head and then to listen to him giving forth on an esoteric conundrum was too great a contrast. Suddenly I saw him as he was, a pseudo, conning himself as well as the rest of us, cynical and captious about everything except his own image of himself in relation to the rest of the world.

Nothing ever happened the way you wanted it to, I thought

101

bitterly. Everything was spoiled and the worst part about it was the feeling that the spoiling was from within me. I wanted to blame Chad but my own fallibility seemed greater than his.

'Do you sleep with the lad?' he asked me.

'Don't call him that,' I said, turning away so I no longer had to look at him. Dan leapt into my thoughts and I almost groaned with the awfulness of the damage that had been done. Everything spoiled. Chad tugged at my hip, pulling me round to face him again.

'You do, don't you, but it's not so good. Nowhere near. He's not enough for you.' His eyes seemed to have glazed over. I stared into them, horrified and frightened by their sudden opacity. He wrenched me towards him and pushing me on to my back lunged straight into me. The cushions had parted and I was lying on the bare floor. Unrelenting, Chad, his full weight trapping me under him, rammed on as if it was necessary to prove Dan's inadequacy with his own fierce thrusting, harsh and painful.

'I love you,' Dan said, awkwardly, the words seeming to catch in his throat.

'Oh, don't say that,' I pleaded, 'please.'

'We'll get married. It'll be all right, I should have been more careful.'

'But it may not be yours,' I repeated.

We were lying in bed, a soft sagging French bed which kept us together in the dip. Dan had his arms around me and I lay against him, still feeling slightly sick.

'But it could be,' he said, tightening his hold.

'Oh, it's all such an awful mess,' I moaned. 'And it could have been so good. I wish I loved you, I really do, Dan. You see I like you so much. I'm sorry, so sorry.'

'You mean you like me, but you don't fancy me any more,' he said, kindly, calmly, as if it had always been inevitable.

'I suppose so,' I answered miserably. 'Although it could be just the state I'm in. They say it changes the way you feel.'

'The baby.'

'Don't call it that. I don't feel like that about it, it's just a condition, like an illness.'

We lay still and silent for a time. The room, narrow and lofty, with faded nondescript furnishing, smelt vaguely of drains although we had pulled open the tall windows which swung into the room away from the metal shutters. Light from the street lamps below filtered in through the horizontal slats and fell across the bed. Sounds came from both out and in, late traffic with the occasional horn blurting into the night and then a sudden groan and gurgle from the hotel plumbing, amplified through the cracked basin by the door. The room, for all its seediness, could have been special, saved from being sordid because it was the very best that Dan could afford.

'What are we going to do, then?' he said, breaking into my despair.

'You still say "we"?'

'What did you expect?'

'I don't know, but I've got no right to expect anything from you. It's my problem, my body.'

'Yes, but it could be something of mine in there.'

He had not asked who else's it might be but then I suppose he must have guessed.

'How does that make you feel?' I asked with shameful curiosity.

He sighed and turned his head away.

'Come on, you said it as if you thought it was rather good,' I persisted, a sense of resentment welling up inside me. He thought he had rights, he assumed them, I thought, unjustly, the resentment gathering force.

'You'd like to think of it as yours, your baby, wouldn't you?' I accused him.

'Yes, I would,' he answered, simply. 'Is that so terrible? Do you find me so repulsive?'

103

'Yes, I mean, no. I just don't love you like that,' I said and overcome with self-disgust felt tears coming from my eyes. I had to let go then and began crying and sobbing into the pillow, obscene visions of Chad forcing themselves from the dark corners of my mind. It had been only that one time, at his flat. I had tried to avoid him since. It had been a mistake, a most awful disgusting mistake that had allowed him to know about me and the knowledge was there, in his eyes, each time we did meet, the worst when we had been in the pub on the last day of term and he had held my head between his hands, forcing recognition.

Dan and I had made love since but the sweetness of his gentle restraint was lost to me. As Chad had said, it was not enough, but I loathed and despised myself for needing more.

Dan took over then and the confusion deepened. Dan, kind and good, motivated by civilised concern, found an abortionist, borrowed the money, drove me in his old Austin to the grey Victorian building in a litter-infested side street off the South Lambeth Road in South London. Perhaps Chad had been right, that there was an element of basic truth in his denigration of this civilisation, although I did not allow myself to think about it then. It was necessary to concentrate on the immediate predicament rather than see it as one created by a supposedly caring civilised society which used labels like bastard and unmarried mother, and appeared to live by a code based on what the neighbours might think. Better to abort, better still to have kept out of trouble in the first place, but better to get rid of the shame and pretend it had not happened. Pay two doctors, civilised men, to sign a piece of paper to say you were in danger of going mad. A social slip of paper.

The room was painted green, pale Palmolive, hospital green. A venetian blind covered the window, black London dust on the grey slats. There had been three other girls and an older woman waiting in the hallway. The girls looked foreign, maybe Spanish, they sat together, their dark eyes cast down, guilt-ridden and terrified. The woman, who was next to me, was thin and nervy with long greying hair, sallow skin taut over a bony face. She kept crossing and then uncrossing her legs and anxiously chewed at her fingers between urgent little puffs from a cigarette.

'Is this your first time?' she asked suddenly, glancing at me.

I nodded.

'You must come alone,' the doctor, who had a middle-European accent, had said. I yearned for Dan. Wished he could have stayed with me.

'Mine too,' the woman said. 'Got five already. Couldn't cope with any more. Doctor's a Catholic. Wouldn't help. Conscience. You know.'

I nodded again. My head ached. I felt a bit faint. My mouth was dry.

The woman fell silent. She had said her piece, explained herself, justified her being there.

A tall, middle-aged woman in a nurse's uniform came out into the hallway and in a businesslike tone said we should all go with her upstairs. The foreign girls looked at one another and waited to see what the older woman and I would do. They followed us up the wide, uncarpeted stairway. There was a pervasive smell of disinfectant and yet the place felt unclean. The stairs opened out on to a wide landing with several doors leading off. The nurse opened the first and indicated that I should enter. I glanced back at the grey-haired woman who had told me her story downstairs; our eyes met and there passed between us an intense moment of shared fate and then the door closed and I was alone in the green-painted room. In the centre there was a high sort of bed with two metal poles sticking up either side at the foot and small slings attached to the tops. The bed was spread with a dark green sheet and beneath it, on the floor, stood a galvanised bucket. Apart from the bed the only other piece of furniture was an upright chair which had a white gown resting on it.

The stark utility of the room made my stomach turn. I went

105

over to the window and pressed down one of the venetian slats. Outside the sun was shining. The day was warm and humid. There was a playground across the street and a group of West Indian children yelping and laughing together as they ran about. The door opened and the nurse's head appeared. She told me to take off my clothes and put on the white gown. The door snapped to and she was gone.

I went over to the chair and picked up the gown, leaving a black mark on it from where I had touched the blind. I undressed and put the gown round me, shivering with cold and fear; the warmth of the day outside had not touched the green room. The nurse came back and told me I had the gown on the wrong way round, it should be open at the back, she informed me flatly as if the mistake was wearisomely common. I was told to get on the bed and wait for the doctor; I wasn't to smoke, she added and went again. I wondered how many other rooms there were. The woman who had spoken to me downstairs was probably in a similar one. Perhaps she had lit another cigarette and the nurse had told her to put it out. I tried to imagine the woman, waiting in a white gown like the one I had on, in a room the same, but she had become remote, like Dan and everyone else, removed as if to another existence. I longed for it all to be over. I just had to steel myself to stop thinking, to close my mind to everything and escape to a sort of nadir in which there was nothing left but mechanical response devoid of feeling. It was the only way to overcome the fear and stop me from grabbing my clothes and bolting.

In this state I saw the masked doctor enter the room followed by another similarly anonymous figure wheeling a trolley laden with chrome instruments. A needle went into my arm and obediently I began to count. I felt my legs being lifted, limp and heavy, and closed my eyes as I saw the slings at the top of the poles appear round my ankles.

When I came to the room was empty. I was lying flat on the bed; the sun, now high in the sky, had penetrated the gap in the blind

106

and streamed across the floor. I lay still as slowly the realisation that it was done filtered through the muzziness of the anaesthetic. A great surge of relief coursed within me and I wanted to laugh out loud as happiness returned.

The doctor and the nurse came in. The doctor no longer wore the surgical mask. He was a good-looking man, quite young, a clean, strong jaw and cornflower blue eyes.

'How are you feeling?' he asked, smiling down at me.

'Fine,' I answered. 'Fine,' and gazing up into his face felt my eyes begin to water. He took my hand in his and gave it a little squeeze.

'It's all over,' he said. 'All over now.'

'I know,' I said, holding on to his hand, and was filled with overwhelming gratitude towards him.

'Thank you,' I said. The smile remained fixed on the handsome face as he extricated his hand and stepped back from me. He went out but the nurse remained. I started talking to her, banal chatter about the sun shining and the injection not hurting.

'You'll have to get dressed now,' she said. 'This room is needed.'

'How's the woman with the grey hair?' I asked, struggling to lift myself off the bed. My legs and arms suddenly felt leaden now that I tried to use them. My head slumped forward as my feet touched the floor. I saw that the bucket was gone.

'She changed her mind,' the nurse told me, still with the same disinterested tone. 'A pity, hers was a genuine case. She should not have needed to come here.'

For some obscure reason I was not allowed to wait at the clinic – turnover maybe and not so obscure. I was not even permitted to use the telephone and had to trudge along the hot dusty street to search for a public kiosk. Dan had said he would come for me at six but it was only a few minutes past four when I left the clinic. He had booked a hotel for the night and said he would be there if I needed him. The telephone and room numbers were written on a prominent piece of paper in my handbag. Dan had put it there.

'Just in case,' he had said.

'Of what!' I said with the dumb innocence I had adopted to carry me through the sordid little arrangement.

'They kill you as well as it. Someone would have to tell your mother,' he said.

The remark was so completely un-Dan-like, harsh and untempered, it made me notice him again, as I had not for the past month since we had returned from France. I had been so miserably preoccupied with my problem I had failed even to go through the motions of the sort of relationship we were still supposed to have.

We had both let the remark pass but I kept hearing it now and desperately wanted to be with him so that I could give him some expression of feeling. Suddenly it seemed as if it might all be too late and the brief respite of relief and false happiness gave way to a ferocious impatience to find a phone and hear Dan's voice.

I reached the end of the street and turned into Wandsworth Road. A considerable way down I could see a telephone box. I began walking towards it, a little too quickly. When I got there I felt exhausted and pulling open the heavily sprung door stumbled into the rank-smelling kiosk. In front of me the telephone receiver hung down, dangling on the end of its wire, the mouth and earpieces smashed in.

Back on the pavement I kept my eyes down. The distance to be covered did not seem so great if I watched the measure of each step. The sun had gone from my side of the street and I began to feel cold. The shivering turned to nausea and in the pit of my stomach a heavy creeping pain kept accelerating into dragging waves.

Eventually I reached the underground station. The rush hour had begun and people hurried by me, accentuating my slow progress. I descended the stone stairs, my head beginning to swim. I thought I was going to pass out and began to be plagued by the thought of making a scene, drawing attention to myself, being

108

taken to hospital and my mother finding out. That was the worst bit. I had been terrified she might guess sooner and that between them she and Dan would talk me into early motherhood. It was too late now, of course, but I did not want her to know; I could not bear the thought of her being hurt because I had not confided in her.

I had to wait for a phone to be free but at least that meant they were working. I walked back and forth to keep myself conscious. Nobody took any notice of me although I felt so awful I feared some kind stranger asking if I was all right.

Dan, I just needed to speak to Dan and it would be better.

A man came out of one of the phone booths and I went in. I took the piece of paper from my bag and dialled the number. A woman announced the name of the hotel and I told her the room number.

I waited.

I put a second coin in the slot.

'I'm sorry, there's no answer.'

'There must be.'

'I'll try again.'

I found a third coin.

'No reply.'

'You are ringing the right room?'

'The number you gave me miss. They are not answering. I'll check the room key if you like.'

'Please.'

'The key is there. The room must be empty.'

'Could you check the register, please.'

The phone went dead. I had no more coins.

It was nearly five o'clock. I left the underground station and began walking towards the clinic. It was not far but seemed a long way. The sun had gone and the street had become windy. I crossed over to the playground I had seen from the window in the clinic. It was deserted now. All the children must have gone home for their tea. I sat down on a swing, the seat was cracked but I did not have the energy to move and they all looked broken anyway. I clasped hold of one of the chains that supported the seats and rested my head against my knotted fingers. The clinic stood in front of me, a vast grey miserable building, reproachable and profane. I shrivelled in its shadow but felt exposed and utterly desolate.

Time seemed to lose its perspective. I just sat on the swing and waited, no longer expecting Dan to come, but waiting because I could not summon the willpower to do anything else. Why should Dan bother with me any more? He had got me out of trouble. It was done. He had every right to hate me. The thought of seeing me again probably repulsed him, maybe not even that but simply indifference now that the baby, which might have been his, was gone.

The wind whipped a flurry of dust from the ground into my face. My eyes stung but remained dry. Everything about me seemed to have dried up, drained away into some pit of emotion I had shut off but which now strained for release. And then I heard a car coming down the street and almost with disbelief saw that it was the Austin.

I watched Dan getting out but remained on the swing, still unable to move. I saw him start up the steps leading into the grey building and then, as if some sixth sense had told him where I was, his head turned.

He hurried across the street.

'I'm sorry I'm late. It's taken more than an hour to get here,' he was saying as he came towards me. 'I got stopped by the police. An MOT check and the damn thing's run out. I'd quite forgotten.'

Tears began to run down my cheeks and a great sob came from nowhere.

'It's all right. It'll only be a fine,' he said, reaching the swing.

He stopped in front of me. Our eyes met but he quickly looked away.

'Come on, let's go,' he said rather awkwardly.

★

In the hotel that night he rang for a hot-water bottle which I clutched to my stomach before falling into a deep and dreamless sleep. The abortion was something we never talked about then or since but three weeks afterwards we went out on a Saturday morning and bought a Victorian ring in an antique shop. It was set with turquoise stones and tiny pearls. In the afternoon we showed it to his mother whom I had not seen for nearly three years.

'That's very nice, dear,' she said to me and looked at Dan, a question mark over her face.

CHAPTER SIX

Friday Night/Saturday Morning – Nick

'Bloody marmalade!' Marion said, lighting another cigarette, dropping the lighted match on the carpet.

She looked down at it in dismay. Her feet were bare. She was wearing only a dressing gown.

'You asked me what I had been doing', I said, stamping out the match, leaning down to pick it up. Marion rarely smoked but the ashtray was full. Had she smoked the cigarettes because she needed them or to make a point and why did I always have to see these indirect little signals and despise her for them?

She had been downstairs when I came in. It was nearly midnight and I wanted to go to bed. There had been little sleep with Charlotte. I was tired.

'All we ever talk about these days is Morgan-Mackie's filthy marmalade,' she said accusingly.

'Well what else do you want to talk about?' I retorted, throwing the burnt-out match to the wastebasket and missing. I got up and picked it off the carpet again, turning my back to her.

'Oh, I don't know, anything. Not marmalade,' she was backing off, as usual.

'We don't actually talk about marmalade, anyway,' I said, falling into the sterile pattern of our rows. 'Never the stuff itself, you may recall but how to sell more of it.'

'That's just as bad,' she said, lamely.

I turned round and looked at her, sitting on the edge of the settee, her knees tight together, her shoulders miserably hunched into her neck, the cigarette quivery between her fingers. My gaze went beyond her. A crack had appeared in the wall. The builder would have to come back. That was in the contract, filling in the cracks.

'I don't know why you bothered to wait up if everything I say is so boring,' I said.

'I'm sorry, Nick. Really,' she said in her pleading tone. 'We'd better go to bed. It's late.'

'Why do you apologise? Why do you always apologise?' I heard myself rounding on her.

'I'm sorry, I didn't mean to.'

'There you go again. Can't you let me do the sorry bit just once in a while?'

'I'm sor . . .' she stopped herself.

I was bullying her. It had to stop. Pointless. The whole thing was crazy.

I crouched down in front of her. 'Marion.'

She lifted her head a little and blinked at me. Her eyes were red and puffy, but I had to go on. There was never going to be a good time to tell her.

'There's someone else. I spent last night with someone else, I'm sorry.'

At first she was calm. There was a pause, she took another puff from her cigarette.

'Is it serious? I mean, are you saying that you want a divorce?' Her voice was unnaturally even, almost a monotone.

'I suppose so,' I said, getting up and turning away from her again. 'Do you?'

'I don't know, I've been expecting something like this but...' She trailed off and then said: 'I always thought that you'd want to leave me one day.'

114

'Don't you want to know who it is?' I asked.

'Oh, I know. I've even seen her. She doesn't look your type. Oh, I shouldn't have said that, I'm sorry.'

Intuitive. Marion was uncannily so. It was one of her greatest assets and weapons.

'How did you know? Who told you?' I demanded.

'Does it matter?'

'Yes, I think it does. Who was it?'

'I'd rather not say. I'm sorry.'

'For Christ's sake!'

She started to cry.

'Please. You're right, it doesn't really make any difference who it was. Don't get upset.'

'Don't get upset!' she yelled, through sobbing and nose-blowing. 'Don't get upset! You bastard!'

She leapt up and threw herself at me, punching her fist hard into my arm.

'Stop it. Don't be silly,' I said, trying to push her away.

'I hate you,' she yelled. 'You've ruined my life. You've ruined everything.' She seemed on the verge of hysteria. I had never seen her show such emotion before; it was raw and hideous and I felt ashamed for having caused it.

She hit out at me again but this time when I pushed her away she fell back on the settee, sniffing hard and gasping for breath.

'Can't you wait a bit?' she asked, the outburst seemingly over. 'Wait and see whether this is what you really want.'

'That doesn't sound very fair to you,' I said.

'Oh, I wouldn't mind,' she pleaded.

'It's no good,' I said, going to her, crouching down in front of her again. 'It's too late. What's the point of pretending otherwise.'

'Fifteen years! Fifteen years just thrown away like that,' she sobbed. 'I don't think I can stand it.'

I did not know whether it would make it easier or harder for her if I said then that Charlotte had not been the first. I wanted Marion

115

to hate me, but I did not want her to think this time was like the others.

'I think I'd rather you had been killed in a car crash than lose you like this,' she said. 'Did you ever love me?'

'Of course.'

'You might again then.'

I did not reply but got up and went over to the fireplace and began running my hand over the slabs of York stone, rough and hard, I pressed my palm into them and tried to feel.

'I saw Phyllis Roberts today,' Marion was saying. 'Her husband has had a stroke. He's paralysed down one side. He can't talk. She's worried out of her mind. Do you know what she said to me though, she said: "He can't speak but we've never been so close. We've never really 'talked' the way we do now!" And do you know, I pitied her, I felt sorry for her.'

'Is he going to recover?' I asked.

'I doubt it, but I envy her now. I actually envy her.'

We were silent for a while. It crossed my mind that if the same fate came to me Marion would nurse and cosset and keep faith whereas with Charlotte I could not be sure. Worthy Marion. Elusive Charlotte; with the objectivity of hypothesis I felt it would be easier to accept the latter.

'Nick, we've been through so much together. I know I'm not very exciting, but all the times we've shared – a lot of them have been good, haven't they?' Marion ventured tentatively.

'Yes, I never said that they hadn't, but things change, we've both changed.' It was easier when she was being unreasonable. She was completely calm now, almost unnaturally so. Her words were measured and distinct.

'I love you so much,' she said, 'more now than in the beginning. I'm sorry if that makes things more difficult for you but I can't help that.'

My back was turned to her but her words hung round me like a cage. Perhaps if she had carried on yelling and punching and venomously throwing hate I would not have felt so desperate to get out.

'What are you going to say to Paul?' she said next.

'Tell him the truth,' I said, snatching my hand away from the stones. I looked at the palm and saw that I had grazed it. A trickle of blood had come and I stood watching as it ran down to my wrist and soaked into the white edge of my shirt cuff.

'It would be Vicky too,' Charlotte had said. 'I couldn't leave without Vicky. She'd have to come too. It would be a package deal.'

'Of course. I never expected otherwise,' I had lied.

'I'm afraid there's a donkey as well.'

I had acquiesced. I did not feel in a bargaining position. Didn't even want to be in one. The donkey could be sorted out afterwards, but how endearingly bizarre of Charlotte to include a donkey. Paul liked animals. He had always wanted a dog but I had not let him have one. Animals were a nuisance and a tie. But how would Paul feel when he found out that I had left him and his mother for a woman with a donkey? My chest ached. My hand began to sting and I took out a handkerchief to press into the blood. Paul was the really hard part.

Marion had wanted a child straight away, fifteen years ago when we were first married and I was earning next to nothing as a journalist in the provinces.

'We'll manage. Other people do,' she said, but it seemed to me that other people did not manage. I saw the evidence of this in the stories I wrote and besides, I did not want children, only a regular sex life and freedom to achieve something in life which, at that time, meant getting to Fleet Street.

Marion, I thought, had understood. She had never mentioned children before we were married, but then we had not talked much, there was never time.

I met her on a story, a strike at a vacuum cleaner factory. 'Sits

117

Vac' the headline – a memorable one – had read, splashed across the front page over a large picture of a group of workers sitting down in front of the factory gates. Marion had been one of them, blonde then and petite, a banner in her hands, her face, like all the others, set in a contrived expression of belligerence.

'Get down there and bring back a story about the little blonde piece,' the news editor had said, studying the row of faces. 'We'll feature her in the late editions, and I want a picture of her on her own with the banner.'

By then the only stories that interested me were those acceptable in Fleet Street. I was jaded with provincial news and spent most of my time on the lookout for *Daily Mirror*-type material. I spent hours in telephone boxes sending copy down to London, twisting stories round and round, bending the truth to get a good angle.

Outside the factory gates Marion, wearing a white mini skirt and pink T-shirt, had abandoned her banner for an enamel mug cupped between her hands. It had started to rain and she was shivering over the steaming tea, her blonde hair wet and lank round her face. She looked very young and had an urchin quality about her accentuated by the tall iron gates she stood against and the rain which seemed to have soaked her scant clothing as well as her hair.

Her banner, which rested against the gates, had slipped down at an angle. 'We need our tea break,' it read. I grabbed the photographer who had come with me and the picture was taken.

I asked her her name and how old she was.

'Nineteen,' she said. 'Nineteen today. It's my birthday,' she added miserably. 'What a way to spend a birthday.'

'Never mind love, at least you won't forget this one,' a tall woman, a notice demanding equal pay strapped across her chest, remarked.

'Come on, let me buy you a drink to celebrate,' I said, feeling pleased with the picture and the story I would write.

She hesitated.

'Go on, love,' the tall woman said, 'and have one for me,' she added, casting a knowing look in my direction.

Marion saw it and looked embarrassed, but put down her mug and we hurried away.

'I hate it there,' she said. 'They're all like that.' She was still shivering and unexpectedly put her arm through mine and huddled against my sleeve as we walked down the street.

The pubs had just opened and I took her to a dingy little place which was the nearest to the factory. The photographer had gone off to process the film.

I bought her a drink, an orange juice was all she would have, and asked her a few questions to pad out the story. It turned out she was leaving the vacuum cleaner factory in a fortnight and had been inveigled into taking part in the strike as it would not matter if she lost her job.

'There are too many tea breaks already,' she said, 'but it's so boring working there I don't blame them for wanting more. My dad drives one of the lorries but it's not so bad for him being as he's out and about most of the time.' She spoke earnestly, her small round face damp and serious.

'What are you going to do in a fortnight?' I asked.

'I've got a job with your newspaper,' she said. 'I'm going to sell advertisements over the telephone. The factory job was just a fill-in.'

She frowned. 'You won't tell them about me striking, will you? It might not sound very good.'

I smiled at her. She was sweet, pretty and naive and her picture would probably appear in most of the popular tabloids the next day.

She started her new job and without much thought I began taking her out, at first with other people from the office when we went to the pub after work. Everybody liked her. She was bright but seemed to have a curiously innocent view of the world which was quite natural and rather endearing. She never knew anything about news stories in our paper or the nationals but listened to our interminable shoptalk and added her own uncomplicated opinions, often more to the point than the rambling complexities the rest of us indulged in to prolong the drinking sessions.

I was living in a bed-sit, a single room with a gas ring, shared bathroom and pedantic landlady. I spent as little time as possible there but could not afford to eat out if it meant buying for two. Marion, instinctively aware of my predicament, persuaded her mother to invite me to share their evening meal two nights a week and I gratefully fell prey to the allure of home cooking. These evenings never varied much, we ate round a high table in a sort of general living room with the television loud and prominent although nobody listened or watched. Marion's father talked at great length about road hogs and vacuum cleaners but nobody listened to him either. There were two sisters, both younger than Marion, and an elder brother. The elder of the two girls never ate a thing while I was there and looked about two stone under weight for her sixteen years. The younger, who was fourteen, ate and did her homework at the same time, books spread out round her plate and splodged with drips of tomato ketchup. The brother, who was slightly simple, read comics and laughed, a low, rumbling sound interspersed with an occasional belch.

It was Marion's mother who dominated the supper table and the family. She was and still is amazingly large to be Marion's mother. But the largeness was not just in appearance, she has a huge personality which can switch like lightning from overbearing affection to manic bad temper and yet people are drawn to her. There have been times when I have loathed her and then despised myself for falling under her spell again. Marion hates her but for different reasons, hers is an abiding hatred probably born out of the sort of thing that happened soon after I got to know the family from those two nights a week against a background of *Coronation*

Street and a strong smell of stale frying fat and Player's Number 6.

One evening Marion said she had to go out for a short while after tea but that I could wait at the house if I liked until she got back. When the meal was over and she had left, her mother accepted my offer of help with the washing up and between us we cleared the table and took the debris through to the kitchen. The house was old and large. It belonged to Marion's grandmother who lived in a geriatric hospital in Birmingham, and little had been done to modernise or improve it. The kitchen was some way from the general living room, down a long narrow passageway, dark and dingy, cracked brown linoleum on the floor. The kitchen itself was a high-ceilinged room with dull red quarry tiles on the floor and a general air of chill.

'Wash or dry, Nick?' Marion's mother, who had insisted I call her Ruby, asked. She smiled at me. It was a sort of leer which at first I failed to recognise for what it really was.

'I don't suppose a good-looking boy like you was ever asked to do any washing up at home,' she said next. 'I'd better wash. If you could just tie my apron. . .' she added, turning her back to me and holding out the two ties for me to take.

'There, dear, that's right,' she said, wriggling a little as I made the knot. Her hair, a faded orangey colour, but thick and wavy, hung down her back. She had been a good-looking woman and was still quite presentable. She took trouble with her appearance, her nails were always painted red and I rarely saw her without make-up. Her biggest mistake was the skirts she wore, too short for a woman her age, but on this occasion she had on a pair of black slacks.

'Marion's a treasure, you know,' she went on, pulling a pair of pink rubber gloves on to her hands. 'She usually does all the washing up. She's a homely little body, but none the worse for that. We can't all be clever, can we, that wouldn't do at all, although I sometimes wonder where I went wrong with my children. Their father maybe!' she added and gave a little laugh

121

which sounded both bitter and collusive.

She plunged her gloved hands into the bowl of steaming water and began passing me the dripping plates.

'Sometimes I feel that I've just wasted my life but if I say that to Frank he just looks at me as if he hasn't heard and goes on talking about his wretched vacuum cleaners. Anbody'd think he'd invented them the way he carries on, when all he does is drive round the country with a silly smile on his face, convinced that he's keeping the nation's carpets clean. He is a fool. We haven't even got one of his cleaners in our own home. Do you know, Nick, he even talks about them in bed. Don't you think that's kinky, because I do?'

I did not know quite how to answer although the question seemed rhetorical. I also had an uneasy feeling that Ruby had only said all she had in order to mention bed.

'You wouldn't talk about your work in bed, would you, Nick,' she continued, on cue. 'Not if you did Frank's kind of job, although I should think your sort of work is a lot more interesting. I've always thought that I could write, you know. I've just never had the opportunity, although I did once have a poem published. I love poetry, Wordsworth, Keats. They're a sort of refuge from all this. I'm sure you understand.'

She was full of surprises. I had no interest in poetry but found it incredible that Ruby had. She gave a little cry and stepped back from the sink, her hands in the pink gloves held out wide in sudden alarm.

'Oh, quickly, Nick. I've just drenched myself. Get a towel, will you, over there. Please!'

I fetched the towel and took it to her.

'Can you?' she pleaded. 'My hands!' She looked at them in dismay. I hesitated a moment and then began tentatively to dab the towel at her blouse.

'You are a dear,' she murmured, 'and so good-looking,' she added wistfully, and leaning forward brushed her cheek against mine.

The gesture was unmistakably sexual and I felt a grotesque sort of excitement. She moved her head back a little and I saw a distinct look of satisfaction in her eyes.

'Careful, dear,' she said. 'You don't want to get wet.' My hand was still holding the towel against her breast as I looked beyond her and saw Marion standing in the doorway to the passage, her thin legs rooted to the spot, her face horribly sad and knowing.

'There you are, darling!' Ruby said, turning her head as she followed my gaze. 'Did you get it all right? Nick's just been helping me with the washing up and like the silly thing I am, I drenched myself. I told him that you usually do all the washing up. Such a treasure.'

She stepped forward to the sink again and continued with the dirty dishes as if nothing had happened although there was a cunning awareness about her. Marion turned and retreated along the passage without a word.

'I'd rather not talk about it,' she said later when I made a clumsy attempt at explaining what she had witnessed in the kitchen. 'You're not the first one,' she added miserably, but with a stoical attempt at dignity that I rather admired. Suddenly it seemed quite insufferable that a girl like Marion should have to put up with a mother like Ruby.

'Where did you go, anyway?' I asked.

'To collect a prescription for her. She asked me if I would.'

What a devious old bag Ruby was, and jealous of her own daughter.

'Why do you stay at home, I mean, why not get your own place?' I taxed her.

'I have thought about it, but it's difficult. Mum would make a fuss.'

'You're bound to leave home one day. She'll just have to accept it,' I said.

'Yes, but my sisters are still at school. It would be different if they were earning. It's the money, you see. I have to give her all my money.'

The injustice of this incensed me. We were sitting in a Wimpy Bar, drinking Espresso coffee, Marion sitting opposite me looking exceptionally vulnerable as she gazed into her cup.

'Why don't you move in with me?' I said on impulse.

She glanced up at me in surprise.

'Do you mean that?' she said.

'I wouldn't have said it if I didn't,' I answered, although I realised that I had perhaps been precipitate, but quickly pushed the thought to the back of my mind.

Marion moved into my bed-sit the following day. She brought with her two suitcases of clothing, a hair dryer and a teddy bear. The sight of the bear, bald and battered and with one eye missing, triggered the same misgivings I had felt the previous night, but again I ignored them and took her out to an Italian restaurant to celebrate our new arrangement.

Weeks went by and it seemed that things were looking up all round. The news editor had a row with the editor and I was offered the newsdesk job. It meant more money and Marion and I were able to move out of the bed-sit into a self-contained flat. I was working longer and longer hours which meant we saw little of one another but when we were together the relationship was easy and undemanding. We had the money to eat out more often but invariably Marion would have cooked a meal for us when I got home. She seemed to enjoy cooking and washing and looking after the flat. She redecorated it and bought net curtains for all the windows. I did not particularly like this idea but saw no point in protesting. Besides, I could not really explain, even to myself, why I found net curtains irritating.

Christmas came and we were invited to spend it with her family. I had not seen my own parents for nearly two years but was grateful for an excuse not to have to take Marion to meet them. The reason did not do me credit but the loss of affinity, if there had ever been any, troubled me little. Marion, I knew, looked up to me, and this was partly due to a certain degree of mystery I had allowed over my background. It suited me to remain somewhat 'unexplained'. I wanted to be seen as I was myself and not against a categorising family background, although the image was probably more for my own satisfaction than any deliberate scheme to present a contrived persona to Marion.

Her family, whom we had not visited since Marion's removal, welcomed us back with their usual indifference as if there had been no break in the pattern of our relationship. The television remained on throughout Christmas day and evening. Frank exerted himself to pour me a brown ale when we arrived and then happily subsided back into his chair and with a look of deep satisfaction announced that he had given Ruby a vacuum cleaner. The elder of Marion's two younger sisters had finally been taken to the doctor who had diagnosed her condition as anorexia, although her parents, who had never heard of the illness, still appeared not to appreciate the seriousness of it and didn't seem to notice her eating a cooking apple while the rest of us had turkey. The other sister and the brother ate enormous quantities and intermittently watched bits of *Billy Smart's Circus*.

Ruby, who kissed me when we arrived and then pointed coquettishly to a twig of dead mistletoe hanging over the front door, seemed the most pleased to see us. She hugged Marion to her bosom and murmured 'my child', just loud enough for me to hear and with an unmistakable edge of tragedy as if Marion were the prodigal daughter. Ruby was the sort to feast upon and magnify emotion. I watched Marion dutifully kiss her mother's cheek but avoid actually looking at her.

'When's it going to be wedding bells for you two?' Ruby asked when we were sitting at the big table feeling gluttonous and bloated after the meal.

She cracked a walnut and looked at Marion and then me. I had not even considered marriage up until that point but now I saw that Marion and her mother had been talking about it, probably in the kitchen when Marion had been helping Ruby with the turkey.

Marion looked embarrassed and helped herself to a Chinese fig. The question was for me but I did not know what to say.

'You're doing quite well now, aren't you, Nick?' Ruby persisted. 'Time you settled down and made me a grandmother,' she added, giving me a decidedly ungrandmotherly look over Marion's bent head.

'Oh, Mum!' Marion murmured incoherently and began collecting up the dishes.

The second week in January the National Union of Journalists called a strike over pay rates for trainees. I resented having to take part in it but the union was getting stronger and I felt I had no choice as I still had hopes of reaching Fleet Street where a reputation for 'black-legging' might be a barrier.

We were out for seven weeks and as the dispute was widespread the union could not afford strike pay. One thin edition of the paper was produced each day by the editor and his deputy and a fair amount of help from the advertising department, which included Marion.

During those seven weeks we had to rely on her money and the day before the dispute was settled, I suggested we might get married. The wedding took place a month later at a registry office. I sent a telegram to my parents but did not hear anything back. We talked about not telling anybody until afterwards and just asking two strangers to act as witnesses. The idea seemed to appeal to Marion at first but in the end her family came, Ruby wearing pillar-box red and a huge white hat and, as might have been expected, quite overshadowing her daughter.

After the ceremony we all went to a hotel. Ruby had too much to drink and becoming maudlin decided to recite one of her poems. Marion was acutely embarrassed, although there was only a waiter and one other couple in the dining room apart from her family. I felt oddly detached from the whole proceedings as if the events of the day were just that and of no permanent duration.

We stayed at the hotel through the afternoon and Ruby insisted on dancing with me to the mournful rhythm of the background muzak in the restaurant. Frank had fallen asleep, untroubled and content. He and Ruby had given us a vacuum cleaner. The sisters and the brother had wandered off to the television room.

At half past five we had to leave as the restaurant needed to be prepared for the evening session. Frank woke up and shook my hand but forgot to say goodbye to Marion. Ruby kissed us both and went home in tears. Marion and I went back to the flat and had our first row.

'For Christ's sake, she's your mother and old enough to be mine too,' I bellowed at her.

'She ruins everything, she always has, and you just let her get away with it. She deliberately monopolised you today – our wedding day. She did it on purpose. She hates me, but not as much as I hate her.' Marion, tears streaming down her face, managed to get out all the pent-up vitriol through the sobs and gasps as she stood by the bed in her tights and slip, attempting to rip up the pale pink dress she had been wearing.

'She was pissed,' I said. 'She didn't mean any harm. And stop doing that. It's stupid. In fact you're being completely stupid about the whole thing.' I was beginning to lose patience with her. I had never seen this side of her before and found it ugly and contemptible. It seemed to me that she had deliberately lost control of herself. Her face had gone red and blotchy and she was actually stamping her feet in temper as she continued to pull at the dress.

'I said stop it,' I repeated, going over to where she was standing to take the dress away.

I took hold of it and she spun round, fetching a stinging slap across my cheek. Automatically I raised my other hand and hit her back.

127

Her eyes widened in horror. She let go of the dress and fled to the bathroom.

For the next hour I stood by the locked door and tried to cajole her into coming out. I apologised. I pleaded. I felt wretched and guilt-ridden but ultimately exasperated. I left the flat and went to the office.

The newsroom was empty, rows of desks with typewriters and telephones, silent and inert, waiting for news. Clatter and urgency seemed to belong to another world. I slumped down at my desk and pulled open the day's edition I had missed by getting married. The main story was about the Profumo affair and there were pictures of Christine Keeler and Mandy Rice-Davies. They did not really look what they were, at least the girl, Keeler, did not. Her face had an almost vacant look about it, naive. She reminded me a little of Marion, as she had been until tonight. I tried to close my mind to the awful mistake I had made. Marion had provoked me and all I felt was disgust with both myself and her, when the contrived little scene might have roused some sort of passion between us that could have been played out and resolved in bed. But I felt no passion for her in that direction. I think I never had and that was the trouble, I had never really thought about it and any qualms over the past few months had been shoved aside for the sake of convenience. What a dreadful admission to have to make to yourself on your wedding night. A lonely and miserable realisation. There was not even sufficient passion to go back and tell her of the mistake and say that we should part, just an awful creeping lethargy which would probably bind me to her for years and years.

I got up and went over to the sub-editors' table where I knew there would be a bottle of scotch in one of the drawers. I found it and took a swig. I put the bottle down and a voice behind me said:

'Is this what they call married bliss?'

I turned and saw one of the subs, Jane Hillier, standing a few feet away, watching me, an expression of mock reproach on her sallow-skinned face. I had never liked Jane. She was an ardent feminist and generally assumed by the rest of the staff to be a lesbian. She was tall and thin and always wore trousers. Her hair was short and straight and her face colourless, although her eyes had an oddly disquieting quality. They seemed to miss nothing, even the goings-on within one's soul.

'Are you planning on keeping it all to yourself or can anyone join in?' she said, glancing at the whisky bottle.

I picked it up and handed it to her as she came forward and perched herself on the edge of the table.

'How did it go today, or is that a rhetorical question?' she asked, her eyes still penetrating my befuzzled brain. I must have drunk a lot during the day and it was beginning to register. Heedless, I took another gulp of the whisky and between us Jane and I finished it off over the next hour as I told her about Marion's mother and Marion and more about Ruby and about Frank and his vacuum cleaners, and the anorexic sister and the idiot brother, the whole lot, poured out in a spate of drunken weakness, and all of it a mournful indirect tirade against poor Marion, locked away in our bathroom, smarting at the unfairness and injustice of it all just as I was with the all-perceiving Jane.

She listened and watched and I didn't care what she heard or saw, only that she stayed to hear me out even though I would probably regret it in the morning.

When all the scotch had gone she got up and told me she was going to take me to her flat and make black coffee. I followed her out of the building and got into her car. My mind and will had gone into a sort of neutral suspended in an alcoholic haze. I think I fell asleep on her sofa while she went to make the coffee and woke up some hours later to find I was lying in a bed with Jane beside me. I sat up and tried to remember how I had got there. I was naked and yet could not recall undressing. I felt Jane's body stir.

'You're not going to be sick, are you?' I heard her murmur drowsily as she switched on the bedside lamp. She eased herself up on her pillow, the sheet slipping down over one breast.

'No,' I said quietly. 'No, I don't think so.' I was staring at her, confused, my mind trying to fill in the gap in my recollection. 'Did I... I mean, did we...?' I asked.

'Yes, we did,' she said, her eyes on mine. 'There seemed no point in trying to get you home in the state you were in although you managed a reasonable performance.'

I felt vaguely alarmed to be told that I had managed anything at all in view of the fact I could not remember a thing.

'But I thought you were...' I began, only half aware of what I was saying.

'That I prefer women?' Jane said, moving back down the bed and switching out the light. 'Let's just say that I'm ambidextrous. Good night, Nick, sleep well and don't confess to your wife.'

CHAPTER SEVEN

Saturday morning – Charlotte

I woke to the sound of the telephone ringing downstairs. At one time we had one by the bed but Dan said it kept him awake even when it was not ringing because he always expected that it might.

I got up. Dan was still asleep, his head barely visible above the cover. I could not remember him coming back to bed.

The phone kept ringing. I hurried, anxious that it should not wake Dan or Vicky but then Vicky was not there and I had forgotten.

Of course the phone would be bound to stop ringing just as I got to it. Wasn't that what always happened, and I had no idea how long it had been going before it had succeeded in rousing me. I glanced at the clock in the hall. It was nine thirty. We had slept late with no Vicky to wake us. I picked up the receiver. No click. No sudden dial tone, the caller was determined.

'Hello.'

'Charlotte. It's Nick.'

His voice sounded tired and battered and yet there was an urgency and insistence there too.

'Marion knows. I told her last night.'

There was a pause.

It felt like a very big moment. A turning point. The crisis had come.

'What do you want me to do?' I asked.

'You must make your own decision.'

'Where are you, at home?'

'No, the office, it was impossible to stay in the house.'

'I'll come to you there.'

'How long?'

'I don't know. As soon as I can.'

I put down the receiver. The house was silent again although beyond the garden I could hear Tamara braying to the morning, carefree and uninhibited. It was a wonderful sound, crazy and funny and sad all at the same time. I stood by the telephone, listening to the donkey and feeling as if my heart might burst out of my chest at any moment.

The stair creaked and a moment later Dan was standing at the other end of the hall, his hands plunged deep into his dressing gown pockets, his eyes filled with certain knowledge.

'Who was it?'

'Nicholas Matthews.'

'What's he doing ringing you on a Saturday morning?'

Why the question when he already knew?

'He's told his wife,' I said, obliquely.

'What?'

'What do you think!' I retorted, unfairly, unkindly. Why should Dan make it easy for me when it was so hard for him to take the truth, even, at last, to demand it?

'I don't know. You tell me.'

'I'm having an affair with him,' I almost shouted. 'No, that doesn't sound right,' I continued less forcefully. 'It's more than an affair, Dan. 'I'm leaving you.' I turned away from him and went out to the kitchen. I started to make toast, mechanically, knowing there was no possibility it would be eaten. In the same way, whenever Vicky had fallen or suffered some minor catastrophe as a baby, I had immediately put her to my breast.

I waited for Dan to come into the kitchen, my kitchen with its expensive oak units I had chosen with such deliberation; the table I had found after months of scouring antique shops and auctions; the floor tiles we had waited six months to be delivered because they were just the right shade. All of it suddenly unimportant and easy to leave, part of all the trappings I had thrown off without a qualm a moment ago by the telephone in the hallway of a house which had been my home. The quick and the dead, and yet the dead had seemed so vital. How strange to be so abruptly cured of materialism.

I made coffee. Put out butter and marmalade. Arranged the table as I always did for a leisurely weekend breakfast. Dan came into the kitchen, dressed but not shaved, the black stubble accentuating the whiteness of his face. Even he seemed removed from my possession. Rights to understanding were forfeited by betrayal, were they not? Besides I did not need him to understand, only to accept. It sounds and is a selfish way of looking at things, but are not we all selfish, even those that martyr themselves to a right course of behaviour? Later I would be called courageous and honest but I always knew that I was selfish. It was simply a matter of degree.

Dan sat down opposite me at the table and then stood up again and went over to the window.

'I don't think I've really taken it in,' he said hoarsely, clearing his throat. 'I knew there was something but I never expected it to go this far. I hoped, I suppose I hoped that it was nothing too much, would blow over. Just a fling. Are you certain, Lottie, that it isn't just a tenuous thing?'

'Tenuous', what a very solicitorish word, I thought resentfully. I was trying to dislike him, even hate him, fending off the vulnerability of a decade spent together, lives and being intertwined day and night and now suddenly severed with bleeding ends to be held in and stopped up before the flow had a chance to drain and weaken resolve.

'No, it's not tenuous, although certainty is another matter. I

133

don't want that any more.'

'You may not want it, but I think you need it,' he said with unbearable evenness of tone, and assumed insight. If only he would fight and be angry.

'There's only one thing that's certain and that's death. I just want to feel alive for a bit in the meantime,' I said, resorting to a sort of desperate and profound cliché which came out sounding like adolescent rebellion.

'Thank you,' Dan said, a totally foreign note of bitterness in his voice.

The gap was widening. I pushed it a little further.

'I'm not ready to do without passion,' I scrambled on. 'Didn't you notice that we never touched one another except in bed?'

'The past tense already?' he said. 'I didn't think that we needed to.' He heaved a great breath, as if there was something constricting in his chest. He was agitated, maybe even a little livid, and yet his eyes still maintained the sad and reproachful gaze of the observer witnessing a tragedy. He thought I was making a mistake, for myself as much as for him.

'Why couldn't we have talked about it sooner?' he said.

'I didn't think it would go this far, but that doesn't mean I wouldn't have left you anyway,' I said, finding it necessary to go on hurting him in order to guard against the possibility of allowing myself to be trapped into staying. Dan had always used understanding and reason to lay the traps. Perhaps if I sounded sufficiently unreasonable and intransigent he would let go now and come to view the parting with a sense of relief. I could not allow there to be any suggestion of hope for us, neither for Dan or myself, although it was frightening to feel so determined to destroy, even something that had felt as if it was destroying me.

'I'd better get dressed.' I said, getting up. 'I have to go and see him.'

'What about his wife? Does she know?'

'Yes, he told her last night.'

'Poor woman, is she all right?'

'I don't know. I didn't ask.'

'I see.'

'That's right! I didn't ask.'

'What time will you be back?'

'I don't know.'

'Damn it all! What have I done?'

'Nothing. I'm sorry, Dan. It's me. These things happen.'

'Don't give me platitudes, please.'

'I can't explain. Not now, I must go. I'll be back later.'

Unfair, so unfair, why had I not shrivelled up in shame? Instead I felt elated, quite undeniably so, driven on by a force transcending guilt and responsibility.

'Are you ready for all those responsibilities?' Frances had asked.

'You make it sound like some sort of sentence,' I said.

'Isn't it? Mortgages, cooking and ironing shirts, answerable to somebody else.'

'It doesn't have to be like that.'

'With Dan I think it will be.'

'You don't really know him. He's all right.'

'If you say so.'

'Please, Fran, I want you to like him.'

'Oh, I don't dislike him. It's just that I think it would be better if you lived together for a while first.'

'You wouldn't have said that a year ago.'

'Perhaps not.'

Frances was in her third year at Cambridge and had fallen in love with a post-graduate student called Leonard, an American Jew whose rooms she now shared. Frances was on the pill. She had taken the precaution before she and Leonard had become lovers.

'Don't you want to marry Leonard?' I asked. We were sitting on the grassy bank which slopes down to the River Cam beyond the smooth expanse of lawn behind King's. It was a warm day for

October but the summer tourists had left and the Backs returned to relative tranquillity. Dan and I had been to Cambridge a month earlier when Frances was not there. We had called at half a dozen estate agents, looking for mortgageable houses. It was how we spent most weekends. Cambridge, Newmarket, Saffron Walden, househunting.

'You should always buy the house you can't afford. It's the best way of saving. A house is the best investment you can make,' Dan's father had delivered sagely after he had come to accept that I had 'turned out all right', after all.

'I haven't thought about marriage,' Frances said.

'But you love Leonard.'

'Yes. Do you love Dan?'

'I suppose so. I haven't thought about it, but of course I do, I must do, mustn't I?'

We lapsed into silence and lay back on our coats which we had spread over the grass.

'I love it here. I hope we get a house in Cambridge. We'll be able to see each other more often,' I said.

'I don't suppose I shall still be here this time next year; Frances said.

'You might stay on. Leonard's been here five years, hasn't he?' I said hopefully. I wanted to live near Frances and felt an odd sense of despair at the thought of moving to Cambridge myself just as she would be about to leave.

'You're not going to finish your course at art college then?' she said.

'Well I can't really, not if we come here. It would be too far and impractical. Dan's new job is more important.'

Frances sat up in a sudden movement.

'You don't really believe that, do you?' she said. 'You can't!'

'Oh. I don't know,' I said, realising how it must have sounded to her, but somehow incapable of rationalising, perhaps because I did not want to have to face up to the new role I had ascribed to myself

136

for fear of seeing it as unacceptable.

'Isn't it strange,' she said next, leaning back on one hand and gazing across the river to a meadow where sheep were grazing. 'I always thought it would be you who didn't conform, not me.'

'Is it such a thin line? I mean, if you get married you are conforming and if you live with someone you are not?' I said, defensively simplistic.

'You know that it's not just the fact of being married, but everything that seems to go with it, self-denial, at least as far as you are concerned.'

'I wish you wouldn't be so direct. What am I supposed to say to Dan, we'll marry on my terms which means you not taking the new job because I've got to finish college and never mind anything else? Doesn't there always have to be a compromise? What would you do if Leonard went back to America and there was the chance for you to go too?'

'I'd finish my degree and then I'd go, assuming there was work for me there and that I could be independent. It would never work between us otherwise.'

'But what would happen if you married and had a baby?'

'That wouldn't change the basis of the relationship. I'd still need to feel independent and having a baby doesn't mean that you have to give that up.'

'Doesn't it?'

'Not at all, although I can't imagine wanting a baby, can you?'

'No,' I said, 'but I suppose one day.' I had not told Frances about Chad or the abortion. Nobody knew except Dan. Perhaps it was the dead baby that bound us together after all. I had not felt the same since it had happened. There was a need to make amends, to retreat and comply, nothing consciously thought out but an overall guiding impulse Frances would probably have understood better than the lame stuff I had given her about practicality. But I could not tell her. Perhaps it was something to do with what had happened years ago on my last day at the convent. That was something we had never dicussed although it seemed so ridiculous and trivial now, but a sin then, a shockingly wrong thing to do, and I was madder and more miserable then than when the two doctors signed me as crazy.

The sun went behind a cloud and suddenly it was cold sitting on the river bank.

'Let's go and have some tea,' Frances suggested. 'I'll even toast you some crumpets if Leonard is back and he's lit a fire. I'm hopeless at them, mine always go out, perhaps I'm not so independent after all,' she said, smiling wryly and taking my arm as we got up and walked back through the colleges.

Leonard was back. We went into the sitting room to find him crouched in front of the old-fashioned fireplace, a sheet of newspaper held across to draw the flames.

'Good. I promised Charlotte crumpets,' Frances said.

'What would you do without me?' Leonard said, standing up and removing the newspaper to reveal a blazing fire. He stood back to admire it and then turned to face us, smiling at me in greeting.

'We've just been discussing that,' Frances said, taking off her coat.

'Sounds interesting,' Leonard said. He was a slightly-built man, with jet black hair, very curly, which he scratched a lot. It was a mannerism. He held his arms high when he talked, as if to give himself extra height. He scratched through his hair with one hand and with the other made expansive gestures to what he was saying. He was not at all good-looking, almost ugly, but attractive as soon as he began to talk. Frances' manner towards him appeared almost offhand a lot of the time but if most sexual relationships between men and women consist of victim and aggressor, Frances was ultimately the victim. She adored Leonard but his intellect intimidated her so she used superficial disparagement as a defence, although Leonard seemed to let it pass most of the time as he did now in not pursuing how she would manage without him.

'I'm afraid it will have to be muffins. I bought muffins,' he said, briefly taking her shoulders and stretching up to kiss her lightly on the forehead as he went past towards the door where I was standing.

'Charlotte. Nice to see you again. How's Dan? Such a nice guy and I understand you and he are to be married. Congratulations,' he said warmly, taking my shoulders and kissing me on both cheeks. Frances followed him out of the room and I went over to the fire to warm up.

The four of us had met in June, about a week before Dan and I went to buy the turquoise ring. It had been in London. A concert at the Festival Hall. Frances had been given the tickets. The music was Prokofiev, and Dan and I, who never thought to go to classical concerts, had surprised ourselves by liking it. Afterwards we had all gone to an Italian restaurant for supper and Leonard had talked about Vietnam although he did not mention the fact that he had been drafted out there and spent two years fighting the Viet Cong; that I disovered later from Frances. Leonard talked about the wider issue rather than his own experiences. He had startling and original ideas which he propounded with clarity and an easy modesty which encouraged the rest of us to form and express views on matters we had hitherto failed to examine or seen only with stereotyped opinion.

The evening was a sparkling taste of what seemed to me like another way of life. I thought I had glimpsed it in Chad, the exhilarating liberation of expansive thinking, but there I had been hoodwinked by a phony and retreated back to Dan and the safety of convention. Listening to Leonard the niggling dissatisfaction was roused again and yet lay dormant for nearly ten years, kept down by kindness and affection and the inertia brought on by material comfort. Selfish again, but perhaps it had been the same for Dan.

Our wedding was to be a grand affair. From the moment the turquoise ring was displayed on the third finger of my left hand the arrangements were set in motion and I was carried along as if on a tide of white tulle with designs for three-tiered cakes, silver-worded invitation cards, flowers, gift lists, guest lists and going-away outfits swept along with me like buffeting flotsam. The ceremony was to take place in Dan's church and the reception at Lakeside. His parents insisted on bearing the cost and my mother gratefully agreed to abdicate the responsibility not only for the expense but the organisation as well.

'Poor Dorothy! It wouldn't be fair to expect her to cope with it all when she's on her own,' Dan's mother said, consulting her diary to find a suitable date for the wedding and prompting Dan to ring the vicar.

It was agreed that I should go and live at Lakeside until we were married and as if Dan's parents were still very wary as to my total conversion to stability and reasonable behaviour the wedding was fixed sooner rather than later. November, to get it over with before preparations began for Christmas, and before the weather was too awful.

I went back to college for the winter term and acquired a moped to get me to and from Lakeside. Chad, who mercifully had been granted leave of absence during the summer term to take up a short fellowship in Mexico, was back but lecturing the new first-year intake and surrounding himself with another group of awed and receptive students. I saw little of him, deliberately as if I was frightened of the hidden dark force taking over again. The sight of him, to hear his voice, filled me with a squirming revulsion, against myself as much as him.

Why I went back to college when I was to leave before the term was over was the one small obstinate rebellion against the tulle tide, although I do not want to give the impression that I was not happy with what was to be my lot. To be surrounded by the kindness, security and decency of Dan's family made me feel privileged and redeemed. Their consideration knew no bounds and Dan's mother, who suspended all her other activities in order to give every bit of her time to the wedding arrangements, showed not a hint of resentment at my daily disappearance while she grappled with caterers and florists and car-hire firms.

'I have always wished that I'd had a daughter,' she told me one evening in the kitchen as she showed me how to make flaky pastry. 'And now I've got one.'

The weekend before the wedding Dan and I went for a walk, beyond the house and across the fields which stretched over the horizon. It was a cold, wintry Sunday afternoon and we both wore wellington boots as it had been raining in the morning and the ground was damp and muddy. When we came to the patch of trees which stood beside the field where the corn had been we stopped and looked at one another.

'Did we come this way on purpose?' I asked him, wondering how he remembered what had happened there three years earlier. With regret? He had never mentioned it directly since.

'It's a pity the ground is so wet,' he said, smiling and kicking at a stray lump of chalk. His hands were thrust into the pockets of his brown anorak. He looked down at the spot where we had been.

'It was the chains that did it,' he said, still smiling but seeming a little embarrassed. 'What about you?'

'Sheer devilment,' I answered, almost without thinking.

'I might have known it,' he said, taking my arm and turning back along the way we had come. 'Tea and Evensong. Mother will be worrying we're going to be late.'

If only he had not said that last bit. I pulled back on his arm.

'I don't mind a bit of mud,' I said, alarmed by the sudden sense of desperation that had made me say it. It was not that I wanted to churn about under the tree in the November dankness, it just seemed necessary to make an attempt at thwarting all the carefully laid plans, if only by making us too late for tea and Evensong on this one occasion.

Dan looked back at me, his expression fleetingly as surprised and bewildered as it had been three years ago.

'How would we explain it? The mud and the wet, I mean. Come on, Lottie, just one more week and we can do whatever we like.'

'Can we?' I said, allowing myself to be tugged away.

'Within reason,' Dan replied.

The following Saturday I stood before the satin-draped altar, my own satin and tulle making me feel like a sacrificial offering. The vicar, a strange little man with that awful pallid and underfed look some clergymen have, stood immediately in front of us, swaying a little, back and forth in his white surplice. He bent his head forward as if he wanted to whisper to us and for an inane moment I thought he might ask us if we had taken the blood tests he had advised.

'My wife and I did,' he told us a month earlier at the obligatory pre-wedding 'little chat'. But what if the tests had shown something to be wrong, I had wanted to ask him, would he and his wife have abandoned one another?

I felt Dan's hand slip over my own, squeezing my fingers. He was trembling a little. He looked amazing in morning dress, the grey and black striped trousers and oddly-tailored black jacket. I glanced at his face but he was staring straight ahead, past the vicar, to the altar. Did he really believe in all this? That the bizarre little ceremony was being watched over by a heavenly God and a Holy Ghost? Perhaps. One never knew for certain any of these things. The trembling passed to me and I was grateful to hear the vicar begin: 'Dearly beloved, we are gathered together here in the sight of God.'

Someone threw rice outside the church. It hit my face and stung, but I smiled on, looking round at all the well-turned-out guests. I did not know any of them. They were all friends of Dan's parents, shooting men, bridge players, men and women of obvious standing in life, who smiled and shook hands and kissed the bride.

Back at Lakeside my mother kept thanking Dan's parents and looking on the verge of tears. Dan's father had 'given me away' to his son. The best man was a cousin from Oxford and the two bridesmaids his twin daughters, identical seven-year-olds who had said they were going to be sick just before we had entered the church but failed to carry out their threat.

I cannot think why Frances was unable to be there, but I remember missing her and gazing with a certain amount of discomfort mixed with pride at her present, a set of pens and instruments used by graphic designers, on display with all the silver and crystal, linen and china.

'What an odd gift, dear,' Dan's mother had said when we were setting everything out. 'Perhaps you will be able to exchange it for something you and Dan need.'

'Lottie, we ought to circulate.' Dan had found me, alone for a moment in the conservatory where the presents were on show. 'What are you doing in here, all alone, gloating over the haul?' He laughed. 'Come on, everyone's waiting for the speeches and telegrams.'

It was the one day to feel special and important and in a way I did, although not as myself but as the bride, a curious creature set apart in her white to be admired and treasured. And Dan seemed pleased with me, even proud.

'It's all right. It's going to be all right. I've done the right thing,' I thought, a secret little sensation of joyous relief settling somewhere within me, warm and hopeful.

The speeches were made, the telegrams read, nothing jarred. There were no intrusions to mar the day. Dan made a joke in his speech and everyone laughed, anxious to ease and indulge. The tears at last sprung from my mother's eyes as we drove away in Dan's new Mini. The sun had broken through the November clouds. An old boot and a string of empty tin cans bounced along the road behind us.

'Thank goodness that's over,' Dan said, and I knew what he meant although the day had been a magical one and we were happy.

CHAPTER EIGHT

Saturday evening – Dan

'Is it because our generation hasn't had a war?'

'I'm sorry?' I said, looking back at Hilary, staring at her.

'We haven't had enough excitement in our lives. Do you think that's why everyone's having affairs?' she persisted, her mouth provocative, her tongue now visible and pressed against her teeth.

'I've no idea. Is everyone?' I said, glancing beyond her to the other side of the room where Charlotte stood, glass in hand, her head held high, talking with a West Indian. She'd lost weight but I had not noticed until now. The ache in my chest became stronger.

'Just about,' Hilary went on, although she too was more aware of someone else in the room and after a few more gins would doubtless be telling me about him just as she had at other parties. His name I could not remember. Perhaps it was another one now and I would have to listen and pretend to fancy her to make her feel better. But no, not tonight. Not possible.

I watched Hilary drain her glass, she was already swaying a little. I had hardly touched my own drink. Maybe it would have helped, numbed the queasy feeling in my gut. Why had we come to this wretched party, just as if nothing had happened and life would go on as normal, although the hope was still there that it would. I had a right to hope.

'Not you and Charlotte, of course. We all know that,' Hilary was saying. 'That's why you're such a challenge, Dan darling. Get me another gin, will you, or I'll die of thirst.'

I took her glass and went across the room to the drinks table where Charlotte was still talking to the West Indian. I caught her eye but she glanced away almost immediately as if she didn't know me. I stood by the table, about two feet away from her although she had her back to me. I unscrewed the gin bottle and started pouring into Hilary's glass. The gin reached the top and overflowed down the sides. Charlotte and the West Indian had moved to another part of the room where several couples were dancing. The lights dimmed still further. I looked for a spare glass to get rid of some of the gin, but there were none left. I started trying to pour some of it back into the bottle but my hand was unsteady and the neck of the bottle too narrow.

Hilary appeared beside me and snatching the glass from my hand took a gulp. Her eyes widened:

'Gracious, Dan, what are you trying to do, get me drunk?' she said, but seemed to like the idea and suggested I ask her to dance.

We moved over towards the other dancers and she threw her arms round my neck and pressed herself against me. She reeked of gin and cigarettes.

'Oh men are such bastards. All except you, that is, darling,' she was saying.

Nicholas Matthews was a bastard. His wife had telephoned me during the afternoon.

'What can we do?' she had said, sounding pretty desperate.

'We could meet if you like, if that would help', I told her, but she said not yet, she didn't want to upset her husband.

'I understand,' I said and she rang off.

I caught a whiff of scent, Charlotte's, as she and her partner moved closer to Hilary and me for a moment. The perfume was distinctive and painfully evocative. Charlotte had only recently started using it again but I had been no more than vaguely aware of this until tonight. It was the same stuff I had bought for her years

146

ago when we were first married and our life together had seemed incredibly good after all the dreadful business a few months before when I had wondered at times whether it could really work. Chad, Charlotte's pregnancy, the abortion, it had all been horrific, but I had wanted her even more than before and pushed things along despite the possibility that she might be marrying me as a sort of escape from the harsher side of life. It was a risk worth taking. The trouble was that you could not live up to that sort of risk over ten years. Caution is relaxed, suspicion gratefully put aside and everyday life takes over.

At first I did things which were, on reflection, subconsciously contrived to secure Charlotte. The same day I was offered the job in Cambridge the firm I was with came up with a similar proposition. In many ways it would have been better to have stayed where I was but going to Cambridge meant moving away, far enough for it to seem impractical for Charlotte to stay at the art college. We bought a tumbledown terraced cottage in the city rather than the modern flat I would have preferred, but a home in need of renovation provided an activity Charlotte and I could share.

For six months we worked on it nearly every evening, stripping the walls and rubbing down fireplaces, ripping out the old kitchen, turning one of the bedrooms into a bathroom. During the day Charlotte carried on alone while I was at the office. She seemed to enjoy it all except when we started painting and the fumes made her feel sick.

By the end of the summer the house was about done and we invited my parents to come over one evening for dinner. It seemed important they should be our first proper guests as they had let us have some money to buy the place which was virtually unmortgageable when we found it. In honour of the occasion Charlotte had bought steak and spent most of the day preparing the meal.

'Lovely, dears, lovely,' my mother said as we took her on a tour of the house. 'You've just got the one room left to tackle then,' she went on as we sat down to eat. 'Those awful clashing colours. They must be a nightmare to have in your bedroom. Don't people have some funny ideas.'

I glanced at Charlotte, hoping she was not upset by my mother's innocent blunder. She did not appear to be but said nothing and got up to clear away the soup plates. I followed her out to the kitchen where she pushed the door to and leaning back against it began to laugh.

'I'm sure she doesn't realise. She would be terribly embarrassed and upset if we told her,' I said, relieved to see she wasn't upset.

'I was terribly tempted to tell her,' she said, still shaking with laughter.

'Her idea of a bedroom is different from yours,' I whispered, hoping my parents couldn't hear us.

'And yours!' Charlotte added.

We had disagreed over the clashing colours.

'No, I quite like it now,' I said. 'It's different anyway and better than pink.'

'Are you sure?' she taunted, smiling at me devilishly.

'No!' I said, catching her mood. 'And for God's sake behave yourself this evening, won't you!'

'Of course!' she retorted with mock indignation. 'Haven't I been good up until now? For the last six months?' she added.

She moved away from the door and bent down to take the steak from the oven. I continued gazing at her for a moment and was conscious of a vaguely worrying inference in what she had just said.

The steak was tough, a real struggle to eat and one that my mother had to give up, leaving most of her meat under her fork as if she had tried to hide it.

'Soup always fills me up,' she said. 'But that was delicious, Lottie, delicious.'

After the meal was over she and Charlotte went out to the kitchen, while my father and I smoked cigars and drank port. That was the order of things with their dinner parties. The old order, archaic, maybe, but pleasant, and if I felt at all uneasy about the way we had automatically allowed their ways to be ours in this, the port and the cigar and the closed kitchen door made it seem not to matter all that much. My father asked me if I wanted to go shooting with him again and as the house was finished I said I would.

'That didn't go too badly, did it?' I said to Charlotte when we were in bed.

'You're joking, aren't you. It was a disaster,' she rounded on me. 'You and your father pompously puffing away like something out of Dickens while your mother told me in the kitchen how to hammer steak with a rolling pin.'

'Why did you stay out there then, and I'm sure she didn't mean anything by it. You know what she's like.'

'That's the trouble, you can't say anything to her. She'd be so hurt, but she drives me mad with her well-meaningness. I wanted to scream and tell her that I'd painted the bedroom but she'd think there was something wrong with me and probably drive over twice a week to "keep me company" and make sure I looked after you all right.'

'She would not. I wouldn't let her.'

'I'm not sure you'd be able to stop her.'

'Oh come on, Lottie.' I switched out the lights and reached for her. 'You do look after me all right,' I murmured, starting to make love to her.

It was late and I supposed that she might be tired but she became almost ferocious as I moved over her. She dug her fingers into my back and when it was over and we had moved apart she remained restless, although she said no more.

The shooting season began and most Saturdays I drove over to Lakeside to meet my father and the other guns before we went off for the day. Charlotte didn't seem to mind. Often she would see Frances who was still at the university, and they'd have tea together. Occasionally, when I got back, we would then go out with Frances and Leonard, but eventually this stopped and I was glad. I found Frances too sharp. Sometimes it seemed almost as if she was trying to 'subvert' Charlotte, in some obscure way to make her dissastisfied. At times I felt as if I couldn't say anything without a sideways look from Frances, hearing what she took to be reactionary. And, of course, the more she did it the more I fell into the trap without meaning to sound at all like that. And Leonard, well, he reminded me rather a lot of Chad.

Charlotte's restlessness became more obvious. Not just in bed, but at other times as well. With no more work to do on the house her days had become long and aimless. She started to look for work but with no qualifications there was nothing very exciting on offer, although in desperation she took a job as a receptionist with one of the many estate agents we had called on. It lasted less than a fortnight before she was asked to leave.

'You know what they say, "the more you do, the more you can do", well, I think it works the other way as well,' she said, justifying the sacking which upset her more than she would admit.

That night she cried in bed. She hardly ever cried. She said herself she was not the type, so that when she did it was all the harder to cope with and I felt awkward and clumsy in my attempts to show understanding.

'Everyone gets the push one time in their life,' I said, my hands hovering and hesitant over her heaving shoulders.

'It's not just that,' she moaned.

'What is it then?' I demanded, more insistent than I had meant to sound.

'I don't know! I don't know,' she sobbed. 'Maybe it's all been a mistake.'

What this meant I dared not ask and flopped back on my side of the bed. The sobbing subsided and after a few moments she moved towards me, her face still turned into the pillows.

'I'm sorry, Dan,' she murmured and slid her hand down my chest. Her fingers closed over me, feeling and pumping. I remained motionless on my back, taking in the sensation of arousal but still perplexed and plagued by an indistinct sort of misery.

It was dark in the bedroom. I felt a rush of cold air as the covers lifted and Charlotte straddled me. I reached up to pull her down but she resisted and grasped my hand, pushing it down to herself, forcing my fingers to jab and knead. The pitch of excitement in my stomach was so strong and exquisite that I lost control but Charlotte didn't seem to realise and almost angrily held on to my wrist. Her body was quivering and insistent and then she went into a sudden shudder and made a deep sort of yell. She let got of my wrist and in the darkness I could just make out the slumped arch of her back, her head hung low. She moved off me and seemed to crawl to her side of the bed, pulling up the flung-back covers round herself like a cocoon.

We were silent. I lay still and amazed, staring up into the darkness, almost disbelieving, a bit bewildered, maybe even shocked. It had been quite wonderful but where had she learnt it? If it had been from Chad then why had she waited so long? I turned over and felt disgusted with myself, analysing and suspecting. It had been wonderful. A gift. An opening up. An expression of trust. I turned again and stretching towards Charlotte pulled down a corner of the sheet from round her back and kissed her shoulder. She seemed to be sleeping.

It was not long after that turning point of a night that I came home one Saturday afternoon to find Chad standing in the kitchen talking to Charlotte. There had been a problem with my gun so I had abandoned the day's shooting and driven back to Cambridge early.

They both seemed surprised to see me, Charlotte even slightly wary at first although I had the impression that she was actually relieved I had come back sooner than expected. Chad greeted me with hearty insincere pleasure, taking my hand, clapping his other on my back.

'Chad's been visiting one of the colleges,' Charlotte said as if she had to give an excuse for him being there. 'He looked up our name in the telephone book and picked the right number first time,' she went on, looking at me directly to make me believe her.

'I was just saying to Charlotte that I can't stop long but it seemed a waste to come here and not look you up,' Chad was saying. They both looked guilty, embarrassingly so the more they tried to appear casual and incidental about it all. I asked Chad how he was getting on, offered him a drink, even suggested he should stay for supper. I seemed to be taken over by a kind of masochism that wanted to indulge the awful jealousy by prolonging the thing. But Chad continued to back off; wary and of no real substance, he had no stomach for it.

'It was like I said,' Charlotte insisted after the front door had closed against him.

'I didn't suggest that it wasn't,' I said.

'Only in the way you looked and spoke and made us feel as if you had caught us out,' she flung at me.

We were standing facing one another. It was an uncomfortable moment and I felt annoyed with myself for allowing a confrontation. Charlotte's direct look had turned into a glare.

'Let it go,' I said, making an effort to smile, finding some small comfort in her aggrieved tone.

Her attitude had been strained and nervous but now she sighed as if it had all been unnecessarily misinterpreted.

'I'm glad you came back when you did,' she said. 'He makes me feel...' she hesitated. 'Oh, I don't know, I just don't like being with him, and you wanted him to stay for supper!' She stepped forward, put her arms round my back, and hugged me.

'I do love you, Dan,' she murmured.

★

A fortnight later I came home to find the house empty, the first time Charlotte had not been there when I got in from work. She turned up half an hour later and announced that she had been to London and got a job with a studio off Regent Street. The introduction had come via Chad I discovered later, but by then Charlotte was well into the job and happier than I had ever known her. Fulfilling herself at last, Frances said, somehow pointedly in my direction as if I had been the cause of the delay. But the jibes – moderated, I noticed, since Charlotte's daily train trips to London – no longer seemed to matter. Our life had come together.

Hilary, divorced and not suited to it, floundering through loneliness from one affair to the next, wanted me to leave the room with her.

'Come on,' she whispered, pulling at my arm, slightly unsteady on her feet, 'I just need to get out of here for a few minutes.'

Charlotte was still dancing with the West Indian, a faster dance now, her body as rhythmic as his. I had not seen her dance like that in years, it was almost abandoned.

I went with Hilary out into the hallway where two couples were talking on the stairs. Hilary glanced at one of the men who saw her but made it obvious he didn't want to. Further along the hall french windows were open to the garden. The night air had a balmy sort of heat left over from the day. Hilary and I went out and began to wander across the lawn, dark and enclosed by mature trees heavy with leafy branches which hung motionless in the stillness of the night. It was in sharp contrast to the house from where the sound of reggae music beat out through the open windows.

Hilary was crying, a tearful whimper that seemed to hold back the big sobs.

'That was him, the one on the stairs, with his wife, of course. I don't think I can bear it, Dan.' She flung her head against me in a dramatic gesture of misery. I think Hilary feared boredom more than heartbreak.

153

'What am I going to do,' she moaned.

'What do you want to do?' I said, wishing now that I had stayed in the house where I could see Charlotte. It was as if she was about to make a long journey and I wanted to spend every moment left with her until she went. That was how it felt even though I was a long way from accepting her going despite the hideous sense of loss.

Hilary was looking up at me, her face quite dry, her eyes bright in the darkness, almost like a cat's, her mouth slightly open. We had stood in that attitude before, the invitation obvious and un-thought-out.

She shook her head, throwing off the pose.

'I give up with you Dan. I just give up!' she said with a little laugh. 'I know, I've had too much to drink, and I'll regret it in the morning and all that, but just once, if I could only get to you just once. You're an anachronism, darling, a faithful husband.'

'Does that make me very dull?' I asked her, actually wanting an answer to the question.

'Not at all, darling, just an enigma these days,' she supplied as we started back towards the house, her arm linked through mine.

'Which is it, enigma or anachronism?' I said jokingly, the ache in my chest suddenly vice-like.

'I always get wordy when I'm sex starved,' she went on. 'It's all the reading I do in bed to get to sleep.'

I liked her. She was honest and open, a good sort under all the overt nonsense she came out with, and I felt sorry for her. Perhaps we could have started an affair and been a comfort to one another, but the thought was only passing. Affairs were not, after all, anything to do with convenience.

That was what Matthews had tried to say earlier, just before we had come out to go to the party. An extraordinary presumption on his part, to come to the house and tell me what he and Charlotte planned to do; as if I had already accepted the inconvenience and of course would be reasonable about it all – just one of those things, old chap, most inconvenient, but I understand.

154

The three of us sitting down in the drawing room being bloody civilised. I even offered him a drink.

'Charlotte and I want to try living together,' he said, declining my whisky as if it would be bad form to take anything of mine. My wife, presumably, didn't count.

He and Charlotte sat together on the tasselled sofa, given to us by my parents, the sofa where Lottie and I had made love. I sat opposite them, the cold sweat of injustice rendering me powerless to argue and reason and making my hands shake.

'I'm sorry, I know it's hard on you, but these things happen.'

Why did people say that: 'These things happen', as if they had had no part in it themselves, using fate as an excuse.

The audacity in what he had said about trying living together had not escaped me. What if it did not work between them, was it assumed that we would all go back as we were before? It was probably no more than an unfortunate turn of phrase. I knew that, and yet I was grateful for it, grabbing at the smallest chink of hope – pathetic, the drowning man clinging on to the boat that has tipped him into the sea.

'We'll have to find somewhere to live which might take a few days, but I'll get a hotel room if you want Charlotte to leave tonight,' he was saying, the practical details like weapons, consolidating and defending the ground already gained.

'No, this is her house as well,' I said with strained evenness of tone, desperately playing for time. 'Wait till you've found somewhere.' I could see the irritation in Charlotte's expression as she glanced at Matthews. She had always baulked against reason, delay, impetuously guarding against her own uncertainty, but delay could perhaps retrieve the situation, for me, and for Vicky.

Vicky. If all this was going to be long term, Vicky I would lose too. Charlotte, of course, would take her, that was a deep, gnawing certainty but something I didn't want to talk about with Matthews there.

Charlotte, maybe aware of this but too defensive to wait until we were alone, blurted it out: 'I'm taking Vicky. I wouldn't leave without her.'

She said it as harshly as possible, to leave no doubt. I wished I could hate her then and despaired at my inability to cause her any pain, but it seemed I had nothing with which to retaliate.

'I appear to have no choice in any of this,' I said, bitterly. 'And I don't suppose Vicky will either.'

'She's too young,' Charlotte said.

'Yes,' I said heavily, seeing that I had again caused irritation. The room was silent for a few moments, thick with dumb emotion. Why had they insisted on this meeting, or had it been my idea? I could not be sure now. Matthews was standing up. He said he was leaving. I found it hard to imagine him as Charlotte's lover. He was quite ordinary really, nothing special. A man with a frown over his eyes, worried, not so very happy to have fallen in love. He would have liked to have done the right thing. I might even have found him quite pleasant in other circumstances.

'Charlotte can come back if it doesn't work out,' I said to him, conscious that magnanimity was unlikely to please either of them at that moment but feeling the necessity to say it nevertheless.

Neither responded. Charlotte followed him out of the room and I saw them through the window, outside by his car, talking, their mouths moving in another language, her hand on his sleeve. It seemed as if they had moved into another sphere quite separate and detached from the one I still inhabited.

When Charlotte came back into the house she seemed nervous, incomplete. She skirted round me as if I posed some kind of a threat.

'What shall we do now?' I asked her.

'Go to the party, I suppose. We might as well.'

'All right.'

'Okay.'

'The party it is. Plenty of other people.'

'Yes. Are you all right, Dan?'

CHAPTER NINE

Sunday morning – Nick

'Where's your mother?' I asked Paul, who was sitting in the kitchen, eating a hunk of fruit cake.

'Gone for a walk,' he said, avoiding looking at me. His back was hunched up. It was an attitude he had inherited from Marion. He sounded morose, but that was not unusual these days. He was still only twelve but big for his age, more a teenager now than a child although the transition had been barely noticeable. It simply had happened, or perhaps I had not been home enough to see it.

'Is that your breakfast?' I asked, going to the coffee pot and finding it empty. I had drunk it all last night while Marion went over all the same old grounds of recrimination, angry and bitter, pleading and tearful until we had gone to bed and found ourselves going through the motions of sex.

'Now you're being unfaithful to her,' she had said, her voice still hoarse from crying.

'Stop it Marion. Shut up,' I said, strangely roused by the erotic combination of her sense of revenge and my own consciousness of finality. She made an effort to be violent. She wanted to hurt me, physically, and I thought I would let her but it wasn't in my nature and in the end I finished it quickly, seeking some sort of temporary release for both of us but feeling nothing, except impatience to get through whatever had to be got through.

I had woken to find myself alone in the bed and the sun streaming through the window regardless. I was neither happy nor unhappy but aware of a new sense of vitality which centred on Charlotte. That was the first impression, the confusion would settle in soon enough.

'Paul,' I began. 'There's something I have to tell you about.' Did it sound too doom-laden? I hoped not. Keep it light. Sell it to him. Fruit cake for breakfast. Perhaps he'd understand.

'You and Mum are getting divorced.' He made the announcement flatly, as if it were old news.

'Well, I don't know about that. Parting, anyway.' I was blustering. 'Your mother told you?'

'No, I heard you last night, and Friday,' he added, without looking up, his tone not accusing but somehow resigned, sad and world weary. He made it sound no more than he had expected for some time. He was so much like Marion, intuitive and imbued with a sense of passive resentment, but they were essentially female characteristics and set me ill at ease with Paul.

'He's sensitive. Please don't bully him,' Marion had pleaded with me in the past when I had reacted to Paul's martyred sulks with exasperation.

'He's never going to get much out of life if he carries on like this,' I had said.

'Maybe he's going to be one of the givers rather than takers,' she replied, implying the virtue of giving as opposed to my own taking.

But I wanted Paul to be a taker. Surely that was natural, to want your child to be a winner rather than a loser, and I could not help going on reacting, driving the wedge of antipathy between us because Paul was in many ways just as I had been as a child, miserably introverted, although for him there was no excuse, no drunken father to beat him silly for wetting the bed, and mother too frightened herself to change the sheets. The stench of stale urine was how I remembered my childhood, and long after I had

158

stopped soaking my own bed, because my father had done the same himself, in the bed he shared with my mother, on the couch in the living room when he had been too drunk to get upstairs. The stench was always there.

Marion was overprotective towards Paul. She excused this by pointing out that neither of us had been allowed particularly happy childhoods and therefore we had to ensure Paul's was different. She would say this as if I did not want just as much for him as she did and the implication would fill me with a furious sense of injustice, because I too wanted everything for Paul but seemed unable to communicate this to either of them.

Once when Paul was in his first year at school Marion and I had been invited to a parents' evening. For some reason I was not able to go and Marion on hearing this had flown into a temper. Our relationship had been at a particularly low ebb at the time and the incident had developed into a full-scale row, one of our worst, bad enough to remember.

'You never wanted a child. You hate Paul. No, not even that, he's just a nuisance to you,' she had screamed at me.

It was the second time that I hit her. A terrifying moment of lost control that sent my hand across her mouth, and drew blood from her lip where the force had jammed it into her teeth. But the blow seemed to satisfy her. Instantly her anger subsided and she was looking for my remorse, hungry to forgive and reconcile. I apologised but I despised her as much as I did myself.

It was true that I had not wanted a child when Marion had started talking about coming off the pill. We had been married less than a year, were still living in the flat and the newspaper we both worked on had not regained the lost circulation caused by the strike. Its survival hung in the balance and none of us knew how long we would still have jobs.

Fleet Street had become a more distant dream, perhaps because the singleminded motivation needed to break in had inevitably lost momentum when I took over the newsdesk. But it went deeper

159

than that. Despondency had crept over the newsroom since the strike. Nobody seemed really to care any more about the stories they wrote, maybe because so many had gone untold during the weeks of the strike and it had not made so very much difference to the course of events during that time. Journalists should not strike. Ultimately such action serves only to create a sense of futility over what cannot be influenced and changed. The cynicism that had previously been healthy we had turned in on ourselves.

For myself the effect was compounded by a continuing relationship with Jane Hillier whose bed I went to on the evenings Marion spent dutifully with her family following Frank's redundancy and a conviction for indecent exposure. Mercifully I did not have to go with her, having been temporarily sent to Coventry by Ruby for failing to keep the case out of the paper. But my visits to Jane, intellectually stimulating and physically adventurous although without emotional involvement on either side, were unwholesome. I still viewed life in terms too black and white to be able to emerge unscathed from Jane's flat, knowing that at other times she shared her bed with a woman. But I couldn't stop it. Jane represented escape from the normal, decent, ordinary and mundane existence implicit in living with Marion, and having a child could only increase the stifling permanency.

So I prevaricated. We should wait until my job was more secure, until we had a better home, until the autumn, until the winter.

'I want a baby,' Marion wailed one night, flushing her pills down the lavatory.

'I don't!' I shouted at her and slept on the couch for a fortnight.

'I'm leaving. Going freelance. I'm pregnant you see,' Jane told me the night Marion conceived. 'I expect you're the father, but that's just a minor detail,' she said. 'My baby will have two mothers. We wanted a baby. We're grateful to you.'

I caught sight of her a few months later, tall and still thin, the pregnancy like a football stuck up her jumper. It was a few days after Marion miscarried.

160

'And I did so long to be a granny,' Ruby blubbered, falling into my arms. 'But there's plenty of time. I'm young yet, still young enough to be a mother myself.'

She came to the flat every day for a week, a look of acid benevolence smeared across her face. Marion stayed in bed, quiet and vaguely reproachful towards the world in general, or so I thought. I felt sorry for her and was surprised to find that I too regretted the loss of the baby.

Ruby fussed around, altering the way Marion had arranged the little furniture we had, setting chairs and table symmetrical, making her presence felt. She turned up each morning looking as if she had spent a good hour in front of the mirror and wearing the sort of outfits not normally associated with comforting mothers. She stayed until I was home in the evenings and sat opposite me at the kitchen table while I ate the huge platefuls of food she had prepared. As the week went on she remained at the flat later and later and on Friday evening she had settled herself in front of the television when I came out of the bedroom after a particularly harrowing half hour with Marion who had retreated further into a sort of inner despair she could neither explain or understand.

'She's very down, the poor treasure, isn't she?' Ruby said, patting the seat of the couch next to her to encourage me to sit down. 'But you mustn't worry about her too much, Nick. It's natural for a girl to be depressed when something like this happens.'

I sat down heavily where she had patted.

'How long do you think it will last?' I asked, throwing my head back against the cushions as a tribe of black and white Red Indians whooped across the television screen.

'She'll be better when she gets another one on the way,' Ruby said, watching me. 'I lost several, you know, before Marion's brother came along. The trouble was . . . well,' she laid her hand on my knee. 'I hope you won't mind me saying this to you, Nick, none of my business I know, but Frank, you see, Frank, he just thought he would carry on as before. Of course he was too insensitive to understand and I had to make him go in the spare bed in the end. I know it's hard for men, you have your appetites. You do understand what I mean, don't you?'

'I'm not sure I do,' I said, too exhausted to want to be bothered with fathoming out Ruby's abstruse attempt to say whatever it was she hoped I wouldn't mind her saying. And then it struck me that she was referring to the relationship with Jane Hillier. Appetites. A Ruby sort of word. Pseudo genteel, sitting too close to me on her daughter's couch, her hand lingering on my leg, her own slightly varicose pair a little too exposed for a mother-in-law. Her chest puffed out. Her lips imbued with a Kathy Kirby succulence.

'How did you know?' I said, the moment unguarded.

'Marion told me. Perhaps she shouldn't, but you mustn't be cross with her. She does so want a baby, your baby, Nick,' she said, adding the last bit with a coy little casting down of her eyes.

'But who told her?' I went on, beginning to feel vaguely nauseated.

'Women just know these things,' Ruby answered obliquely. 'I knew that was the problem when I miscarried, but Frank wouldn't see it,' she added with vitriol. 'Too selfish, that was his trouble. Still is. I told him,' she went on, her tone softening again, 'that I didn't mind if he went elsewhere if it was so important to him, anything so long as he left me alone until the baby had, well, settled.'

I realised then that we were not talking about Jane and mercifully, Ruby was too intent on having her say to be aware of the divergence in our trains of thought.

'You do understand, don't you, Nick,' she said.

'Yes, Ruby. No sex for nine months.'

'Just a little consideration,' she said, 'that's all that's needed, but if you find it too much of a strain I'm sure that Marion would turn a blind eye. She needn't even know. That would be best.'

'You are amazing!' I said, getting up. 'You're her mother, for Christ's sake!'

162

'I know that, Nick.'
'Coming out with all this lascivious nonsense.'
'There's no need to use bad language.'
'You are amazing.'

Marion stayed in bed for another week to recover from Ruby's looking after. Uneventful months ensued although we were each suffering from a growing sense of panic, of time slipping by, Marion over motherhood and me over the direction, or lack of it, my career was taking. Marion made love only with a purpose and became preoccupied with dates and temperature charts she brought home from the doctor. Our bed seemed to take on a clinical air and the performances within it a mechanical routineness. And then one afternoon when I was at home and Marion was at work a delivery van drew up outside the flat and a pram was wheeled out.

'It's unforgiveable. Thank God my wife wasn't at home,' I stormed down the telephone to the firm who had arranged the delivery.

'But the pram is paid for Mr Matthews, and we have no record of cancellation.'

I slammed down the receiver, left the flat and drove to the address on the delivery note, the months of frustration and guilt suddenly concentrated into this one unfortunate incident. The pram had come from a dingy showroom painted on the outside in pink and blue, faded and peeling. The display area fronted what turned out to be the factory where the prams were made. It was nearly five thirty and the office staff were getting ready to leave. I stood by a frosted glass partition with 'Reception' painted on it. Someone had stuck a piece of paper with 'Con' printed on it over the 'Rec' although it had slipped and the paper was starting to curl. I banged on the glass. The place was seedy, almost run down, the two rows of prams flanking the strip of floor in front of the offices dusty and unappealing.

'Yes?' A girl's head peered round the side of the glass, insolent and out of patience.

'I want to speak to the manager,' I demanded.

'We're just finishing for the day. You'll have to come back tomorrow.'

'I'm not leaving until I've spoken to someone in authority. I've got a complaint,' I said, glaring at the mean-mouthed little face.

The girl disappeared without speaking again but with a look of officious exasperation. A few minutes later she reappeared. She had her coat on and evidently was about to leave.

'Miss Parkin will see you in a minute,' she threw at me and stalked off past the prams.

I waited about a quarter of an hour and was about to start hitting the glass again when a fair-haired woman of about forty came out and addressed herself to me.

'I understand you want to make a complaint,' she said, her hands were clasped together, the knuckles white with tension although the rest of her appeared quite calm and in control.

'Yes,' I began. I explained what had happened and waited for her reaction. She looked at me hard for a moment and said: 'Don't I know you Mr Matthews? I'm sure I've seen you somewhere before.' Recognition came into her face. 'I know, you're Nick Mathews. I always read your column in the paper. I thought it was such a pity when it finished.' I'd stopped writing the column when I moved on to the newsdesk: it had appeared once a week for a couple of years, latterly with a head and shoulders photograph of me under the heading, although this was the first time anybody had recognised me from it.

Miss Parkin's knuckles were regaining their natural tone. her anxiety seemed to have been replaced by a sort of relief, even pleasure. She invited me to her office which was sparse and drab but looked as if it had only recently been cleared out. There were marks on the walls where furniture had stood and a pile of old files was stacked by the waste bin. We sat down and she offered me a cigar from a tarnished silver box on her desk.

'My father's idea,' she said, holding the box open in front of me, 'cigars for the men and a cup of tea for the women. "Complaining customers cannot be too cross if they're drinking your tea or smoking your tobacco", he used to say.' She smiled hopefully and watched me take a cigar.

Miss Parkin, large of bust, slim-ankled, smartly dressed and only just past her prime, had inherited the business from her father two months earlier, she told me. A heart attack had made the transition rather sudden, she explained, although he had been ailing for some time and the business had naturally suffered. She talked on, enumerating the problems surrounding the prams. It was as if there was no one else she could tell all these things to so I listened, content to dwell on somebody else's troubles for an hour, if only as a release from my own. And then the conversation took a new and more positive turn. Miss Parkin was not after all telling me all this only with a view to unburdening herself. She knew what the business lacked, she had been in commerce of one sort or another all her working life, she knew what it was about. Her father's pram business basically lacked marketing and that included public relations, and public relations included customer relations, did it not, and wasn't that what had been lacking in my particular case?

The hopeful smile appeared again.

'Perhaps you can help me, Mr Mathews? I need someone to write about Parkin's Prams – to get us more publicity so that we can take a bigger share of the market and afford to run a business that doesn't make insensitive mistakes.'

'How old is she?' Marion asked warily when I told her about the job.

'What's the woman's age got to do with it?' I snapped.

'Nothing, I'm sorry, I was just curious,' she replied. 'If this job is what you want then you must take it.' She sounded doubtful, her tone echoing my own misgivings over quitting newspapers.

'PR pays well, a lot better than journalism,' I justified.

'Even in Fleet Street?' Marion asked.

'You don't want to live in London anyway,' I retorted.

'I would if I had to. I wouldn't mind.'

'You'd hate it,' I insisted.

'I'd rather move to London than be accused of holding you back.'

'It's a little late to be saying that,' I said unfairly. The look of hurt that I had come to know so well appeared in her eyes, but its familiarity had bred contempt and I had become incapable of responding other than by compounding the injustice with the guise of indifference.

A month later I left the newspaper and started working for Parkin's Prams. 'Selling your soul to commerce,' one of the reporters said and I had an uneasy sense that he was right, but PR, about which I knew nothing, quickly became an all-engrossing obsession. I lived and breathed Parkin's Prams, not so much the prams themselves any more than it was Morgan-Mackie's marmalade that turned me on in years to come, but the challenge of convincing a fickle public to choose a Parkin's or a jar of M-M's rather than anyone else's. Image creation, at its best achieved by subliminal influence – the process fascinated me and the fascination meant that I spent more and more time at work. Often in the evenings I would go to Dorothy Parkin's office, now refurbished in elegant style, and we would scheme and formulate new departures for Parkin's, diversifying, under her influence, into collapsible bicycles and a new streamlined wheelchair designed by a famous racing driver.

Dorothy was a shrewd businesswoman who knew enough about the mechanics of PR to guide me through the early months. We got on well, respected one another, and shared the same passion to succeed.

'You will have to let me take you and Marion out to dinner,' she said one evening when we were still in her office at nine thirty.

166

'She must get fed up with all these late sessions.'

'Marion understands,' I said, but nothing could have been further from the truth. She was obsessed and depressed over her efforts to conceive again. I endured deaf and dumb meals, the food on my plate as dried up and shrivelled as the state of our marriage.

'Why do you bother to come home at all?' she asked accusingly one night when I came in after midnight.

'Stud duty and sleep,' I said, unconcerned as to how it sounded.

'Well you can forget the first bit, there doesn't seem to be any point any more, does there?' she said, her mouth twisted down into a bitter expression that held a strong element of Ruby.

'Not really, no,' I said wearily, too tired for an argument but sensing the inevitability of one.

'There's someone else, Nick, isn't there?' she said next. 'That woman you work for, it's her.'

'Don't be ridiculous,' I said, walking past her towards the bedroom, but she caught hold of me from behind, throwing her arms about my waist and pressing herself into my back.

'I'm sorry, I'm sorry,' she whispered urgently. 'I didn't mean any of it, please,' but the sudden contrition only added to the great lump of irritation I had allowed to build up and prising her arms from me I walked on into the bedroom, feeling cold and mean.

The level of work staved off the sense of loneliness, filled for me the great aching gulf I had put between us. I did not really want it to be like that but I could not allow time to dwell on emotional problems and the longer I avoided the issue the less able I seemed to talk to Marion at all, although in a strange way I needed her and even began to be aware of a sort of possessive jealousy as we drew further apart. I wanted her to be in the flat when I got home even though we had nothing to say to one another. It seemed that by distancing her I was realising the need and yet I remained incapable of communicating this to her.

Marion had been pregnant with Paul for nearly four months before she told me. The revelation came one morning when she inadvertently left the bathroom door unlocked and I found her standing naked by the bath, her hands flying to her stomach as if she had something to hide. I was surprised by the sense of elation within me when she said it timidly, almost apologetic, as if I might be angry, but still I was unable to show her any sign of feeling. To have responded would have been like an atheist admitting to belief in God. It was a humility I could not give, maybe because I saw Marion half hoped, half expected it.

A month before the baby was due I went to California for a week to attend a public relations seminar and also to look into the possibility of the Parkin's bicycle being manufactured under licence in America. Dorothy Parkin was convinced that the Americans, with their craze for fitness, would really go for the Parkin's collapsible. At the end of the seminar, which was full of esoteric and pretentious stuff relating little to the reality of business, I took a plane from Oakland down to Burbank, hired a car and drove into Beverly Hills, past the huge and immaculate houses, which made me think of Ruby, larger than life, almost unreal.

I turned into Rodeo Drive and began looking for a gymnasium called Gym and Tonic run by a woman Dorothy had known at university and who, intermittently, had kept in touch over the years. I found it near the end of the drive, a candy-striped awning over the door which was squeezed between a boutique and a chocolate shop. Ruby, as a Hollywood star, was still in my mind, and on impulse I went into the chocolate shop and bought a large and vulgar box of sweets with her name painted on.

The idea behind my visit was that Dorothy's friend, who already knew about the bicycle project, should help promote it through her fitness programme at the gymnasium. A good proportion of her clientele were Hollywood names and the publicity possibilities seemed immense.

A waif-like Filipino girl in a white track suit directed me to the boss's office and there I met Germaine Hartnell, blonde, bronzed

168

and a glowing, glistening advertisement for her gymnasium. As I went in she was standing by a wall of glass which looked down into the gym. She stepped towards me, her hand outstretched, a smile across her wide mouth exposing a set of dazzling white teeth.

'Nick,' she said. 'You must be Nick. Dorothy warned me you were gorgeous.'

'I was given the same warning about you,' I lied, amazed at the possibility Dorothy could have said any such thing, and at my own instant response; I had become more the P R man than I realised.

The next two days were dominated by Germaine's teeth, flashed at me every time I looked in her direction and seemingly ultimately set to eat me which they nearly did on a vast round bed in her vast house a few hours before I was due to leave.

'Dorothy said you could do with a bit of fun,' Germaine informed me, her firm forty-year-old breasts pressed against my side, 'and I guess she was right!' In the two days it had indeed been all 'fun', no business at all which, with a plane to catch first thing in the morning, was beginning to concern me.

'I know this doesn't seem like the appropriate moment Germaine, but I wouldn't like Dorothy to think I hadn't done any work.'

'Ah, don't you worry about it, me and Dorothy, we fixed the whole thing over the phone. I guess she just thought it would be nice for you to come along down here for a bit of a break.'

'An expensive break,' I murmured, an uneasy sense of having been benevolently manipulated creeping over me.

I flew straight back to London, driven to the airport at six a.m. in Germaine's white Cadillac, the hire car left outside her house. She did not wait to see me off, that was not her style, a final flash of teeth, a blown kiss and she was gone. I got on the plane and as it taxied for takeoff realised I had nothing to take back for Marion, not even a box of chocolates.

I telephoned the flat from Heathrow but there was no reply and I assumed Marion had gone to Ruby's but felt disinclined to call her there. It seemed to take longer to get to Birmingham from London than it had to fly the Atlantic and when I eventually reached the flat I had lost track of the hours, jet-lagged, time-zoned and paying with exhaustion for the two sleepless days and nights spent with Germaine. I went into the kitchen and found a note by the sink, Marion's small, neat handwriting: 'Gone to the hospital', and as if she had known I would not remember which hospital, the name and address were on the card under her message.

I had not spoken to her for three, it could have been four days, I was not sure; a brief, terse telephone call from the hotel in Oakland before I went down to Los Angeles. The line had been as clear as if she had been in the next room but the distance between us had seemed even greater than the thousands of miles it was. Neither of us had known what to say, so out of practice were we, if there had even been a time when we had said anything very much to one another; we no longer communicated even when we were together so what hope was there over a trans-Atlantic telephone link? Not that I had tried very hard although it had seemed necessary to make the call. The problem now was I could not tell when her note had been written, I could be a father already and unaware of it. I rang the hospital number, a sudden sense of panic and impatience getting through the confusion of tiredness.

'Mrs Matthews, wait a moment please, I'll check for you,' an efficient-sounding impersonal voice told me.

'Are you a relation?' it came back a few seconds later.

'Her husband, for Christ's sake,' I shouted, my heart thumping in my chest, 'I've just got back from America.'

'You had better come immediately, your wife is in the final stage of labour. She's been here two days.'

'But it's a month early,' I heard myself saying as if to justify my absence.

'Babies don't always come when they're supposed to, Mr Matthews,' the voice said with a long-suffering note. 'I suggest you put the phone down and hurry if you want to be here when the birth takes place.'

170

I ran out of the flat and found my car parked down the road. I got in, started the engine and pulled out into the dark, empty street. It was the middle of the night and I had gone about a mile before I saw another car and realised I had been driving on the wrong side of the road. I swerved over, the lights of the other car blazed on to full beam and I nearly hit a parked lorry. A sudden vision of Germaine's smile on Ruby's face flashed through my mind; I rammed my foot down on the accelerator and tried to subdue such involuntary rovings of my mind's eye by concentrating on speed.

At the hospital all was quiet, the aura of night time and sleep seemed to engulf the place and yet babies were often born at night were they not, screaming out of the dark into the dark; the hospital was silent. I found a solitary nurse and followed her along corridors to the place where Marion was, a single room with a piece of glass in the door so that I could see her, lying on her back, her body distorted, a mass of hospital equipment and green-gowned people clustering about the bed.

'You'll have to be quick.' The nurse was holding out a similar green gown for me to put on. 'You're not a fainter are you?'

'I don't think so,' I mumbled.

'In you go then.'

'Nick!' Marion smiled at me and then her face contorted, she closed her eyes and I saw her bite into her lip. Her hair was wringing wet, the limp strands hanging round her face making her look vulnerable and pathetic in the same way I had seen her the first time, outside the factory gates, rain-soaked but with a stubborn determination that dismissed the discomfort.

'One more big push, dear,' somebody said encouragingly. 'Prop her up a bit more, will you,' another voice said to me. I fumbled with the pillows. 'No. Hold her. Support her shoulders,' the voice ordered. Marion seemed to be concentrating hard, gathering her remaining strength. 'Now, dear, now!' the other voice insisted.

'Come on. Come on. There's a good girl. A little one now, just a little one.' It was like arriving at a party stone cold sober while

171

everyone else had been drinking all night; I felt awkward and out of place, an interloper on the scene, uninitiated, unprepared; and then the baby was born.

'You've got a son!' someone said.

'I can't believe it,' Marion whispered, straining to see him, absorbed in joy.

I looked at the baby and then at Marion's face and was almost overcome by a piercing sensation of love, a single, crystal-clear moment of emotion that seemed to scoop a hole within me which then filled up with a pride I had not expected or realised possible. Gratitude came next, a feeling even beyond that towards the people in green gowns and over the fact that I was capable of this new joy and able to respond to instinct after all. The blockage had been removed and I could love Marion. But something else was happening. Through the reverie of it all I became aware of concern, heightened all around the tiny room, a resurgence of busyness.

'I think it would be better if you left for a few minutes,' someone said, their face, relaxed and smiling a few moments earlier now taut and the eyes suddenly distant. Marion, her white face composed and content, seemed as unaware of the sudden change of atmosphere as I was to understand it.

In the corridor I was told to go and sit down and to wait. The baby, in a small canvas cot, was wheeled by and a moment later a large trolley swiftly shunted into the room where I had left Marion, white and inert, sunken in the bed.

The whiteness of her filled me with terror and a guilty sense of helplessness. Drained of life blood, the skin on her face had been almost translucent. More people came along the corridor, their pace alarmingly hurried. A red light had gone on above the door of Marion's room.

'She's going to die,' I thought. Morbid pictures of having to hand over the care of our child to the tender mercies of Ruby loomed up; and then the awful remorse of time lost, guilt over the

172

years of indifference and deliberate hurtfulness, at least it seemed now as if it had been deliberate. If Marion died now she would be a haunting spectre for ever more.

'Where have you been?' I looked up and saw Ruby scurrying towards me. 'Two days my little girl's been in here and where were you?' she demanded aggresively.

'America, Ruby, remember?' I told her, momentarily indignant, rising to the aggression, using it as a sort of relief.

'You should never have gone, not with Marion in her state, but I suppose it's too late for all that now, the baby's here and that's that. Where are they?' she continued along the corridor, peering in through the glass doors.

'No! Ruby!' I called after her, 'something's gone wrong. Marion's... ill, something, I don't know. We've got to wait.'

The prospect of waiting with Ruby was too awful to contemplate. She came back to where I was sitting: 'What's wrong with her? The baby, the baby's all right?' she asked insistently, a note of hysteria in her voice.

'Yes, I think it's all right.'

'It! He's your son and you only think he's all right? And Marion, what's wrong with her?' she was almost shouting.

'I don't know!' I shouted back.

'You men, you're all the same, pathetic in a crisis, and it's all your fault. Don't think I don't know how miserable you've made my daughter. Oh, she told me, I know.' Her voice had gone low and venomous. She almost spat the indictment at me.

'Shut up, Ruby!' I said, looking up into her face which was puffy with anger.

'I think I've held my tongue too long,' she went on. She looked old. She had come to the hospital without her make-up, but she had chosen the moment well, I was in no mood to fight her.

'Marion told us, Frank and I, that you didn't really want the child, and how you punished her with silence all the time she's been pregnant. You don't care at all, do you? The only reason you're sitting here now is because it wouldn't look too good if you had stayed away.'

'Please Ruby, not now,' I implored her.

'I'm inclined to agree with you, Nick. It's all too late now, far too late.'

A doctor came out of Marion's room. I stood up, expecting him to speak to me, but he hurried by, his head down, as if he might be prised of some secret.

'Oh, doctor. Doctor!' Ruby called after him. The man hesitated and turned back to us.

'Yes?' he said, impatiently.

'What is happening to my daughter?'

The doctor, his expression haggard but impersonal, looked at me. 'Are you the husband?'

'Yes.'

'Your wife is very weak. She's haemorrhaged but I think we've managed to stop the bleeding now.'

'She's going to be all right?' I asked, incredulous but with a great surge of relief passing through me.

'In all probability,' the doctor reassured.

'Can I see her?' I asked.

'Just for a few moments.'

I dashed past him. Outside the door I paused and looked through the glass. Marion was lying flat with her eyes closed, an array of tubes sprouting from her body, her face still drained of colour. I pushed open the door and then I was aware of Ruby immediately behind me. She brushed me aside and was by the bed.

'My little girl,' she murmured mawkishly. Marion opened her eyes.

'Mum. Have you seen him? Have you seen my baby?'

'Yes, darling, and he's lovely – just like you.'

I stood watching them, by the door, separate unnoticed by Marion, pushed out by her mother. In default. Too late. The hospital hush made it impossible to tell Ruby to bugger off, although Marion might have. The wonder was spoiled, the moment destroyed.

I went home and changed. I had not slept for I could not remember how long and had fallen victim to the unjustified self-pity symptomatic of overtiredness. I drove to my office and wrote out a letter of resignation.

'So you're buggering off,' Paul said with a defiant stab at indifference.

'I don't like to hear you speak like that,' I said.

'You won't be around to hear it,' he retorted.

'Of course I'll be around. Your mother and I are parting but that doesn't mean I won't see you any more.'

'Darren Jones' mum and dad are divorced. He never sees his dad.'

'Will you want to see me?' I ventured, suddenly afraid that he might not.

Paul's gaze remained fixed on his plate of fruit cake crumbs, as if he was counting them.

'Suppose so,' he murmured, but the admission seemed to embarrass him and he got up, taking the plate of crumbs which he put down on the grass outside the back door.

'Birds like fruit cake. Did you know that?' he said, still not looking at me as he came back into the kitchen.

'No, I didn't,' I said.

'They like Mum's best, the ones she makes.'

'I didn't know that birds had such highly developed palates.' It sounded as though I was making fun of him although I had not meant it to come out like that.

Paul's expression remained closed. We stood facing one another across the kitchen, neither of us able to think what to say.

'Paul,' I paused, 'we'll be able to spend weekends together, we'll probably see each other more than we do now.'

'Darren Jones' father said that to him.'

'I'm not Darren Jones' father,' I said.

'He doesn't like his father anyway.'

Again silence.

Paul turned to watch the birds taking the crumbs. I could hear them squabbling over the tiny morsels. The back of Paul's thin body looked stiff and defensive.

'Couldn't you and Mum sort of share this house, but not be married any more?' he said, without turning.

'I don't think that would work. Would you really want us to stay together even if it was making us both unhappy?' I asked. In the instant of saying it I realised the terrible unfairness of such a question, asking the child to make the sort of sacrifice the parent had abdicated.

'No, I suppose not,' he said but it had cost him a lot to say and by accepting the burden suddenly had made it less easy for me to leave.

CHAPTER TEN

Sunday Midday – Charlotte

'It's the children that suffer,' Audrey was saying. 'Poor little Amy, she's become sullen and she can't stop telling fibs.'

'It seems to be an epidemic, half our friends are either divorced or separated,' James said as he sliced through the Sunday joint, beef, tender and succulent, cooked as only Audrey knew how. I felt my stomach contract and knew I would have difficulty eating anything. It crossed my mind for an instant that Dan might have said something but then I dismissed the thought, I had never known him to be devious and Audrey and James were too straightforward to play games of innuendo; if they had known they would have said, as soon as we arrived, before we had to start putting on a show.

'I don't like cabbage,' Vicky announced. She seemed rather tetchy, which wasn't like her. She had pushed away from me as I bent to kiss her when Dan and I arrived. Dan had hugged her overlong and eventually she had scrambled away from him as well, anxious to get back to her game with James and Audrey's children.

'Just try to eat a little,' I said.

'Well I'm not going to taste it. I'll just put it in my mouth and swallow it whole,' she persisted.

'Cabbage makes your hair curl,' James said.

'That's carrots,' somebody said.

'No, stupid, they let you see in the dark,' Vicky countered.

'Don't be rude,' I said, glancing at Dan whose face was still unnaturally pale. When he spoke he seemed to make an effort to appear as if nothing out of the ordinary was happening, but the effort made him sound almost hearty in sharp contrast to the way he looked now, wrung out but his eyes a little crazed as if he was only just beginning to fathom the full meaning of what had been done to him. I couldn't look at him for long. The show had to go on. The ritual played out in front of the people who were our friends because they assumed that we all shared the same values and lived by the unspoken code of decent, honest behaviour.

James and Dan had met one another through shooting and when Frances had gone to America and Saturdays had become the loneliest day of the week, Audrey had materialised like a rescue party, full of wisdom and tolerance and the wondrous ability to make the best of things. She would pick me up in her Mini and whisk me off into Cambridge; once or twice we went up to London, although that was not so easy with Vicky and her children still in pushchairs. We would try on clothes we could not really afford and then spend a fortune on lunch.

'James is always so mellow on Saturday nights after a day out in the open, he never complains about the money I've spent,' she told me, and the sprees continued although I hated not having my own money to spend, hated the new dependence upon Dan following the arrival of Vicky and the consequent termination of the daily train trips to town where I had in fact earned barely enough to cover the cost of the fares. But it had felt like independence and would have been had I not been forced to live so far out due to Dan's job. That was the justification and the resentment, although the latter was so well implanted by the time Vicky was born that it fed upon anything that came to hand: Dan's shooting, his parents and their stifling solicitude; the move out of town, which at first I had wanted, only to find myself alone and isolated in the eternal quiet of the countryside where I knew nobody and nobody appeared to want to know me.

'I've come to cheer you up,' Audrey would say, calling round twice, sometimes three times a week, 'and myself as well. Let's go out to tea. Let's take the children swimming. Let's go to the church bazaar.' Let's. I missed Frances and thought how little she would have in common with Audrey. But Audrey was there and Frances was not and we were able to share the effortless bond between women whose lives have been put into abeyance by babies.

'I went to church with Rupert and Clare,' Vicky said, a lump of cabbage balanced on her fork between the plate and her mouth.

'We thought you wouldn't mind,' Audrey said quickly. 'Vicky wanted to come and we couldn't leave her here by herself.' Religion had been one of the topics over which we had not agreed. Audrey was well into the church and in the early days of our friendship had shown signs of missionary tendencies towards me, but she had long ago given me up as a bad job in that respect and even managed to joke about it in spite of her own earnest beliefs, which of course encompassed the full moral spectrum including love, honour and obedience.

Suddenly I felt wicked to be sitting at her dining table but irrationally possessive over Vicky's soul.

'Why don't we ever go to church, Daddy?' Vicky said, the cabbage back on the plate, shoved under her knife; the question was, I knew, no more than a smokescreen to divert adult attention from the green lump.

'We will if you like,' Dan said. Our eyes met briefly over Vicky's head. I remained silent.

'Mummy says church is a leaning post for people who need one but I don't understand,' Vicky went on.

'Get on with your lunch, darling,' I said, regretting my tendency to plain speaking when Vicky and I were alone and she asked big questions. I supposed I ought to have been full of regret about everything, but that was as far as it went. I had looked at Dan and

179

been unable to stop myself from despising him, devious after all and at such a moment with accusation and guilt, strength and weakness, confusion, giddy uncertainty, roaring desire, revulsion, all rushing and receding and rushing back, crashing through me like tidal waves, crashing through him too. I felt his presence, physical and mental, stronger than ever before, quite over-poweringly there as if Vicky was the conductor between us, linking us and then shooting us apart in shock waves. Love and hate so close, so confused and compulsive. I had tricked myself into believing that I never really loved him and yet to hate with such piercing intensity, even for a moment, was surely indicative of an equal emotion, felt with fierce tenderness at some point during ten years.

'Shall you take Vicky or will I?' Dan was saying.

'I will of course,' I said, mistaking his meaning and then knowing the ambiguity had been deliberate.

'Oh, Charlotte, I'm so pleased,' Audrey exclaimed.

I was constantly amazed and gratified over the way I felt about Vicky. Her conception had been unwitting, the result of a contraception muddle over which I behaved very badly, largely because I could not find anyone to blame but myself. I brooded over it, feeling cheated and, of course, trapped, my old phobia manifest as my abdomen expanded and I became petulant and unreasonable over the little things of life. My main regret once I had come grudgingly to accept my new situation, was that Dan and I had not been aware of 'doing it for real'. It seemed to me that it would have been rather magnificent to have made love with a purpose so permanent in mind, the ultimate gratification of the creative instinct, and I had missed it, been quite oblivious. It was a regret Dan and I shared.

As the time drew near for the birth I started going to relaxation classes. They were run by a spinster in her fifties, a health visitor who arrived at the village hall in a Land Rover with three black labradors falling over her.

'What's it like?' we asked her, me and the other rotund expectants.

'Like passing a giant vegetable marrow, I'm told,' she said airily, 'but I'll show you a film.'

The film was of the stuff nightmares are made of. Down to earth, in full colour and shot at the angle from which none of us would ever have to see when it came to our turn.

The night Vicky was born it dawned on me as I lay counting the minutes and seconds between contractions that I had never held a baby, never wanted to and still was unable to countenance the one inside me as a living being to whom I would be expected to relate. Dan was by me, a tedious fondness radiating through the fear and anxiety to the point where I wanted to bite his hand on its way down from mopping my sweating brow. I said things to him, bad, unkind things that rose up and out of me from an uncontrollable anger that also seemed to generate the positive energy needed to accomplish the wretched business. But Dan was impervious to my vile tongue and I became more angry.

'Beautiful angry person,' he murmured and I almost spat at him.

Vicky was born and all was well. I feasted upon the sight of her, every tiny bit of her little body, so appealingly yellow with the touch of jaundice she had developed.

Dan's mother came to see us and said she expected it would be a boy next time. I cradled Vicky in my arms and felt serenely protective, loving her, if it was possible, even more. I told Dan what his mother had said.

'You know what she's like. She doesn't think what she's saying. She'd be upset if she realised,' he said.

'You're not disappointed, are you?' I asked.

'Of course not, and besides I've always rather fancied a large family.'

After he had gone and Vicky had been put away for the night I subsided into my pillows and succumbed to the blues, storing what he had said in the subconscious reservoir of indictments I had been building in my mind.

I had decided that I was not going to suffer from post-natal depression, but the decision was made long before the event and during that twilight period of retreat into the exclusive little world of pregnancy; but the sudden overwhelming reality, the great void previously filled with a sense of wellbeing, defied all such resolution. Vicky was not a difficult baby and I marvelled at how I might have coped at all had she been. But even an easy baby will deprive its mother of sufficient sleep and thus the problem is compounded with broken nights, broken spirit, and broken nails as your own share of calcium and survival is sucked away.

It was dear, kind, interfering Audrey, and by that I don't wish it to sound as if I was not grateful for her interference, who came to my rescue with her wisdom and experience and propensity to reduce everything to practical level; solving emotional trauma with a cup of tea and a home-made biscuit.

Audrey assured me that she had been through it all herself, although I did not believe her, nobody could suffer so; it was my own unique isolated misery because that was the nature of the malady. But Audrey, who read a lot of women's magazines, made me believe that my problem was chemical rather than psychological which, illogically, made me feel a great deal better. I suppose it was a comfort knowing that the chemistry was out of phase rather than the much more fragile psyche.

When Vicky was six months old, established and smiling, and I began to feel that I was emerging from the vegetable patch, Audrey suggested we should all take a holiday and promptly booked a castle in Scotland.

'It's not quite as grand as it sounds,' she told me, but Saddell Castle, isolated and resplendent at the mouth of a small river and facing out towards the Isle of Arran across Kilbrannan Sound, seemed pretty splendid with its battlemented tower, endless spiral

182

stairway, baronial fireplaces and massively thick walls.

Audrey and James had been there before, the previous spring, just after its conversion from near ruin:

'We couldn't believe our luck,' James said enthusiastically, 'what a place!'

It was indeed everything they had promised us during the evenings we had spent together planning the great sojourn, although arriving there at dusk, with a cloud-veiled moon casting an eerie light down the pale grey walls, set us in awe rather than enthusiasm while Audrey and James energetically vied with one another to point out the more amazing snippets of history attached to the place.

'Do you see the floor, here by the main door. It's removable. They used to take it up when unwelcome visitors were expected so they'd fall down into the prison beneath.'

'And do you see up there, that corner of the battlement? That was where the woman in white stood and watched her husband murder her father and then threw herself over the edge in despair.'

'No, it was her father who murdered her husband,' James corrected.

'I don't think so. I think I'm right on that one,' Audrey insisted.

'Well we can check it, can't we? There's a book upstairs with the whole story.'

'Does it matter very much which way round it was?' Audrey retorted.

'For the sake of historical accuracy I would say, yes, that it does,' James continued pendantically.

The four of us were still standing in the cobbled courtyard, the gentle roar of a night wind building momentum through the tall, densely planted trees beyond the far side of the tower. The children, James and Audrey's pair and Vicky, were asleep in the cars. Rupert's dog, Pineapple, a rough-haired fox terrier, had started to bark at the strange and unfamiliar sounds.

'Come on, we'd better get the children in and get sorted out,'

Audrey said, stalking off towards the car, her back stiff with bad temper.

Dan and I, mute and vaguely embarrassed, set to with our own unloading.

'Oh dear,' he murmured to me as we pulled out our bags and the general paraphernalia that goes with new parenthood. He glanced in the direction of the other two and I knew what he meant, although we were, perhaps, enjoying the touch of smugness that goes with seeing another couple at odds.

We transferred Vicky to the panelled bedroom that was to be ours, spent half an hour making it so, another twenty minutes exploring the upper levels of the great stone building and then descended the spiralling steps to join James and Audrey in the main living room where they were still engaged in the argument that had begun when we arrived.

Sniping at one another from either side of the vast fireplace they made an effort to restore civility when we appeared but the atmosphere between them remained densely hostile.

'How about a drink?' James said terribly brightly, rubbing his hands together as if to create a spark. 'Scotch seems like the most appropriate thing.'

'Yes, lovely,' I said.

'Yes, fine,' Dan said.

'I'd rather have wine,' Audrey said. 'Have you seen the view from this window, Charlotte? Look, before all the light goes,' she continued as I moved forward to gaze out across the deserted beach edging the black water which looked as dense and heavy as treacle. Nothing stirred. The wind had died in the trees behind. Night was falling like a blanket, smothering movement, forcing calm.

'It looks so peaceful, doesn't it?' Audrey was saying. 'It seems hard to believe that there's been so much turmoil here in the past.'

Having admired the tranquillity, Audrey and I went to the kitchen to prepare supper while Dan and James went out to find driftwood to make a fire.

184

'Of course it's going to be much too dark to find anything but you can't tell James anything like that, he's far too pigheaded,' Audrey muttered after they had gone. 'He's dragged poor Dan out there too, I am sorry, Charlotte.'

'Oh please don't apologise,' I said hastily, 'I'm sure Dan doesn't mind.'

'No, I don't suppose he does. He's so good-natured, the lamb. I'm afraid James is always like this at the start of a holiday. It takes him two or three days to unwind and the rest of us just have to suffer in the meantime.'

'I'm sure it's not that bad,' I said.

Audrey let out a scoffing sort of snort and in the process, which seemed to involve her whole body, knocked over the bottle of wine. There was another row over that when James returned with a handful of damp twigs and the ensuing meal was eaten with Audrey and James at either end of the long dining table, scoring points off one another while Dan and I sat in the middle attempting indirect mediation. As if to emphasise their dislike of one another, the acid jibes thrown up and down the table were interspersed with solicitous comments and questions to Dan or to me, face muscles contorting from one extreme to the other, from a frown to a beam in a bizarre comedy of manners that had to be played out to a captive audience, Dan and me, who had also become part of the play.

It went on after the meal was over and we had all four settled in front of the fire, which kept smoking because the wood was so damp. We were to play cards, Newmarket and rummy.

'Someone hasn't put their penny on the ace,' James said. 'Come on, pay up whoever it is.'

'Don't be so officious,' Audrey snapped at him.

'I wasn't!'

'You were!'

'I think it must be me,' Dan interrupted, placing another penny on the card.

'No. I remember seeing you put yours down at the beginning,'

James said. 'It's Audrey that hasn't paid.'

'Well, if you knew it was me why didn't you say so in the first place!' Audrey accused him.

'I didn't want to embarrass you!'

'That was nice of you,' she retorted sarcastically.

'Well, you've always been a duffer at cards,' James said, a soothing edge to his voice.

'Since when!'

'You know you have.'

'How dare you call me a duffer!'

'Look, I'll leave my second penny on the ace and that makes it all square,' Dan interrupted again.

'You see, he had already paid!' James declared.

'Excuse us,' Dan said, getting up and reaching for my hand. 'I'm feeling a bit full after the meal. I think Lottie and I will take a stroll along the beach.'

'Oh! . . . yes, of course. Careful of the birds though,' James said as we left the room. 'They nest on the beach, lay their eggs in the sand. Oyster-catchers. Might be an idea to take a torch.'

'Know-all!' we heard Audrey say as we made our escape.

The beach was soft-sanded and still slightly warm from the day's sun, although the air was cold and Dan and I huddled together as we moved along with the torch beam a few inches in front of our feet.

'They say you should never go on holiday with friends,' I said.

'Yes, but I always thought that meant you were likely to fall out with them, not that they would with one another,' Dan said.

'D'you think we'll be able to stick a week of it?' I asked.

'I suppose we'll have to.'

'I'd no idea they were like that but then it's not often I've seen them together.'

'I don't know which of them is the worse.'

'Both as bad.'

'Glad we're not like that.'

'Umm.'

When we got back James and Audrey were in the kitchen locked in a passionate embrace, the electric kettle shooting a cloud of steam over their heads.

'Sorry,' Audrey said sheepishly when they drew apart and saw us just as we were about to make another hasty exit.

'Yes,' James said, switching off the kettle. 'A couple of silly chumps, aren't we?'

'It should have been us that had to go for a walk, not you,' Audrey continued.

'No really, we wanted a walk, a bit of fresh air,' Dan said.

'I'm not surprised with all that smoke from the fire. I knew it would do that with the wood sopping wet,' Audrey said.

'Hardly sopping,' James interjected.

'Well, pretty damp at any rate. Coffee?'

'No thanks. I think we'll go to bed,' Dan said.

'Where was I supposed to find dry wood?' James was saying as we disappeared again.

In bed, the light out, our room was so densely dark I could almost feel the weight of it. Dan had fallen asleep but I lay awake, unable to dismiss the steamy little scene we had witnessed in the kitchen. My heart ached over it. I couldn't put it out of my mind. I lay there in the dark and felt alone and inexplicably envious.

'We're thinking of taking the castle again this year, maybe for Christmas,' James had said.

'Yes, how about us all going?' Audrey added. 'It must be lovely there in winter and with any luck we might get snowed up and have to stay for weeks!'

'Can we get down?' one of the children asked.

'Okay, we'll call you when the pud's ready,' Audrey said.

'I don't think you should allow them to keep jumping up and down during mealtimes,' James said with disapproval. 'Apart from anything else it's bad for the digestion.'

'Oh, don't be so pompous,' Audrey snapped at him.

'We're not going to start that again, are we?' James went on. 'Audrey has this notion that anyone who doesn't agree with her is pompous,' he announced to the room in general, although there were only the four of us left.

'That's not quite true, my darling,' Audrey countered, her voice like silver acid. It's only you that's pompous.'

'That's rich, coming from you, President of the W I, Chairman of the Mothers' Union, Treasurer of the Parochial Church Council, pomposity personified!' James laughed, a quick, embarrassed chuckle for our benefit, to make it seem that he, at any rate, took none of it too seriously.

'I hardly call it pompous to do one's bit in society,' Audrey said with simmering indignation.

'Well if that doesn't sound pompous I don't know what does!' James retorted emphatically.

'We won't be coming to the castle with you at Christmas,' Dan suddenly interjected.

James and Audrey fell silent, looked at one another and then at us.

'Oh we are dreadful, and I don't blame you a bit for not wanting to spend Christmas with us – we'd probably ruin it for you, arguing all the time,' Audrey said. 'I can't think why you put up with us at all.'

'It's not you two,' Dan said, avoiding my agitated gaze. 'It's simply that Lottie and I are parting.'

'What did you say?' they both said, almost simultaneously.

'Lottie and I, we're separating,' Dan repeated, lightly, as if it was a matter of small moment, but the only way he could say it a second time without the 'bad form' melodrama so alien to his nature.

The room seemed to contract, the air stop moving.

'But you get on so well,' Audrey said quietly, as if to herself, and then: 'You're not serious?'

'Unfortunately, yes.'

I had said nothing but all three were now looking to me for some kind of explanation. Their eyes accused me, sent daggers into my soul. Traitor, destroyer, revealed at last as of no moral fibre. Suddenly it seemed quite unbearable that I might never again sit with Dan and listen to James and Audrey argue. Yet another facet to the pattern of familiarity endured, ever nurtured, through years. I had lost count of the number of times Dan and I, driving home after lunch or dinner with James and Audrey, would marvel at the degree of antagonism between them and fail to understand what kept them together – or maybe we had an inkling but chose to dismiss it for fear of recognising what they had and we did not. In truth, far from finding their company in any way irksome or even embarrassing after the familiarity had set in, it was like being in a darkened room and suddenly having the light switched on to be with them: and their glow reflected on us; made us feel fortunate and privileged to have them as friends, real friends, sharing the same conversational wavelengths, implicitly assuming understanding, and yet not now, because I had shattered the basis of that understanding, destroyed the foundations that had made it possible.

'I don't understand,' Audrey said.

'Neither do I,' said Dan.

CHAPTER ELEVEN

Letters to America –Frances

The year Charlotte's daughter was born I was in America with Leonard. Struggling round the shadow of his brilliance, I set about achieving the independence I had urged upon Charlotte during our conversations in Cambridge, sitting on the banks of the River Cam and later toasting muffins and crumpets over Leonard's fire. The ivory towers of Berkeley, which seemed to hold no intellectual terrors for him, presented a formidable psychological barrier to me, although the self-doubt, even fear, I kept to myself.

It never occurred to me to tell Charlotte, still my closest friend even though years could pass between our seeing one another. I have never shown myself to her as I really am even though she has always seemed able to do this with me and I see it now as a failure on my part. Taking is as vital to friendship as giving and in that I have failed Charlotte. I've kept all her letters but I shouldn't think mine to her were worth a second read. I didn't write to her as she to me with such candid assumption of tolerance and understanding.

When her first letter arrived it contained the suspicion of pregnancy and, to my private shame, I felt envy. I wanted Leonard's child. This desire had been with me ever since that first conversation with Charlotte when we had shivered against the river bank on the Backs outside King's. I kept it, like a special treat for the future, allowing it to the forefront of my thoughts every now and then to be imagined over and savoured before being put back into store in the corner of my mind that was hope. Lately, in Berkeley, I had allowed it an increasing number of silent airings although, unable to deceive myself, I recognised the attraction of having Leonard's baby to have become something with an ulterior motive to the way it had begun in Cambridge. There it had been an unencumbered sort of reverie because I loved Leonard. I still loved him, sometimes to a point of distraction I could barely tolerate as I watched him amidst the university hierarchy, revered, respected, sought out, and totally unaware of all this himself. I suppose what frightened me most was that one day he must realise the extent of his worth and find me wanting, and against that eventuality, I had begun to place the bond of bearing his child.

So it was that I read Charlotte's letter and, while I saw motherhood as a bad thing for her I still felt the awful pang of envy. The letter, written on two crisp white sheets of water-marked paper in black ink, Charlotte's words almost drawn as opposed to written – graphic designers' script fighting large rounded letters to produce an uncertain style, did not reach the momentous news until the second page, although when I reread it the signs of despair could be seen in the first sheet.

In the next letter, received just a fortnight later, the writing was more restrained, the fierce individuality less apparent; some of the letters were only partially formed:

My dear Frances,

This should be a happy letter, I think even joyous is the word people use. The news is that I am expecting a baby having 'passed' the positive test – is everything in life determined by things associated with the lavatory? It seems that all I do in the next few months must be. Everything has to be regular – I really hate that word, especially as I feel so irregular at the moment, sick and worn out and trapped. What is the matter with me –

why can't I be pleased and glowing like everyone else?

Dan is positively puffed up with the expectation of it all, but he tries to hide it because he knows I'm not pleased, although the more he pretends the more irritating he becomes – I'm being horrid to him and I can't stop even though I would much prefer to be nice. Oh well, I suppose it will pass, as they say, and I will come to accept it, although inevitability has always been hard for me to accept. Sorry to go on so much about me – how are you – and Leonard? I long to hear all your news and wish there were not so many expensive miles between us. Is America as it seems on television or even better? Do you think you will ever come back? Questions, questions, I ask them all so you will have to answer – please write soon to restore my sanity.

love Charlotte

The next letter came after a further two months:

My dear Frances,

I am fat. Everything about me has become fat; feet, fingers, arms, legs, face. I look like a parody of the Michelin man. Why is nature so cruel, don't all women hate being fat? Dan says it's beautiful (note – not me but it). I've never felt less beautiful but what is worse is that I am beginning to accept – I read the *Daily Telegraph* births column searching for names although all the best ones are in the deaths. Do you like Mirabella – I feel it will be a girl because I want a boy. You will be her godmother, won't you – no doubt Dan's family will insist on a christening, in fact his mother has already proposed Lakeside for the bunfight afterwards and I wouldn't be surprised if she hasn't already made a shortlist of caterers.

I still travel to town each day although Dan keeps making noises about there being no need to stay the course, but I must hold on. The studio is making people redundant and I have the terrible fear that I might have been one of them had I not been leaving anyway. The baby has saved me that, for which I am grateful.

I read the openly selfish sentences and felt a mixture of irritation and affection. I wrote back, describing life at Berkeley but too aware of Charlotte's growing despondency to be able to make it sound as interesting and stimulating as it was. The process of tempering my enthusiasm gave the letters a tone of detachment which I wondered afterwards if Charlotte had read as a deliberate distancing of our friendship. The last letter from England before Vicky was born was worryingly subdued:

Not long now, but waiting has become a way of life. I don't go out much any more I've become so big that people seem to stare. Dan's working very hard at the moment and weekends he relaxes by going shooting with his father. They're planning a holiday in Scotland after the glorious 12th – a fortnight's grouse shooting by which time the baby should have arrived and Dan's mother will be at home with me. She says it's better for the men to be out of the way but I don't know whether I agree. Either way I don't suppose it will make much difference. I can't imagine what life after birth will be like. Dan's mother says busy. She's been a great help – bought a lot of blue things for the nursery. I hope none of them will be too disappointed when Georgina (latest name) arrives.

'She sounds okay,' Leonard said after I had shown him the letter.
'The fighting spirit seems to have disappeared,' I said. 'There are bits that sound like Charlotte but overall she seems to have been engulfed by her condition.'
'You never say the word baby or anything approaching it,' he said then, unexpectedly. He was watching me with too much attention. He had seized upon this moment to bring into the open the thing that had been hovering between us for a long time and to

which I had thought him oblivious.

'Does it get to you, this baby business? Is it what you want?' he asked.

'I thought so,' I began and then told him what I had imagined and hoped and come to reject.

'What changed your mind – all those letters from Charlotte?' We were sitting in the white-pillared dining hall of the Claremont Hotel in Oakland. It was a Sunday, midday, the remains of a Californian brunch in front of us. Our table was by a window, looking out across the bay towards San Francisco, ethereal even at this time of day, with its veil-like mist softening the outlines of the city. Leonard had been in New York for a week, increasingly he went away but I never went with him, I had my teaching job at the school in Piedmont and besides, there was no reason for me to go.

'Maybe the letters a little, but not really. I couldn't do it now unless I was certain it wasn't for the wrong reasons,' I said, a sense of finality, of talking about what might have been but now would never happen, giving me a strange feeling of relief.

'I guess we've drifted,' Leonard was saying, still watching me closely. 'Frances,' (he laid heavy emphasis on the 'a' when he had something important to say) 'I've been offered a post in Israel.'

'Offered, or did you apply?' I asked, quite calmly, needing the facts.

'Offered but I would have applied anyway.'

He reached his hand across the white tablecloth and lightly touched the curve of my neck. I swallowed against his fingers.

'The British reserve,' he said, his eyes full of tender regret. 'It's more than I can handle.'

I noticed an involuntary quiver gathering momentum in my hand and withdrew it from sight, clenching my fist under the table. I felt a little sick, because the despair was so great, but my mind was dreadfully clear, wretched objectivity released from the well-maintained safety valve fixed next to the corner that had been hope.

We didn't say any more, although the 'whys' and 'what happens now' bulged and bulged as if I had not tormented myself long enough with that destructive notion of intellectual inferiority. That was it, I had no doubt, listening to his voice but not hearing what he said about New York, devouring the moments left in which I could watch his face and hands and neck and hair. That afternoon I wrote to Charlotte, a bright breezy letter urging her to be happy but not to lose her identity or purpose to motherhood. I ended:

'I think you should call your daughter Victoria – it's a name that sounds full of hope and achievement.'

I moved out of Leonard's apartment the week before he left for Israel. Against instructions I went to the airport to say goodbye and found another girl, Jewish, darkly beautiful, kissing Leonard by the departure gate. Masochistically, although there was curiosity there too, I offered to share a taxi back into the city. The girl's beauty was quite intimidating, but she had no brain, at least none that was apparent, and I wondered at my own lack of sense and perception. I had been wrong from the start – had never known, or even greatly thought about what Leonard really wanted.

There was a letter from England in the mail box when I got back to the new apartment. Redirected from Leonard's old address, it announced the arrival of Victoria three weeks earlier.

My dear Frances,

Victoria is a reality and already she has lived up to her name. My sense of achievement in having produced such a perfect little person makes me feel quite heady. And the hopes I have for her seem to know no bounds.

Motherhood has proved a revelation and I have hopes for myself – perhaps I can after all be something good to somebody. I feel wicked now to think how I resented Vicky's coming and dreaded her arrival and must apologise to you for all those

196

wretched letters I've sent over the past few months.

I would like to describe Vicky to you in minute detail but I suppose that would be too tedious of me, and besides I want you to see her for yourself – will Leonard let you come? My love to you and him.

Charlotte

PS   Dan is away in Scotland blasting the grouse.

PPS   His mother has accepted Vicky's gender very well, although she still buys blue.

I reread the brief letter and rushed out to buy something pink, before I had a chance to weep.

I decided to remain at the school in Piedmont for a further year. I was not sure what I wanted to do and therefore determined that it was better to make no changes until I did. The letters kept coming from Charlotte but I no longer read them more than once. They spoke in a language I could not understand and made me feel sad with a sense of loss I felt it would be wrong to try to explain in the letters I sent to England. I had been grateful to be spared the lurid details of birth I had expected from Charlotte although after a while I came to see this sparing as symptomatic of the loss. I wanted to write: 'Where are you, Charlotte – is it really you that writes those long paragraphs about the nuts and bolts of getting through one day to the next?' There was a lot about a woman called Audrey, who sounded stiflingly kind and crass and jolly. I wondered whether I was jealous and decided that maybe I was as I could think only menacingly towards this woman whom I had never met and hoped never would.

'Write me a horrid self-centred letter like they used to be and tell me that you've been wretchedly rude to Audrey,' I scribbled in despair after reading a particularly inane letter from Charlotte; but I screwed up the piece of paper and dropped it in the empty silver ashtray Leonard had once filled three and four times a day with the pungent knockings from his pipe.

And then the letters changed again. Their tone became aggressive and while I was relieved to read the re-emergence of Charlotte as opposed to the serene and mindless mumsy-figure, I began to fear that she had lost the new sense of purpose expressed in that first letter after Vicky's birth.

'Frances,' the last but one began, no 'my dear' or even 'dear'.

I am afraid I am in no mood for endearments – not even to you – in fact especially not to you – for if our situations were reversed I would not have abandoned you for so long. Today I think I have gone a little mad – I took Dan's gun, loaded it and fired it, not at anyone or anything, I hasten to add, I just simply felt in need of making a loud noise, although I don't think that anybody heard, at least, nobody came to see what was going on but then gunshots are not so very uncommon in this neck of the woods – this God-forsaken literal neck of the woods where there is no life except the birds and the bees – even Audrey has disappeared – gone camping with the Brownies – do you remember when we went camping and spent all week emptying latrines – it sticks out in my memory as one of the best weeks of my life. I think I wrote to you once before that everything comes back to the lavatory (excuse vulgarity) – but what else are we here for – my life has been governed by nappy changes for the past year, I think it has been my most important function. Life is shit.

I read the letter three times and then wondered why I always felt so sorry for Charlotte. The aggressive tone had made me react with the old feelings of affection and irritation plus overwhelming gladness that Charlotte was still Charlotte after all, but when I came to analyse her situation I could find nothing that warranted pity. She had a kind and long-suffering husband, a baby, a nice home and no financial worries. Perhaps feeling sympathetic and protective towards her was still due to the awful time when her

198

father had died and she'd been expelled from the convent, but even before all that Charlotte had always been her own worst enemy. Satisfaction with anything in life, the possibility of peace of mind, would ever elude her. She rubbed up against life like a spitting cat attracted to a fire, scalding itself needlessly over and over when it could have stood back and basked in the warmth.

'Charlotte could be quite something,' Leonard had once said. 'But there's something bugging her.'

'Dan?' I had suggested as at the time I was more than usually anti-him.

'No, Dan's a good guy, I like him. He's wrong for Charlotte, too nice, but he's not the root of her problem. It's something in herself.'

America without Leonard was like remaining in an enormous theatre after the show was over. I tried to find satisfaction in teaching my bright-eyed, toothy pupils but I went on feeling hollow inside and the void seemed to grow rather than diminish. To my surprise, the people I had met with Leonard at Berkeley went on inviting me to their houses and even asked me to join their intimate little supper parties at the various ethnic restaurants they favoured. Weekends they wanted me to go with them to Sausalito to their boats that bobbed about on sun-speckled water and where we would spend the day messing about on the deck and the night sunk below in nests of cushions for long conversations arising out of obscure topics – the health-giving properties of seaweed turned into the re-emergence of China, the lack of Havana cigars in the US became an analysis of America's part in twentieth-century wars, hot and cold. They were nice people, modest intellectuals delighting in the discovery of crazy notions in relation to serious issues; and through it all I felt the absence of Leonard even more keenly than when I was alone, and could not believe that they did not feel the lack of his being there as well, like a departed guru.

The final letter from Charlotte was waiting when I returned from one of these weekends.

My dear Frances –

I have acquired a donkey. Her name is Tamara and she views me with suspicion and mistrust, as well she might. We glare at one another across the field like new-found sparring partners and when I can think of nothing else to do, which is quite often, I go out and watch and wait for her to make her wonderful noise, so discordant and crazy – it makes me feel better.

Dan is away shooting. Vicky has measles – I didn't have her vaccinated for fear of brain damage – but I'm so worried about her I feel as if the damage is done anyway – in my own head. No one comes near – I won't let them. Vicky and I must sit it out alone, malignant terror keeping the world at bay – not that anyone much comes near anyway. Audrey telephones but I can't think what we say. Her children haven't been vaccinated either but she says going blind or deaf is better than being a cabbage.

'Charlotte is going mad!' I said aloud. 'I must go back to England.'

CHAPTER TWELVE

Sunday Afternoon – Nick

'I don't understand, Nick, I just don't understand at all,' Ruby said.

'It's strange, but I thought you might,' I said. 'And I felt that I should tell you myself, partly because I wasn't sure Marion would say anything. I thought she might delay it.'

'To come all this way and to tell me this, and look at the state of you – you look as if you haven't had a decent night's sleep for weeks and you don't even look happy – downright miserable in fact. Can I get you something to eat?'

'No, thank you, Ruby, nothing. I just wanted to tell you.'

'At least a cup of tea?' she insisted, retaining a strong note of disapproval.

But if Ruby was angry she was also flattered that I had come to tell her myself although the decision to do so was more calculated than she realised; a PR exercise the purpose of which would never occur to her – not after all the years of seeing me as the reluctant father.

It was more than five years since the last time I had been to the house in Birmingham, although I had seen Ruby, two or three times a year, when she came to stay with us, uninvited, but too potent a force to refuse when she declared her impending visits over the phone to Marion, who would bemoan her mother's domineering ways and had even indicated a reluctance to let her know the new address and telephone number when we moved house. Ruby, incurably divisive, would arrive and the visits, which always left their mark on Marion's tentative ego, were somehow endured and even enjoyed at times because for all her old wickedness Ruby was never dull, and Marion and I, each in different ways finding her infuriating, ultimately accepted her as inevitable. Paul, of course, adored her, Ruby made sure of that.

'We can't stand here in the hallway,' she said, brusquely. 'You go along in there and nod at Frank. I'll make the tea.'

I had delivered what I had come to tell her straight away before the telling could be diluted and blurred by the television and the rest of Marion's family who doubtless were eating some sort of meal in the general living room. I went in. The scene was as I had imagined, food, hard to categorise as lunch or tea, remained half eaten on the big table. The brother, who was still poised to eat, knife and fork vertical in his hands as he gazed at the television (colour now and with a vast screen) sat nearest the door. He glanced round when he heard me come in and gave a lopsided half-smiling grimace revealing a mouth full of masticated chips. The elder of the two sisters actually spoke. She was no longer thin, in fact she had become quite fat and appeared to be growing a moustache. The younger sister was no longer part of the scene, having married five years ago – the last occasion I had been to the house, but a child, presumably hers – the one that Ruby looked after since the break-up of the marriage – sat beside the thin-cum-fat sister, its face smudged with tomato ketchup. Frank, in his usual armchair, acknowledged the five-year interim with a nod; that was all he did these days Ruby had told me, since vacuum cleaners went out of his life.

The room, which all those years ago, the first time I entered it, had transmitted a careless kind of warmth, now seemed suffused with a stultifying air of hopelessness. It felt like the concentrated source of what it was in Marion that I wanted to leave, and it occurred to me that maybe I had only come here to reinforce the decision to do so.

I sat down at the table. In front of me stood a jar of Morgan-Mackie's with the lid off – perhaps the meal had been breakfast as well – although it had been my idea to launch the campaign promoting marmalade as the bitter/sweet flavour to go with any meal at any time; breaking down the tradition of marmalade as a breakfast-only food. Perhaps it had worked on Ruby. The notion that Ruby could be swayed gave me heart, and yet, if I had not already believed this possible why had I come? Ruby and I had long ago come to terms with 'understanding' one another, at least that was what I hoped and needed to believe. There was, I felt, the possibility of trust between us, and some sort of pact, but I had to be sure.

To have any hope of certainty where Ruby was concerned was perhaps somewhat asinine. There may appear to be a strong degree of predictability in what she does, but at close quarters she has always seemed to me totally unpredictable. After Paul's birth and the heavy indictment she hurled at me with all the force of indignant mother-in-lawhood, her attitude changed again in the following months. My resignation from Parkin's Prams, hastily written and delivered in an unbalanced mood of destruction, was, somewhat to my chagrin, accepted without discussion by Dorothy Parkin. Much later, after I had left and eventually come through the early struggle to succeed on my own, Dorothy, whom I had come to view as a friend as much as an employer, did explain the reason for her early acceptance of my departure.

'It was time for you to strike out on your own, even though the timing itself may have been bad, and besides, no one can go on writing about prams for too long,' she had said, presenting Marion and me with the new Parkin's pushchair.

'I always thought that maybe you'd upset someone in America,' Marion said after she'd gone.

'So did I, although it seemed all right at the time,' I told her.

An uneasy calm existed between Marion and me as if we were putting off some undefined but inevitable crisis until a time when we would both be more able to cope with its consequences. Two months after Paul was born we had to leave the flat and move in with her family, the nightmare suddenly transformed into reality as Marion went back to her job with the newspaper and Ruby took over the daily care of our son.

Recrimination barely held back, mother and daughter rallied, stoically 'keeping things together' in the face of wanton irresponsibility as they saw it on my part, while everything I had, every penny, went into my new venture, a headlong, obsessional investment in a hard to envisage future. It was six months before I got my first account, a plimsoll manufacturer in Northampton resentfully battling against cheap imports from Korea. He was equally resentful about having to waste any money on public relations but his advisers were adamant and my fees undercut everyone else's, and this time the timing was right. Everyone started wearing jeans, and with them, variations on the plimsoll theme. As fashion took over, price was no longer the criterion and my client's plimsolls became the expensive sneakers everyone wanted.

I had rented a small office in the centre of Birmingham and spent more and more time there, in the evenings especially, when I could catch up on the more mundane paperwork and at the same time avoid the reproachful atmosphere of the general living room at Ruby's. The acrimony, I felt, sprang from her, but then I was not there enough to realise for some time that the source was Marion, Ruby having long since found it unnecessary to go on harbouring spite and rancour all the time her daughter was prepared to do it for her. I hardly need to say that I was far from happy with the situation. If I allowed myself to think about it I felt wretched and guilty over my failure to provide a proper home for Marion and Paul, and if Marion showed her resentment I saw it magnified because it was what I expected and yet could not accept.

Most of the time she said nothing, which could be even worse. She was getting very tired, working at the newspaper all day and still weak from the haemorrhage after Paul's birth, and yet she insisted on being the one who always got up to him in the night. The baby would wake twice, sometimes three and four times a night, his desolate cry piercing through our sleep until we found we were anticipating it and no longer able to sleep at all except in brief, fitful spells laced with muddled dreams, sometimes hearing the relentless grizzle before it had even started.

The dreams were all that we shared. Marion, understandably, was too tired for sex, but my own need grew beyond understanding and one night I virtually forced her to make love in a desperate attempt to find a vestige of harmony between us. Marion, who had been zombie-like for days, began to whimper as I pressed myself over her and suddenly I was incapable of doing anything, the pathetic miserable sound rendering me impotent. I flopped back on my side of the bed and turned my head towards the grey dawn edging through the thin curtains.

'I'm sorry,' Marion murmured.

'So am I,' I said harshly, which was not how I had intended it to sound. At that moment I would have been content just to hold her, to draw comfort and maybe give some to her in a gesture of tenderness, but, as always, I held back and the moment passed, leaving us both even more wretched and alone.

The house in Birmingham had seven bedrooms and the following night I found that Marion had removed herself and Paul to one of the other six.

'I think it's better that way for a while, Nick. There's no reason why both of us should have broken nights,' she explained evenly, without looking at me.

'Maybe you're right, but it seems a bit unfair on you. We could take turns with Paul,' I suggested, knowing she would never allow it. She seemed to wince every time I went near him, which was not often, as, if I was honest, the baby frightened me. His fragile softness was like fingering a peach and I feared bruising him, and setting off the alarming fierceness of his cry.

Marion looked up at me then, her eyes briefly scanning mine.

'That's nice of you to say that,' she said. 'Nick, I don't want you to feel that Paul and I are shutting you out, you don't feel that, do you?'

'Of course not,' I lied.

That night I slept no better than before, and the nightmares were more vivid. It was also the first time I dreamt the murder dream, waking in a cold sweat with the terrible conviction I had killed somebody, an anonymous figure tortured and mangled and then buried in a grave dug out of slimy clay, me with the shovel frantically trying to keep back the heavy orange clods long enough to heave the leaden body into the fast-diminishing hole.

The third night alone the dream came a second time and I must have shouted out loud because I came to at the sound of rapping on the door. A small but insistent little rapping, almost like an animal scratching to come in. I got up and moved across the room, stumbling against a chair, uncertain as to whether I was asleep or awake. I opened the door and saw Ruby standing in the hallway silhouetted against the white moonlight coursing down through the skylight over the stair well. She came towards me, into the bedroom, closing the door behind her.

The nightmares were abated and life became more tolerable even if the new arrangement was beyond toleration outwardly, but then nobody knew or at least the others in the house all feigned not to know.

'A civilised, rather sophisticated sort of arrangement,' Ruby called it. 'If we can't help each other out a bit then we might just as well not be a family,' she said with airy smugness, 'and after all, what harm are we doing, none at all, and if it stops you gallivanting.'

How easily I had allowed it to happen. The grotesqueness of sleeping with Ruby was too huge to contemplate so it just went on happening like a bad habit one would give up tomorrow but not today. Lying in the bed, our arms and legs intertwined, we would hear the baby start to cry in the room down the corridor, and then the sound would stop as Marion got up to him.

'No harm done,' Ruby would say, again and again, until I almost believed her.

Guilt, I discovered, was finite. The sum of my transgressions against Marion reached such enormous proportions that it came to the point where remorse was so inadequate as to be impossible. It was as if I had swum against the tide of honour and decency for so long and found myself in such deep water that it no longer made any difference to struggle, even a little. I might just as well succumb to drowning in the murky depths and wait to see whether I would surface again.

Rescue, from the more immediate whirlpool of Ruby, came in the unlikely form of Germaine Hartnell. Germaine, glowing like a brown beacon of health, turned up at my one-room office one morning in grey, wet November and gave me my second large account. She had come to England to set up a Gym and Tonic chain in the home counties and wanted me to look after the PR.

'Bodies are my business and bodies my criteria, so you get the job Nicky-boy darling!' she said, letting out a ricochet laugh.

I took her to lunch, spent a fortune on food she barely touched, signed a contract and ordered a bottle of Taittinger to celebrate.

'So you see, darling, California was worth the ride,' she said, with wry lack of subtlety. 'Old Dorothy's quite a fixer.'

'Dorothy?'

'Yeh, Dorothy. Who'd you think's my partner in Gym and Tonic UK?'

'I thought it was all finished with her,' Marion said when I told her the news.

I wanted to laugh then, at the absurdity of her suspicion, at the enormity of her unknowing, but instead I went over to where she was standing, in the tiny bedroom she had escaped to with Paul. She had her back against the cot in a subconscious attitude of protection, standing between me and the sleeping child. She straightened as I approached, her eyes widening a little as if it had become second nature to view me as a predator, but that night I was too full of hope for the future to react with the old form of dismissal and retreat. She flinched as I put my arms around her shoulders but it was not in her nature to resist and we accomplished some sort of reconciliation, a temporary repair.

Ruby, inscrutable, energetically helped us move the cot and Paul's paraphernalia back into the bigger bedroom and enigmatically put a vase of flowers on the dressing table. Marion gave up her job and six weeks later we moved down to Hertfordshire, a new house attached to one exactly the same, cloned twins, repeated and repeated a hundred times in a maze of cul-de-sacs laid out on a bare hillside like virulent suckers climbing an empty trellis. The houses filled up and we had neighbours, all with young families, maximum mortgages and the single common aim to move as soon as possible off the estate. We wanted houses with four walls of individuality, not three; double garages instead of single in a block, and gardens around which we could erect fences as opposed to the open plan imposed by the developers of Meadow Fields.

Hertfordshire was Dorothy's suggestion: 'I think it would be a good idea for you and Marion to live in the Home Counties. People are different down there and we need to know what they want.'

So Gym and Tonic paid for the move and we compromised with an office in Cambridge as I didn't want to lose sight of my plimsoll manufacturer. But Home Counties life on Meadow Fields was not as I had imagined. Our neighbours did not have enough money to worry about health and fitness, their lives were dedicated to the appearance of their houses, but within lurked an unexpected taste for debauchery.

'The people at number three are having a pyjama party on Saturday,' Marion told me soon after we had moved in. 'They've invited us.'

208

'Do you want to go?'

'Not really, but then we ought to make some friends.'

'It sounds a bit silly, pyjamas, and I haven't got any.'

'This is not how I want to live,' I thought, on Saturday evening as I drove in to the village to collect the babysitter. At half past nine Marion and I walked down the road to number three, the pyjamas she had bought from British Home Stores flapping round my legs, a bottle of Nicolas wine shoved under my arm.

'I'm Ralph and this is Edwina, glad you could come,' a prematurely balding man wearing a frilly nightdress greeted us, shaking my hand. Edwina, tall and thin and with a hook nose, was wearing the pyjamas.

'You're number seventeen aren't you?' she enquired.

'Drinks in the kitchen. Help yourself,' Ralph said.

The Beatles' 'She Loves You' was coming from the living room. It ended and the Beach Boys started to sing.

'What do you do, I'm with ICI at Welwyn, a sort of troubleshooter you know,' a man in a black and red nightdress told me in the kitchen. 'What number are you?'

'Seventeen.'

'Ah, we must be neighbours! Fifteen. Our wives have met over the proverbial fence. You're the chap who makes wine, or is that nineteen.'

'Must be nineteen. No wine at seventeen.'

'Ah, got it wrong have I. Are you interested in model trains?'

'No.'

'I've got a complete set of first-edition Hornby double "O" set out in the loft. You'll have to come over and take a look.'

'How long do we have to stay?' I murmured to Marion as we pushed our way out of the kitchen.

In the living room there were just three or four couples standing around in semi-darkness, sipping drinks and wondering what had happened to the party. Somebody asked me if I played cricket, another what sort of car I had. Marion found number fifteen's wife and started talking about Paul. I moved away and was confronted by Edwina who thought we should dance. After that the room seemed to fill up. More and more people arrived including the winemaker whose vintage elderberry was passed round until we were all pissed out of our minds. Edwina twirled about in front of me, Ralph's pyjama jacket flying open at every spin. I had lost sight of Marion but wasn't looking. Somebody produced a reefer. 'Oh my turn, my turn,' Edwina said as I took a drag.

'Whose is it?' I asked.

'Number five, he's a policeman,' Edwina said, taking the cigarette, holding it with her fingertips.

The party seemed to shift into slow motion and then began to disseminate. At some time during the night I found myself in number fifteen's loft, in among the Hornby double 'O's on the floor with Edwina, going like an express as the trains sped around us. 'I can't stop the damned thing,' I shouted, trying to reach the control panel above our heads. 'Stop now and I'll kill you!' Edwina screamed.

Just before dawn I went back to number seventeen. A wind had blown up, icily whipping round the houses on the bare hillside, chilling to the bone. Edwina had scurried off up the road, furtive and liverish, her face a deathly shade of paste. The front door was bolted. I went round to the back of the house and climbed in through a window. It had not occurred to me until then that Marion might not be alone. The notion twisted a nerve in my gut and I crept up the stairs in an agony of jealous expectation. I paused outside the bedroom, wondering what I would do if Ralph or number five or number fifteen lay snoring next to my wife. I flung open the door. Marion, alone in the bed, did not stir. I stared down at her and felt vaguely disappointed, even let down.

I threw off my clothes and got into bed, lying down with my back towards her. 'Bastard,' she murmured in a barely audible whisper.

'Yes,' I said.

There were more parties. We said we would not go but we did.

The wind kept blowing and the hillside remained bare. Nothing would grow properly because there were no fences, no chance of consolidation. The estate developed patches of superficial scrub grass but it couldn't hold the dust which the wind blew up into the face. You couldn't see where you were going.

There were two, nearer three, of those dusty years, a bleak lump of time in which I worked harder and longer than ever before, the effort seeming to achieve very little other than the meeting of monthly bills. There were times when I looked around at my neighbours with their new company Cortinas parked in their drives, water sprinklers on the front lawns enticing the scrub, spare time for golf and cricket, trains and winemaking; time to tend allotments away from the hill where the earth was rich and fertile. Their lives depressed me and yet at the same time filled me with a sense of futility over my own existence. Such moments still come to me. I fear them more than anything else, although now I realise they have been useful. The scramble to escape that pit of despair has forced me on, produced the drive to succeed, the negative achieving the positive, and still I scramble on, afraid of time to stop and think and see the wider futility of it all.

I got up and went to find Ruby in the kitchen. She was standing in the middle of the room, vigorously rubbing a blackened cloth against a tarnished silver teapot. She started when she saw me, as if she had been caught out, discovered doing something furtive.

'Nick! I was just about to bring the tea through. I thought we'd have it in the front room.'

Her attitude had changed. She was almost shy, not calculatingly coy as I had seen her in the past, and no longer disapproving in the way she had been when I told her why I had come. She finished the polishing and filled the pot with tea bags and boiling water, placing it on a tray with two bone china cups which had dark red flowers and gold leaf painted on them. I noticed she had rearranged her hair and her lips were newly red. She had gained more weight since the last time I had seen her but her figure was still good although the clothes she wore these days were less revealing: she had gone a bit ethnic in style. Her skirt was not unlike the one Charlotte had worn the night in London.

She handed me the tray and we proceeded through the house, past the room where the rest of the family were, to what had once been termed the front parlour. The door was stiff and she rammed her hip against it as I stood waiting with the tray. Inside, the room had a musty unused atmosphere but it had escaped the ever-present cooking smells that lingered everywhere else. Ruby closed the door behind us and took the tray from me.

'I'm sorry to have taken so long,' she said, setting it down and starting to pour, avoiding my gaze.

'What's all this in aid of?' I said, watching her fuss with the cups and saucers. 'Silver teapot, best china, front room. What are you playing at, Ruby?'

She stopped what she was doing and glanced up at me, her eyes soft and watery.

'You can't do it, Nick, you really can't,' she made a little sob and put her knuckle to her lips.

'It's done, Ruby. It's too late,' I said.

'No it's not,' she countered, regaining a little of her fierceness. 'You wouldn't have come here like this – come all this way to tell me, if that was the case. You would just have gone off with this woman and left it at that.'

'But why the silver teapot treatment?' I asked without denying what she had suggested. 'I might have expected a good rollicking from you, but not this. The soft approach isn't like you, what are you trying to achieve?'

'I'm not sure I know myself,' she said, continuing to pour the tea. 'Do you know, I haven't sat in this room for years. Perhaps if I had, perhaps if I had let Marion and the others in here a few times they might have turned out differently. It's a beautiful room, don't you think, elegant, refined.'

The room was in the past. It had stood still and unused for too long. Its colours had faded and its furnishing and decoration gone out of fashion.

'We haven't done right by you, Nick,' she continued after a heavy pause. 'You've become a success like I always thought you would and I suppose we're just not good enough for you any more. What's this other girl like, clever and posh I dare say?'

'Please Ruby,' I tried to stop her, but she carried on:

'I can't say I blame you for wanting to leave us behind now that you're in the money, big house, fast car, smart clothes.' She sighed and glanced at me again, only this time I caught a gleam of something else in the sharp grey eyes.

'Of course, I know exactly how you feel. There have been times when I've wanted to escape, but I've stuck it out, you have to, and there are always the compensations along the way. You were one of them, Nick,' she added. Her tone, which had been mournful was gathering an edge.

'What are you getting at Ruby?' I asked. 'Are we playing some sort of game?'

'You're the one that's playing games,' she said, 'fun and games, isn't that right, Nick?' Her mouth had gone into a hard line.

'Come on, Ruby, we've always been able to talk,' I said.

'Yes, we have, so tell me what it is that you want, my approval? Is that it?'

'I don't even expect you to understand. I have no right to expect that. I've simply come to tell you and to ask that you won't make it more difficult for Marion and Paul.'

'Ah ha!' she exclaimed. 'Now we have it. You want it all nice and clean and tidy.'

'I don't want Paul growing up in an atmosphere of bitterness and recriminations.'

'You are a hypocrite,' she snapped. The pretence of subdued bewilderment and regret had disappeared, but I felt more able to deal with her in her present mood.

'Okay, so I'm a hypocrite, but what's gone wrong between Marion and me has nothing to do with Paul, and I don't want him poisoned against me because of it. I'm asking you, Ruby, pleading, if you like, not to say anything to him that will turn him against me.'

Ruby leant back in her chair in an attitude of matriarchal power.

'I never thought you cared all that much about Paul,' she said with icy satisfaction. 'There's something especially dear about a child whose father can't be bothered with him. I suppose that's partly why I've always been so fond of the boy.'

'That's unforgivable,' I said, feeling hot with loathing.

'But true,' Ruby sang out.

'I shouldn't have come here,' I said, standing up. 'I've wasted my time.'

'Yes,' Ruby said. She remained still as if she knew I would stay and hear what she was to say next.

'Your trouble, Nick, is that you think if you've bedded a woman she'll ever after do as you say. A lot of men think like that but it's more often than not the other way round.'

I sat down again. It was the first time she had ever referred to what had happened between us.

'Another cuppa?' she said lightly, stretching forward towards the silver pot. I did not reply but she refilled my cup all the same.

'If you'll take a bit of advice from an old friend,' she began, the recent victory having softened her tone. 'That side of life becomes less important as the years go on. You and Marion have weathered a few storms. I know she's not a glamour girl but she's stuck by you in the bad times and she must have helped you a bit to get where you are now. Have a little fling here and there but don't break up what it's taken all these years to build.'

'It's gone too far,' I said. 'Ruby, wouldn't you have left Frank if you'd fallen in love with someone else?' I felt compelled to try to reason it out with her and unable to leave until we had reached some sort of pact. At one moment I hated her, felt revulsion and disgust, and the next found myself drawn to her again as if I needed her to understand.

'I did fall in love,' she said, 'but there was never any possibility of leaving Frank. You see he wouldn't have coped by himself and the other thing was impossible anyway.'

'Who was it?' I asked.

'Don't you know,' she said.

CHAPTER THIRTEEN

Sunday – Early Evening – Charlotte

'I wish I had a brother or a sister. We'd be a real family then,' Vicky said, without warning, on the way home from James and Audrey's.

'Aren't we already?' Dan said, keeping his eyes fixed on the road.

'Families have to have four people, don't they, otherwise they don't count?' she persisted earnestly.

'Don't count for what, darling?' I said. 'A family can be just two people and anyway, if you count grannies and people like that we are more than four.'

'I didn't know that grannies counted. I still wish I had a brother. Can't I have one? Couldn't you make one for me? You said you and Daddy made me.'

'I don't think so, darling. It's not as easy as that.'

'Why not?'

'It just isn't.'

'Why isn't it?'

'Please don't start "whying" Vicky. Not now.'

'When can I?'

'Vicky, will you stop it,' I snapped and she went quiet for a moment before starting to cry.

The car crunched on the gravel in front of the house. Dan

switched off the engine and got out. He opened the back door and Vicky, her arms stretched out, scrambled into his, burying her face against his neck as he lifted her against him and carried her towards the house.

I followed them but inside I went through to the kitchen while Dan carried Vicky up to her room. An interminable half hour went past before he came down again and I heard his footsteps coming through the house. I waited for him to come into the kitchen where I sat in the silent stillness, a feverish expectancy burning inside me as if Dan could somehow put everything right, as if it wasn't up to me any more.

'Is she all right? Did you say anything to her?' I asked him quickly when he appeared.

'She's asleep. I think she was overtired. All the excitement over the weekend,' he said wearily. He went across to the window, his hands in his trouser pockets as he stood with his back to me, looking out over the garden.

'You didn't say anything to her then?' I repeated.

'No,' he said, the word sounding a little constricted in his throat.

We were silent for a few moments as he remained by the window. I was frightened of him, unable to continue with all the things that needed to be said and sorted out because I feared any manifestation of emotion from him; that he might break down terrified me more than his anger. Dan angry would be strange enough but emotional, that I could not handle. Everything seemed to depend upon his strength; even now, when I had no earthly right to expect or demand anything from him, I was still relying on his wisdom and understanding, his friendship.

I pictured Vicky, asleep in the bedroom that had been empty the night I had come home. Dan could always soothe her, soothing was a gift. Dan, the comforter, the soother, with no one to soothe him. The poignant thought welled up in me.

'Oh Dan, why does life have to be so difficult?' I said. 'So complicated?'

'It doesn't have to be, not for everyone,' he said. He coughed, a pretence of a sound followed by a muffled sniff that nearly broke my cold, selfish heart.

He turned then, to face me, and came across the kitchen to where I was sitting at the table, but the daylight was fading and he appeared shadowy so that I could not properly see his eyes and expression.

'Shall I turn on the light?' I said, stupidly, against my will, as a sort of diversion, something positive to do.

'No, not at the moment. Leave it for a bit,' he said, sitting down heavily.

'And you're sure Vicky's all right?' I said.

'She senses that something's wrong.'

'Do you think I should go up and make sure she's alseep?'

'She was exhausted. Leave her. She's all right. Children are very resilient.'

'I wasn't when I was a child.'

'Yes you were. I remember.'

'All those years ago. We've known each other so long.'

'Do you really want to leave?' he said then and I recognised it as the question behind my fear.

'No, not at this moment,' I said.

'But you will tomorrow?'

'Yes.'

'I think you're making a terrible mistake.'

'It's a risk.'

'If you stayed things would have to change. We'd be together more. Do things. Maybe we should sell this house and move back into Cambridge.'

'What about Nick?'

'Ah, Nick.' Dan paused for a moment. 'What worries me Lottie is that you are using him as a catalyst.'

'How do you mean?'

'You're fed up with your life here ... Oh, I don't know. I

suppose what I'm saying, asking, is would you want to leave me anyway?'

'I don't know any more. I might not have had the courage to leave by myself.'

'I see.'

'Please don't say it like that.'

'Do you think you ever loved me?'

'Of course. Of course!'

'But not as you do Nick?'

I did not reply. At that moment I could see the worthiness of Dan and the unworthiness of Nick so clearly, and of course I identified with Nick.

'Why couldn't we have talked about it sooner?' Dan was saying.

'I don't think it would have made any difference.'

'You know, I had my suspicions but I hoped it would pass, that you'd get it out of your system.'

'I think I felt the same at first. I know it was wrong but I thought I could have an affair with him and nobody would know or get hurt.'

'The worst part, Lottie, the bit I find hardest to take, is the sense of waste.'

I got up then and went across to the window. The house was so terribly still and dead and I wanted to see something move to break the intensity. I looked out across the familiar scene, bathed in the eerie light of dusk, making it look somehow remote and unreal. The sky was darkening but still coloured by the sunken sun with a violet sadness that seemed to throw a shroud over the land. An emotional scene, that it had always been. I had gazed out at it with my head full of bitterness and resentment, depression and despair, excitement and hope, the episodes of my life daydreamed over against the backdrop of trees and grass, flowers and field beyond, the horizon blurred one day and clear another. Tonight I could not see it at all.

'Lets go out in the garden,' I said on impulse.

Outside the air was still warm but a shiver ran through me and instinctively I moved closer to Dan, putting my arm through his and a hand down into his pocket. I went to withdraw but he put his other hand across and held it against mine. We started across the grass, walking slowly, as if to eke out the time. At the far end of the garden we stopped and leant against the gate that led into Tamara's field. The sweet smell of grass cuttings pervaded the night air, fresh and pungent so that you wanted to breathe it in to keep and savour.

'I didn't notice you'd cut the grass this weekend,' I said, finding refuge in the mundane.

'Yesterday, while you were out. It didn't really need it. I'm afraid the lawn is almost bald in parts.'

'Never mind. It'll recover.'

'I expect so.'

'Can you see Tamara? She normally knows when we're here and comes over to the gate. Tammy – Tamara,' I called out. The field remained still. 'She's not there, Dan. She must have got out again. We'll have to go and look.' I scrambled over the gate, stumbling the other side. My heart was beating wildly, out of all proportion to the disappearance of the donkey.

'Tamara!' I yelled. An awful sense of doom had come over me. Perhaps she had been stolen. Guilt raged in me. Somehow it was my fault Tamara wasn't there.

'Easy does it, Lottie,' Dan breathed in my ear. I had not heard him behind me, had not realised he was so close. 'She could be in the next field but if you yell like that she'll run off. You know how contrary she is.'

We hurried across the uneven grass but it had become too dark to see into the next field which dipped at the far side anyway.

'She's probably hiding down by that hawthorn hedge that runs this side of the brook,' Dan said comfortingly.

'Do you think she could be?' I said without much hope.

We went down the length of the boundary with the dipping

field searching for a gap in the hedgerow but the light was going so quickly we could barely see and had to get out on to the road which skirted both fields and led down to the ford a few hundred yards on. And then a car came by and the murkiness of the lane was dispersed in its headlights. The unnatural sound of Tamara's bray hooted nearby. The car veered, its lights sweeping across Tamara who stood, stock still in the immediate line of its swerve.

'I'll be good, God, if Tamara can be saved,' I thought with the simplistic clarity brought on by panic.

Dan had run forward, through the lights. The car careered off down the lane and I heard it splashing into the ford and then the sound of its engine pulling away and up the hill the other side.

The lane had gone dark and silent again. I stepped forward, my arms and legs trembling.

'Come on, you ridiculous creature. Let's get you back where you belong,' I heard Dan say. He was leaning against the donkey on the other side of the road, his back pushing her up against the thick hedge.

'It didn't even stop,' I said, crossing the lane. 'Dan, you could have been run over.'

'But I wasn't,' he said and for a moment we stood facing one another but just out of reach. I couldn't go any nearer, an overwhelming hollowness that was lack of generosity and an uncompromising, heartless sort of honesty, held me where I was. I heard Dan take a sharp intake of breath.

'Fate got it wrong again,' he murmured with a bitterness I had never heard before.

He set about manoeuvring Tamara.

'Dan, no,' I pleaded, going forward now to help him with the pushing and shoving. 'However would I have managed without you, I just can't imagine . . .' I trailed off.

'You will,' he said, breathless with the effort of moving Tamara. 'You'll have to manage, Lottie. People do when they have to.'

'You want me to leave?' I said, an unreasonable desolateness running through me.

'I think you've already left.'

Tamara bit me before we got her back to her field. Her teeth didn't break the skin but I could feel the heavy bruise threatening in my arm. Cantankerous creature that she was I couldn't feel angry, only sad at her perception. She had bitten me before but never Dan. Dan she recognised as good.

'Silly old girl,' he said, kissing her big heavy head and patting her neck as we left her for the night. We walked back across the field and through the garden to the house. It was earlier than it seemed, still only eight o'clock.

'What do you want to do?' I asked Dan.

'Have a bit of time to think.'

'Yes, I feel the same. I don't think I can bear so stay in the house. If you don't mind I'll go out for a little while.'

'Take the car,' he said. 'It's too dark to go wandering about in the lanes.'

I glanced up at him in the bright light of the hallway.

'Ah, I see,' he said, reading my intention.

I drove the car into the village and went to the public phone box outside the post office. I dialled Nick's number and after a moment heard his voice, strong and positive, the slight hint of northern accent more noticeable down the phone.

'It's me. Can you talk?'

'Yes.'

'I want to be with you, Nick. Soon.'

'Is it bloody your end?'

'Yes, but not in the way you mean.'

'I'll meet you somewhere. Say twenty minutes.'

'Nick, do you wish we had never met?'

'No. Do you?'

'No.'

CHAPTER FOURTEEN

Sunday Night – Frances

I had spent the weekend in Cambridge, an unplanned, spur-of-the-moment visit to American friends who kept open house in the tall Regency terraced property they rented overlooking Parker's Piece. They had seemed pleased to see me but their pleasure was vague and preoccupied. They were always involved in something pressing, the latest, all-absorbing frantically interesting and important project – currently the saving of a county council primary school in one of the smaller villages. I spent Saturday collecting signatures for a petition and then screenprinting 'Save our School' on a batch of T shirts down in the basement of the house where an assortment of printing equipment and a very old Roneo duplicator were kept for just such eventualities. Barbie, whose children attended a private school in the city, came down every now and then with a flagon of red wine. The third time she had a glass for herself as well and with a casual sort of energy began folding the shirts that were dry.

'You ought to come see us more often, Frances,' she said. 'We still miss you and Leonard, y'know. Do you ever hear from him now?' Barbie asked these sort of questions in the tone of a social worker, her deep concern for the welfare of others justifying her tendency to pry.

'No, not for more than a year, but I think he's still in Israel,' I said, smudging one of the slogans.

'You two should never have drifted. You were right for one another,' Barbie went on.

'Maybe, but it's too late now,' I said, trying to sound philosophical and wishing that Barbie would mind her own business. Why had I come to Cambridge, I asked myself, when it was a cast-iron certainty Leonard would be discussed.

'It's never too late,' Barbie continued. 'I don't wanna interfere, Frances, but Jack and I could arrange something. You see, Leonard's coming to England next month. He'll be staying with us. I think he'd like to see you.'

I felt my heart begin to pound and willed it to be still. Hope pressed in on me and then reason tried to banish it.

'He knows my address in London,' I said dismissively.

'Well, the offer is there,' Barbie rejoined kindly and picking up the flagon, made a move towards the door. 'I must go fix supper,' she said.

Sunday passed slowly, a long day full of earnest talk about the school campaign with half a dozen assorted hangers-on – no, I should be more charitable, other guests, maybe even friends, although Barbie and Jack didn't really have time for friends, only causes, and I could see myself becoming one of them. At some time during the afternoon Jack, who has the lumpy good looks of a retired baseball player, high cheek bones, sandy hair, a faded Adonis, spoke of Leonard. Immediately Barbie glanced at me and clumsily contrived to change the subject. I had been about to leave but had to wait then or risk appearing upset. It was too silly but I had not wanted to give a wrong impression that might further encourage Barbie to set something up when Leonard came to England. So I sat on in the high-ceilinged drawing room, its walls plastered with Art Deco posters, shelves bulging with books that had all been read, and everywhere, singly and in clusters, little earthenware pots with weedy-looking sproutings which I recognised as the prime ingredients of Barbie's herbal remedies. I looked at it all, the sound of Jack's enthusiasm droning on in the background beyond concentration. It all added up to a kind of honesty that was overall rather endearing. It was sort of naive and yet not, the naivety of those who had been to the other extreme and rejected it in favour of a 'home-spun' way of life. It was a very American thing to do, I thought, and saw with a sudden surge of affection the newly-naive pair. 'Dammit,' I almost said aloud, 'I wish like hell they would set up something when Leonard comes.'

I went to help Barbie prepare a vat of soya-based chilli con carne but left without staying for the meal.

'I really must go. You see there are some friends I promised to call in on before going back to London,' I said to extricate myself. It was only half a lie, Charlotte and Dan had been as much in my thoughts over the weekend as Leonard; perhaps that was why I had gone to Cambridge, but to Jack and Barbie's because it would have been too meddlesome to have gone straight to the other house. It went against the grain to interfere but there were times when it seemed one was not meant to stand back, not if it was possible to help: Barbie's philosophy, but what would happen to the world without the caring Barbies?

At the top of the steps that led down from the front door Barbie and Jack in turn hugged and kissed me, the only people I knew who did that. Their open-heartedness was infectious and I hugged them back.

'Thank you for a lovely time.'

'Come again soon. You know you're one of our favourite people.'

I didn't. It had never occurred to me. I glanced back at them as I went down the steps, side by side, arms around each other, both heads slightly tilted in an attitude of affectionate sympathy as they watched me go.

'I'm not that unhappy. I've got my own life,' I thought a little peevishly as I drove out along Trumpington Road, but even the kindest of people seemed to draw strength from the supposed unhappiness of others, and it struck me that I was in danger of doing the same myself.

It was a quarter to nine when I pulled up outside Dan and Charlotte's, and getting out of the car immediately heard screaming. The house stood dark and solid before me, the alarming, terrified screech and wail seeming deep inside but so piercing it could not be contained.

It was a child, I knew that by the timbre and level of abandonment. Vicky, and there were no lights coming from the house. I went up to the front door and pressed the bell but could not hear it sound inside. I pressed again and then went round to the back of the house. The back door was standing open. I went in. Everywhere was dark, I moved down the passageway towards the front of the house where the stairs were. I couldn't find a light switch but the insistent wailing coming from upstairs didn't allow time to search. I came out into the front hall and hurried up the stairs. On the landing one of the doors stood ajar, Vicky's room, a dim, flickering light playing against the wall. I pushed the door wider. In the far corner Dan was sitting on the bed, the convulsive child quieter now but still sobbing as he held her close against him, soothing, stroking her head.

The flickering light came from a candle standing in a jam jar on a small table by the bed. I stood in the doorway for a few more moments and my heart ached.

When I said Dan's name he didn't start or look up straight away, but turned his head in a slow, even movement as if nothing could surprise him or matter very much any more. His eyes glistened in the candlelight and there was moisture on his face but perhaps it was from holding Vicky's tear-drenched face against him.

'Frances!' he exclaimed, seemingly making an effort to reduce the poignancy of the scene. 'There's a power cut and Vicky's had a nightmare. The two would have to coincide. I was in the garage, searching for a torch and she began screaming. You must have wondered what was going on. How did you get in?'

228

'The back door – you left it open. Is Vicky all right now?' I remained in the doorway, an interloper, that was how I felt.

'I think she's gone back to sleep. I'll get her back into bed and then we can check whether it is a power cut or just a fuse in the house.'

I watched him gently ease the child back under the bedcovers. She seemed to have fallen into a sudden and dead sleep which gave her an oddly rag-doll appearance.

We came away from the bedroom, and treading softly and with caution in the darkness, I followed Dan down the stairs. I waited in the drawing room while he went out to the garage and found the torch and more candles, two of which he lit and placed in dishes by the fireplace. Then he went to the fuse box and I still waited, convinced I was too late and Charlotte had already left. But too late for what? What had I hoped to achieve by turning up, unannounced, to interfere in their lives; and Dan must have known I had lied to him on the phone and been an accomplice in the break-up of his marriage. I felt wretched about it and angry with Charlotte for having drawn me into the conspiracy. Selfish, silly Charlotte; unhappy, desperate Charlotte to leave all this and that little girl. The rag-doll image of Vicky persisted. I pictured her asleep upstairs and then remembered what a pain she could be when she was awake. She had a tendency to be precocious but I had always felt it was something that went unnoticed by Charlotte whose adoration and spoiling had probably caused it. And Charlotte did adore her daughter, of that there was no doubt. Surely she would not have left without her. I began to rethink the situation and the scene I had interrupted in Vicky's room. I stared into the flickering light of one of the candles and could see Dan's white, damp face; such desolation and despair. Why did people mess up each other's lives so harshly?

The telephone started to ring and having lived by myself for some time I knew that meant the lights were out because of a fuse in the house. Dan was still buried somewhere in a cupboard so I went out to the front hall and answered the call.

'Who am I speaking to?' the voice at the other end demanded, a woman's voice with the strange infection, sing-songy, of Birmingham.

'A friend. A friend of the family,' I said, slightly taken aback by the brusqueness of the woman's tone. 'I'll fetch someone.'

'No, you'll do,' the woman said quickly. She sounded quite hostile. 'Your friend,' she continued accusingly. 'Charlotte's her name, isn't it, well I think she ought to know something about her new fancy man.'

I listened to what the woman had to say and then put the receiver down. The lights came back on and I returned to the drawing room. As I was blowing out the candles Dan came in. The room was filled with the acrid smell of burnt-out wax.

'Who was that?' he asked.

'She didn't give her name,' I said. 'Dan, where's Charlotte?'

He looked at me. His eyes seemed to have sunk into his head. The skin around them was as dark as bruising.

'She's gone out.'

'I took a breath. 'Will she be back?'

'Probably, tonight.'

'But after that?'

'Probably not.' He looked away then, dismissively, to cut the strain. 'D'you know, I think I preferred the candles, I've often felt the light in here was too much, but Charlotte likes brightness, she says dim light bulbs are depressing, it's one of the few things we disagree over.'

'I am sorry, Dan,' I said. 'I shouldn't have told you that lie on the phone. I hate lying.'

'Oh, the fictitious bath. Don't worry, Frances. I don't know what else you could have said.'

'Well, the truth, I suppose.'

'I can see that you were in a difficult position,' he said acquiescently.

'Don't you ever get angry?' I asked him.

'Yes, of course,' he said, still sounding unnaturally reasonable. 'I used to get very angry with you in those early days when you tried to persuade Charlotte not to marry me. Perhaps you were right after all.'

I gazed after him as he went to leave the room. He came back a moment or two later with two glasses and a bottle of scotch. He put them down and then relit the candles and switched out the main light. We sat down then, next to one another on a rather out-of-place old sofa, goldy-coloured with fraying tassels.

'Why did you come here tonight?' Dan asked and then quickly added: 'I'm sorry, that sounds terribly rude.'

'No, perhaps I shouldn't have come, but it's been playing on my mind the last few days – since that telephone call – the fictitious bath. I could tell you knew something.' I went on then to tell him how the call had set me thinking about events of the past, in particular the awful time when Charlotte's father had been so ill. I was surprised to discover Dan knew nothing of the episode with the convent or that Charlotte had been expelled: 'And I never said anything, when I could have. I should have done,' I told him.

'I don't suppose it would have made any difference,' he said. 'My God, those nuns!'

'I just felt that it might have done and I suppose that's the same sort of feeling I had after you phoned.'

'It's a pity we've never really talked before,' he said, refilling the glasses. 'We're both concerned for Charlotte. We're the two people who know her best, and somehow that's put us at odds over the years.'

I thought then how very nice and sane and good he was. A person to value. I had been so wrong about him, but kindness and tolerance were not virtues you recognised as making good husband material for your friend, not when you were in your early twenties. Leonard had been neither kind nor particularly tolerant in personal affairs but I had disregarded this and seen intellect and

231

original thought as the only possible basis on which to choose a partner. And how miserable it had made me. I had told Charlotte, so emphatically, that everyone had to be their own person, and then fallen into the trap myself. Charlotte, Charlotte, I felt a strong surge of exasperation with her. She should have been able to realise herself – her potential as an individual, with a partner like Dan to share her life. I couldn't imagine that he would ever put her down in the way Leonard had me, smiling, cruel, just a word here and there, placed with the accuracy of a poisoned dart piercing the jugular vein.

Poison. The ugly telephone call I had taken in the darkness of the hall. The great lump of evil in the woman's voice. Who was she? A madwoman? I wished I had told Dan straight away, but the old reserve, the sense of complicity with Charlotte against him, it must have been that which had stopped me.

The feeble candle flames burned on. Dan, seeming absorbed in his own thoughts, stared into the emptiness of the fire grate, swept out clean and cold, his eyes caught in the glimmer like liquid mercury.

'That telephone call,' I began, 'I must tell you about it.'

'No need,' he murmured bleakly, still half lost in thought, 'although she shouldn't have asked you to lie.'

'I don't mean that call, Dan. The one I took while you were mending the fuse. It was a woman, she said something about this man Charlotte's seeing.' The words came with difficulty. It seemed so blunt and cruel to speak openly to him of Charlotte's lover.

'Matthews. Nicholas Matthews is his name,' Dan said, suddenly alert and defensive.

'I think I must tell you,' I went on. 'It might not be true, but she said he had slept with his mother-in-law – although she didn't put it quite like that.'

There, it was said. A piece of malicious tittle-tattle, that was how it sounded, perhaps that was all it was. Nasty, defiling, diminishing the tragedy with an element of farce. I thought then I should have said nothing, that by saying it I had only damaged Dan further; but it was too late, and even if true had I supposed such a revelation could restore the marriage?

'Why not his sister, or his own mother!' Dan exclaimed, lifting his hand and slapping it down on the edge of the sofa to emphasise the preposterousness of the whole thing. 'And you've no idea who the woman was?'

'She wouldn't say. Middle-aged. A slight accent – not foreign, regional, I mean, Birmingham, I think. Dan, it sounds ridiculous, stupid, malicious, but she was in earnest. Do you suppose it could have been her – the mother-in-law?' I persisted as it was impossible to leave it alone now.

'God, I don't know. I don't know anything about Matthews, not really, only that he's got a wife, a pleasant, timid-sounding woman – I've spoken to her on the phone. She's terrified of her husband. How about that! Perhaps I should have made Charlotte frightened of me – do you think she would have liked that?'

For a moment I was afraid that the gentle man sitting beside me was about to lose control. I saw him then as angry, with a deep, intense anger that startled me; but it had been there all along, even at that moment when I had intruded on the scene in Vicky's bedroom and seen him fiercely clutching the child. It was the injustice, I could see that now, feel it myself.

'I wonder how she got our number, this anonymous caller?' Dan was saying. He had flung himself back into the corner of the sofa, one leg over the other, the ankle resting on the knee, his head hard against the ridge of the back-stay, his face turned up to the ceiling. 'We're ex-directory, you know – had to do it – kept getting these anonymous calls. Ha!'

'Please don't!' I pleaded.

'Where did I go wrong, Frances? You're her friend, the one she talks to, where did I fail her?' he cried out.

Instinctively, I wanted to touch him in order to reach him in

233

some way, but the recognition of what I felt as pity stopped me. Pity never helped anyone, I thought, remembering Jack and Barbie's sorrowful hugging of me, but it wasn't hard to understand how easily it could be indulged.

I thought then of the letters Charlotte had sent me in America. Maybe Dan had failed her, but I didn't see it as a failure he could have much helped. People couldn't change themselves, or each other, not in the long term. Failure, reason, logic, none of it had much bearing on the vitality of being in love and how could I say to Dan that his failure was in not sustaining Charlotte's love? Charlotte, who seemed to need more than most and had the capacity to give a lot herself but had never really given, except, perhaps now, to a man who sounded unworthy, but then wasn't that always the way? I wondered whether I would have told her about the telephone call had she been there instead of Dan. I began to think that it had, after all, been a kind of abdication to tell him and by doing so spread the responsibility of such knowledge. I did feel what the woman had said was true, but could it really change anything or just further confuse the wretched business, adding more pain for all of them?

It was then I realised my own dilemma and the subconscious reason why I had told Dan. If nothing had been said I would have served badly the long friendship with Charlotte wherein truth had always been vital, but at the same time I knew that the telling was in a sense divisive and as such would probably be seen by Charlotte as betrayal.

'I can't say,' I said, answering Dan's question. 'Perhaps it's better not to see it in those terms. I think what you have to decide is whether what you and Charlotte had has run its course or whether there is something worth saving, something left to fight for.'

'There's Vicky. That's what I really can't accept, losing Vicky,' he said. 'I'm not sure of the dividing line any more, if you know what I mean – Charlotte and Vicky. When they say that a child complicates a marriage break-up it's understating, it really is.

God, I've said it enough times myself, to clients, aggrieved people fighting for custody, saying their concern is only for the child when all it amounts to is another weapon of spite. That's the trouble, I know all the tricks. It would be so unfair.'

I had not realised that his acceptance of Charlotte's going had reached such a point; perhaps that was another failure – conceding to easily. Unfair! The notion seemed invalid in the circumstances.

Later, on my way back to London, I knew Dan would say nothing to Charlotte of the telephone call. Decisions such as the one she was making had to be unclouded, as far as was possible. That I could understand. It was free will that counted, although such restraint on the part of people like Dan and me could reach masochistic proportions. Leonard was coming to England but Jack and Barbie must not interfere or manipulate. It would be unfair.

CHAPTER FIFTEEN

Monday Morning

In the early hours of Monday morning Charlotte was driving to Heathrow. The roads were empty, bleak and chilling in the silent stillness preceding dawn, but inside the car it was warm, a little too warm, she edged her hand forward and fractionally altered the heating control, and then with a suddden jerk pushed it on to 'cold.' An icy blast immediately came into the car and after a few more minutes her passenger stirred and became irritable.

'It's too hot. I was feeling drowsy,' she said before he could comment.

He said nothing, but altered the knob back to warm and pushed a tape into the cassette player. Opera, at five o'clock in the morning!

They'd had a row, the second or maybe the third really big one and she'd only just realised that Nick liked them, he enjoyed the flow of adrenalin, while she couldn't stand them, the viciousness in him or herself. It took two to quarrel, she knew that, but what was she to do, just accept the hurt and let him get the upper hand? She couldn't do it. It wasn't that she had to win but she did not see why she should have to lose either.

They had been together almost exactly a year, the most traumatic of her life, during which the full spectrum of emotions had been experienced, one following on from another in no logical order, sometimes crashing in together, the possessive intensity of loving, the sudden sharp acidity of guilt; wretched, poisoning hatred, aggression, ambition, discovery, sometimes regret, but overall a sense of being alive, for that there was gratitude.

At times her attitude to Nick was one of 'why should I be grateful to you for anything', but at others she would fawn on him, kissing every part of his body, licking, caressing. 'I could eat you,' she would say, 'I love you so much.' 'And I love you,' he would respond. 'We did the right thing?' she liked that, the moment when he doubted her, and always when there seemed least cause. It gave her a feeling of power which she stored and guarded with small expressions of reserve. When he asked her if they had done the right thing she would not answer but to stop him searching for meaning in her silence she would put her arms around him, dispelling his need to know. It was better that he should never be entirely sure of her. The element of uncertainty had to be sustained.

In fact she preferred not to think too much about the right or the wrong in what she had done. She had left Dan quickly, within days of the weekend when it had all blown up; 'unseemly haste' he had accused her of in a brief and unexpected moment of anger that had thrilled and frightened her. The fear was that he might after all put up a fight to make her stay and while the notion had undeniable appeal to her vanity she wanted to remain definite over her decision to leave. From that she could draw strength. And so she had packed her things, the more immediate necessities of life and by no means all that belonged to her in the house, collected together Vicky's clothes and toys, and left at the civilised and unromantic hour of three o'clock in the afternoon, fetching Vicky from school on her way to the furnished house Nick had rented for them. In the end it had all been remarkably straightforward. Or had it?

Charlotte, although as yet not fully aware of her discovery, was coming to realise that nothing in life, her life anyway, was ever going to be straightforward. There was an automatic tangling process that went on inside her head and her heart with relentless regularity. Her problem was that she had always looked to other people to sort out the confusion, first Dan and now Nick, when the sorting could ultimately be done only by herself. Perhaps that was what Frances had meant when she had urged her to live her own life. It went deeper than the obvious avenues of independence – having a job, financial freedom, all that sort of thing. It was independence of spirit – to be able to determine how you were and what you did from a core of certainty in self. It was the greatest and only real strength and did not have to be accompanied by selfishness or any of the other vices that caused hurt to other people. The realisation was dawning in Charlotte, hard as she tried to put it aside; it still seemed easier to live according to others.

The first intensity of living with Nick had pushed out everything else. Their mutual determination to indulge themselves in each other provided a consuming interest that left little time for doubt or regret. They talked a lot about their previous lives. Each separately and silently determined not to consider the shortcomings they inevitably began to see in one another. They spent a great deal of time making love. In the daytime Nick would suddenly appear at the house and Charlotte would leave her drawing board in the tiny spare room and go downstairs to meet him in the narrow hallway, delight in his presence producing an exquisite ache in her chest. They had to touch one another, they couldn't not. They made love in the hallway, standing up. They tried it on the stairs. In the evenings, after Vicky was asleep, they would sit in the poky little living room drinking black coffee and large brandies. They didn't watch television, not at first – watching television had been one of the shortcomings of those previous lives. At night in bed they worked hard at performance – another area of previous shortcomings. Nothing was taboo in the headlong need to prove they had a better thing than before.

There were difficulties. Nick found it impossible to relate to

Vicky who cried rather too easily and often. He made an effort but he was awkward with children and Vicky was morose with him. She had an unfortunate tendency to stop talking when he came into the room and if he told he to do something she informed him that he was not her father. The second time she did this he smacked her leg but it was Charlotte who felt the sting more than Vicky. Maternal instinct rose up in her and for an instant she hated Nick.

'Well you ought to discipline her more,' he retorted to the unspoken rebuke as Charlotte bore holes in him with her raging stare.

'You're a fine one to talk,' she said venomously, clutching Vicky, who for once was not crying. 'You're son's manners leave rather a lot to be desired.'

'Paul's at that age.'

'And Vicky's at another!'

Vicky was better after that, but Charlotte's somewhat over-fierce mothering at that time did not blind her to the look of triumph on Vicky's little face. Matters were also helped by a friendship struck up between Vicky and a child the same age who lived next door.

'You didn't have a friend to play with where we lived before,' Charlotte said to her and then felt mean for drawing the comparison. Somehow it was underhand.

Vicky saw Dan every other weekend. He came to collect her, whisking her away as quickly as possible. He was, of course, polite to Charlotte – even pleasant, but he had bandaged his emotions, wrapped them up tight to conceal the rawness. Charlotte felt the barrier with relief and regret but she preferred not to think about that.

Vicky never said anything about the outings with Dan. There was something old and wise in her silence. She was split between two camps and would betray neither. In the early weeks Charlotte had sometimes asked her about her father, wheedling little questions to find out how he lived now that she was gone, but

Vicky would cast down her head and find absorption in whatever was at hand, murmuring non-committally to Charlotte's enquiries.

Charlotte gave up asking, but as the weeks of separation became months she began to feel the absence of Dan with a growing awareness of loss. Being in love with Nick was entirely different from the old loving of Dan. She found there were times when she disliked Nick intensely but still felt in love with him, whereas she had never not liked Dan. It was the friendship that she mourned. She had discovered a new desolation in loving and not liking.

During those first weeks alone Dan had felt numb. He lived and breathed, worked and slept (deeply unconscious sleep produced as an aftermath of shock) and ate – a little. He lost nearly two stone in weight and was forced to go out and buy new clothes. Hilary went with him and he found himself buying styles and colours he would not have considered had he been by himself.

Hanging on to his arm, she pulled him from shop to shop, eager and nervous, trying too hard. She went to the house in the evenings, dropping in to make sure he was all right, offering to cook his meals, wash his clothes. The more she tried to be intimate the further he backed away.

'We're the losers of the world,' she said to him. 'The failures,' and he knew he must stop her coming round. But it was not easy. He did not want to be unkind. He began to go out in the evenings. He joined things. A squash club, a theatre group, the Conservative Club. His parents, who were mercifully silent about Charlotte's departure, suggested he take a holiday with them, but the local council elections were coming up and he found himself suddenly immersed in organising the Tories' campaign. He accepted every job that was going in order to fill the hours between work and sleep. The constituency members, many of whom were old friends of his parents, were impressed by what he achieved. He had the sort of dedication they were looking for and at the end of the year they approached him with the idea of putting his name forward to Central Office as a prospective parliamentary candidate.

He was neither flattered nor pleased. He felt nothing, but accepted their offer and worked on. He could not avoid noticing that other women besides Hilary were interested in him. He was genuinely surprised by the realisation but kept them all at a distance, unwittingly creating a magnetic aura of mystery about himself. He had hardened without knowing it, survived, changed, become a success, but it would take longer to find joy. The ego which had been suppressed all the years he had lived with Charlotte had emerged as a potent force – more badly bruised than he would have thought possible in those selfless times, but strengthened now that he had lost what he had most feared losing.

He actually began to enjoy electioneering. At first he had forced himself into it but a sense of challenge grew in him and he liked calling on people, talking to them, hearing their concerns. One evening he called at a large house on a small exclusive development of neo-Georgian-style houses. A boy, in his early teens, opened the door and invited him in. The drone of pop music filled the house and the smell of baking wafted into the hallway. The place was warm and pleasantly cluttered. It was not as he had expected from the outside; two of the other houses he had been in were of the Ideal Home image, pristine, un-lived-in, houses that were not homes but status symbols.

A woman, presumably the boy's mother, came bustling out of the kitchen, her hands floury, an ample apron covering her dress. She was of indeterminate middle age. Her hair, a faded blonde, looked slightly damp from the steam in the kitchen. An untidy but pleasant-looking little woman, Dan thought.

He told her why he had called but before he could introduce himself had been offered a cup of tea. Normally he politely refused anything like that – it took up too much time, but on this occasion he accepted. The woman asked the boy to take him into their living room. Dan sat down beside a pile of ironing and looked about the room. In the corner opposite him there was a great heap of toys – things for very young children – there was a plastic tricycle the same as the one Vicky had when she was a toddler. On one of the walls childish paintings, daubs of bright poster colours, had been stuck up in a row. Dan noticed that one of them partly concealed a crack in the plaster.

The boy sat opposite him. He had a quiet, serious look about him, a sensitive face. His mother came into the room with the tea and a plate of fruit cake. 'Will you have some – it's not been long out of the oven,' she said, setting the tray down, and then to the boy: 'Budge up Paul, make room for me.'

'I hope you'll excuse the mess,' she went on to Dan. 'I run a playgroup, you see. It's something I always fancied doing but it wasn't possible until recently and I'm still trying to get things properly organised. Paul helps me with the clearing up but we just don't know where to put everything.' Her enthusiasm had a naive sort of charm.

Dan bit into a slice of the warm cake and regretted not telling Marion Matthews who he was from the outset, it would be more difficult now. He wondered why he had come to the house at all, why he had not simply missed it out. Was there an element of mawkish curiosity in what he was doing, or a desire to recognise his own suffering (no longer so acute he now realised) in a fellow human being – to indulge it by sharing and hearing how she had survived and coped?

The boy Paul, was studying him. Unaccountably Dan felt that he knew who he was even if his mother didn't, but he remained silent, silent and watchful. Marion was chatting on about her playgroup, she had taken a course, done it all properly she assured him, as if he was some kind of interfering official.

'Have you still got the donkey? Dad said there was a donkey,' the boy suddenly asked, as if that was what had been preying on his mind.

Dan looked at Marion. Her posture had stiffened.

'I'm sorry. I tried to tell you at the beginning. I'm Charlotte's husband,' he said.

'But I thought you were ...'

'The Tory candidate? Yes, that as well. As I said, I'm sorry. I'll leave now if you like.'

'The donkey?' Paul urged him.

'Ah, the donkey. Yes. I still have that.'

'I'd like to see it.'

'Paul!'

The boy leapt up and ran from the room at his mother's sharpened tone.

'Oh dear,' she sighed when he had gone. 'He gets upset so easily, over nothing sometimes.'

Dan stood up to leave.

'No, please. I didn't mean to be rude – it was just the surprise of it being you, sit down and finish your tea.'

'I'm sorry if Paul's upset.'

'Oh, he'll get over it. I worry about him a lot but when all's said and done he's going to have to toughen up a bit – like his father always said. The world's so full of knocks and bumps, isn't it?'

Dan noticed that she used the past tense when she spoke of Nick, as if he were dead – no longer living and breathing now, at this very second, as they were. Nick and Charlotte, their existence had become remote.

They talked then, Dan and Marion, discovering each other's disguised survival tactics, urging one another to believe how they had conquered misery, and perhaps they had.

'Do you know, I never thought I would say this, but it's been a relief in a way. I can do as I like now. My life is my own,' Marion said.

Cosi Fan Tutte, Charlotte switched it off.

'I thought you liked opera,' Nick yawned, stretching his arms in the constricting space inside the car and bringing one hand down to rest on her leg. The conciliatory gesture.

'I do, but it's like shepherd's pie – I usually like it when I have it but I'd never choose it,' Charlotte said, 'and certainly not for breakfast!'

It was getting lighter. Another twenty minutes and they'd be into Heathrow.

'You can turn out the lights now,' Nick said.

'Not yet.'

'Come on, you don't need them now,' he persisted and lifted his hand from her leg towards the switch.

'Who's driving, you or me!' Charlotte demanded, she was excited and edgy and Nick rose to the bait he had laid for her, spoiling for a fight without even knowing it.

They snapped and snarled at one another for ten, fifteen minutes.

'You're a bloody awful driver anyway,' he said finally.

'And you're bloody rude,' Charlotte retorted, stopping the car with a squeal of brakes. 'You drive if you're so bloody marvellous.' She got out and stalked round to the passenger door. Nick levered himself across into the driver's seat and when Charlotte had got in jerked the car forward. He waited for her to pass some sarcastic comment but she stayed quiet, and he felt all the more irritated, denied of any satisfaction in their quarrelling.

At length he said he was sorry and called her darling. She leant across and kissed his neck, but the mood was still on him and they would fight again before the day was out. He had to push it until he got to her and made sure the spark was still there, to consume and engross him. When he had time he wondered at the nature of love.

'I hope Vicky will be good while we're away,' Charlotte was saying, oblivious to her husband's continuing bellicosity.

'She'll be all right,' he murmured as they approached the terminal building.

'Ruby's wonderful with her. I know we shouldn't have to worry.'

'Then don't,' Nick said.

On the plane Charlote plugged into the film but Nick had work to do. He pulled out the file he needed to study, opening it at Germaine's last letter, congratulatory about his achievements with Gym and Tonic (Europe), about his new marriage. He allowed himself a brief sense of pleasure and wondered how Charlotte would get on with Germaine. Her relationship with Ruby amazed him. Ruby, as inescapable as a cancer, he thought, it was she who was amazing, unfathomable, devious. She had come to see them, quite unannounced and unexpected, turning up one afternoon to find Charlotte alone in the house. He had come home late that evening, and there they were, the two of them, as friendly as could be. Ruby had put Vicky to bed, read her a story. It was incredible, Charlotte told him in the kitchen, the three of them, she, Vicky and Ruby, they'd had an instant rapport, and who would have thought it possible!

'I like her. She's a character. She's had a hard life,' Charlotte said when they were in bed and Ruby lay in the spare room beside Charlotte's drawing board. 'And it was kind of her to bring back the diary. She needn't have. She said you must have left it there a long time ago but she only just found it.'

'She could have posted it,' Nick grunted.

'I'm glad she didn't. It's not nice to feel there are people you've never met who may hate you.'

Ruby had met Nick's eyes only once but that had been enough to put him on his guard. 'If you can't beat em – join em,' she had seemed to say but Nick knew Ruby of old and was chilled by what might be beneath her magnanimity.

He found it impossible to make love to Charlotte while Ruby was in the house, an occurrence which grew in frequency; and he felt unable actively to discourage the association for fear of reprisal. But Nick was not a man to be cowed for long. The condition went against his nature and so he told Charlotte what Ruby might if she had a mind to. He couldn't think quite how to put it but in the end he just told her straight: 'I used to sleep with Ruby.' No justification. No excuses. It seemed better to be blunt.

'Really?' Charlotte said, an odd tingling sensation in the pit of her stomach. 'You mean you fucked her.'

'Don't be vulgar, it doesn't suit you.' They were lying in bed, in the dark, side by side, each alert to the other, but still, as if neither wanted the air to move.

'You do mean that though, don't you?'

'Yes.'

'What was it like?'

'I'm not telling you.'

'Go on!'

'You don't mind then?'

'I'm not sure – no, I don't think so. It's rather a turn-on.'

'Not jealous?'

'Not of the past. Why, do you want me to be?'

'You are extraordinary!'

'Am I?'

And so it was said. Charlotte brooded upon it for a while, Nick was sure of that, but if she mentioned it to him her interest was wickedly prurient.

'What a kinky person you are,' he told her.

And she answered that yes she was, and wasn't he glad. Neither of them ever suggested that he was of the same ilk. Men had a right to be kinky.

Despite her acceptance of what had happened Nick felt the friendship with Ruby might abate, but Charlotte continued to allow the visits and amazed him again by asking Ruby to stay at the house and look after Vicky while they were in America. His new wife was impossible to understand he concluded, and yet his understanding of her was greater than he realised. They were

247

alike and that was why they fought and struggled against one another but always realigned. He felt that Charlotte was impossible to understand and yet he had never understood himself. They shared a destructive instinct that made them tear into one another but they were both survivors so the destruction would always be thwarted and perhaps each knew it deep down and they were therefore able to play their game with impunity.

The conundrum of Charlotte, of himself, held him, entranced him, angered and frustrated him, but he no longer felt boredom or despair. A part of the puzzle of his life had been solved – for the time being, because, like Charlotte, he did not possess the quality of constance.

In times past Nick would have been termed a bounder and he knew it and sometimes felt an odd quirk of resentment against himself and the world for making him so. But not for long. He did not have time to ruminate over his own shortcomings or consider where he was categorised by his fellows. Achievement was not finite, it was a continuous state and above all Nick needed to achieve.

His attention concentrated on the contents of the file in front of him and he quite forgot that Charlotte was there.

The sound quality from Charlotte's earphones was poor and after a while she decided to abandon the film. Her mind was too full of her own life anyway. She was in a mood to think.

She got up and went to the lavatory to sort out her face. The plane's atmosphere had made her sweat and she had sucked off most of the red lipstick she had bought for America. Little things, but they affected her psyche. She reapplied the make-up and gazed at herself in the mirror. She pushed back her hair and smiled a bright, happy smile, her chin well up. It was how she wanted to appear to Frances and Leonard when they met them at the airport.

She swung her way back through the aisles of seats and slipped into her own next to Nick, who was engrossed in his reading. She gazed across him at the emptiness of the sky, at last she was going to America and she wanted to savour the realisation of a so-long-held desire. She concentrated her mind on it, urging delight, but there was something missing, a void she wished she could dismiss from her thoughts. It was tied up with her sense of unreality about herself, a purposelessness that had begun to grow within her since the inevitable abatement of the initial all-absorbing intensity of her relationship with Nick. She longed to talk with Frances again, and yet it was the prospect of their imminent meeting that had heightened her awareness of her own situation. Frances was in a sense her oracle although she had never fully heeded the philosophy that had sprung from their conversations. Her muddled fallibility had prevented that. She wondered whether Frances' life had changed now that she had returned to Leonard. In essence probably not – that was Frances' strength, Charlotte thought with envy; envy even now – would she for ever feel envious of her friend? Would she never be satisfied with what she had herself?

She rested her head against the aircraft seat but the tangled thinking ran on and pockets of clarity began to emerge. She was going to America but she wished the going could have been by her own achievement as was planned before she knew Nick. She could not for ever live by dint of other people's doing. Envy was a shallow emotion, counterproductive, niggling, the result of frustration with oneself, unrealised possibilities.

Charlotte sighed within herself. Nothing really changed unless it happened inside your own head, independently of others. She had never really got started, not yet. With Dan, with Nick, with neither. It should make no difference. Be true to yourself, Frances had said, but she had never fully understood until now. But how to start? That she had still to determine.

In California as Frances and Leonard greeted Charlotte and Nick it was still Monday morning. In England the afternoon had faded into evening. Dan had allowed himself a long weekend after the solid weeks of campaigning. The by-election was to take place on Thursday and he was expected to win. Paul, who now regularly cycled to the house after school, had just arrived and together they walked through the garden to the field where Tamara lived, but this evening she was determined to ignore them.

'I wish she belonged to me,' Paul sighed, leaning forward against the gate. Dan had noticed that the boy's face seemed to clear when he saw the donkey. The mask of moroseness lifted and his innocence was exposed.

'Tamara's a stubborn creature but she's got a free spirit and I don't think she could ever really belong to anybody,' Dan said to him.

'Doesn't she ever try to get out of this field?' Paul continued.

'When the mood takes her,' Dan answered. 'She did once about a year ago. She got out into the lane, she was very nearly run over. Whether that made any impression on her one can't be sure, but she hasn't tried again. Perhaps she's realised that one field is very much the same as another.'